FOR WORSE
AND
FOR BETTER

A Pride & Prejudice Variation

ALEXA DOUGLAS

BLUESTOCKING
PRESS

For information contact :

Alexa Douglas

www.alexadouglas.com

Cover design by ebooklaunch.com

ISBN: 978-1-7354461-3-4

First Edition: August 2021 by Bluestocking Press LLC

10 9 8 7 6 5 4 3 2 1

For Bruce,

until death do us part.

Since There's No Help

Since there's no help, come let us kiss and part;
Nay, I have done, you get no more of me,
And I am glad, yea glad with all my heart
That thus so cleanly I myself can free;
Shake hands forever, cancel all our vows,
And when we meet at any time again,
Be it not seen in either of our brows
That we one jot of former love retain.
Now at the last gasp of Love's latest breath,
When, his pulse failing, Passion speechless lies,
When Faith is kneeling by his bed of death,
And Innocence is closing up his eyes,
Now if thou woudst, when all have given him over,
From death to life thou mightst him yet recover.

– Michael Drayton (1563-1631)

Part One

Elizabeth

One

An Impossible Choice

ELIZABETH BENNET had no sooner made it through the front door of the parsonage than she was accosted.

"Cousin Elizabeth!" Mr. Collins cried, hurrying toward her from the front parlor. "You must dress quickly if we are to be in time for dinner. You know Lady Catherine cannot abide tardiness."

Elizabeth schooled her features. *I care not a whit for Lady Catherine's good opinion,* she thought.

"I must beg leave to be excused, cousin," she said. "I feel very ill this evening." This was no exaggeration. Thanks to the information she had just received from Colonel Fitzwilliam, she was in such a state of fury — which, of course, she had been obliged to instantly conceal — that she now boasted a throbbing headache.

"My dear cousin," he began, "I beg you would consider —"

"Why, Lizzy, you do look very ill indeed!" Elizabeth's dearest friend Charlotte entered from the hallway, linking her arm through Elizabeth's and directing a brief, quelling glance at her husband. "Lady Catherine is such a charitable woman, I have no doubt she will agree you must stay here at the parsonage and rest while we dine at Rosings."

Mr. Collins nodded sagely. "Very true, my dear, very true. Lady Catherine is the soul of generosity and condescension. When all the circumstances are fully explained to her, she will not be angry."

Elizabeth managed to wait until she was in the hallway before rolling her eyes. Her cousin seemed to believe his primary duty as the parson for this parish was to extol the virtues of his patroness, the Right Honorable Lady Catherine de Bourgh. Lady Catherine appeared only too pleased by this behavior.

Likely why Her Ladyship granted such a valuable living to such an inexperienced clergyman, Elizabeth thought. *She may enjoy his gratification of her vanity for the rest of her life. Well, until Papa dies and Mr. Collins inherits Longbourn, at the very least.*

Charlotte propelled Elizabeth to the back of the house, bidding the maid to bring a fresh pot of tea. The morning-parlor was a comfortable room, warm and cheery, with none of the stuffy formality Mr. Collins seemed to find necessary in the front parlor. It was Charlotte's favorite room and had quickly become Elizabeth's as well in the month she had been visiting the Collinses in Kent.

Elizabeth's shoulders relaxed as she was seated in the cozy chair before the fire. "I thank you," she said, her gaze taking in Charlotte and Mr. Collins together. "I am quite certain the combination of tea, quiet, and solitude shall soon set me to rights. Please convey my regrets to Lady Catherine."

Charlotte's tiny smile was the only outward sign that she was not deceived by Elizabeth's entirely imaginary regret. Indeed, Elizabeth rather suspected Charlotte would have offered to stay with her had Elizabeth not signaled her desire to be left alone. But Charlotte had chosen to marry Mr. Collins with her eyes open. Tolerance of Lady Catherine was her self-imposed lot in life.

"We shall certainly convey your most particular regrets to her Ladyship and all her family," Mr. Collins said with a small bow. "And —"

Before he could wax eloquent on the subject of his noble patroness, Charlotte said only, "My dear, the time."

Soon afterward the front door closed, cutting off Mr. Collins's exclamations about the many pronouncements Lady Catherine had made on the sovereign importance of punctuality. Elizabeth slumped against the chair. *Blessed silence.* The maid brought in the tea-tray and departed on light feet; the only sound that remained was the crackling of the fire.

It was exceedingly unfortunate: Elizabeth would have invented a headache to avoid dining at Rosings Park this evening, but it seemed she was to suffer one in truth. It was not even the officious Lady Catherine she sought to avoid. Elizabeth had no desire to see either of the great lady's nephews tonight — or ever again, really. If Mr. Fitzwilliam Darcy and Colonel Richard Fitzwilliam were suddenly to vanish entirely, it would give her not a moment's concern.

In fairness, when Colonel Fitzwilliam told me of Mr. Darcy's recent triumph in separating an unnamed friend from an unsuitable young lady, he could not have known the young lady in question was my sister.

Jane was too angelic to suspect willful interference in her courtship with Charles Bingley. Elizabeth's lovely, sweet-tempered sister was unable even to blame her former suitor for his abandonment! Elizabeth, of a less forgiving turn of mind, had thought it likely Mr. Bingley had been persuaded to stay away, but until today had laid the blame at the feet of Mr. Bingley's socially ambitious sister Caroline.

The colonel no doubt meant to impress upon me Mr. Darcy's fine qualities as a friend. Were Elizabeth not already party to the particulars, she might even have agreed. *But Jane is the daughter of a gentleman. Hardly an ineligible match for the son of a tradesman, for all his newfound wealth! And Mr. Bingley was so clearly attached to her! Or so we all thought. Had his attachment been genuine, surely his friend could not have put him off so easily!*

Sighing, Elizabeth pulled Jane's latest letter from her pocket. She had no wish to think on Mr. Darcy a moment longer. He had already proved himself the most arrogant man of her acquaintance a dozen times over. Besides, her unexpected encounter with the colonel this afternoon had diverted her from her primary goal, which had been to settle beneath her favorite tree in the tiny grove near the parsonage and read her letter. She selected a biscuit and curled up in the chair, determined to enjoy all the news from home.

Minutes later she was on her feet, unable to remain still as she read the letter a second time. Unlike their mother, Jane was not prone to hysterics. And if *Jane* was worried…

Elizabeth's thoughts were interrupted by the sound of the bell. *Who can be calling at this hour?* she wondered. She was certainly not dressed to receive visitors — she still wore her walking-dress and muddy boots!

She heard a man's deep tones, followed by the thud of booted feet striking the floorboards. *It can only be someone I know. Colonel Fitzwilliam, perhaps, come to inquire after my health?*

Hurriedly she tucked Jane's letter under the blotter on the writing-desk and sat on the nearest sofa. Despite her attempt to compose herself, she was entirely unprepared to see the gentleman she had so recently banished from her mind. "Mr. Darcy!"

"Good evening, Miss Bennet. I am sorry to disturb you. I hope you are feeling better."

"I am, thank you." It was a lie, of course, but she desired no artificial concern; rather, she wished him to depart. Instead, he stood about looking agitated and avoiding her gaze as long seconds ticked by. *Why leave his aunt's table to come here, only to ignore me?* It was incomprehensible. "Will you not sit down?" she asked.

He started, as though just recalling her presence. "I thank you, no," he said, pacing to the fireplace and staring into the flames. The silence stretched. Finally, he seemed to come to some sort of decision; back straight and shoulders squared, he came to stand directly before her.

"In vain I have struggled," he said. "It will not do. My feelings will not be repressed. You must allow me to tell you how ardently I admire and love you."

What? Elizabeth stared, open-mouthed. *Impossible!* She had come to expect many things from Fitzwilliam Darcy in the course of their acquaintance, but a declaration of love was not among them.

"You may well be surprised," he said. "I confess I have long endeavored to shield you from awareness of my regard. The relative social position of our families is so disparate that my relations must surely disapprove. I am expected to marry into nobility, or at the least a lady of my own class."

He appeared to speak as much to himself as to Elizabeth. "And that is not the only consideration. Your family's social inferiority would be offense enough, but the behavior of your mother and younger sisters cannot be deemed acceptable by any polite society." He gave a small shrug. "But it cannot be helped. Within a month of our acquaintance, I knew myself to be in danger. Your beauty, wit, and vivacity brought you constantly to my mind. I thought I escaped it when I quitted Hertfordshire in November, but meeting you again here in Kent has shown me my folly."

Elizabeth sucked in a breath. Mr. Darcy continued when she would have spoken, however, dropping to a knee and taking her hands in his.

"From the moment I saw you in this parlor, I was forced to concede defeat. All my former feelings, which I believed I had conquered, rushed forth with an intensity that would not be denied. Elizabeth, I beg you to relieve me. I cannot be easy until you tell me you will be my wife."

She had never been this close to him. His eyes, the warm brown of cinnamon, shone with unwavering confidence. *For all his talk of uneasiness he has no doubt of his success,* she realized. *As though the favor of his suit alone must sway me, no matter my feelings!*

She looked away, jaw clenched tightly. Her eyes fell on Jane's letter, half-hidden under the blotter; she took a slow, steadying breath and carefully reclaimed her hands.

"Mr. Darcy, I confess myself greatly surprised by your application. I must beg some time to consider my answer. I would not wish to be hasty."

His eyes widened a fraction before his usual disdainful expression returned. "Of course, Miss Bennet. Perhaps we may speak again tomorrow. Shall I find you walking in the grove?"

"Yes. I hope to have an answer for you by then."

The moment he was gone, she retrieved her letter and escaped to her bedchamber. Charlotte and Mr. Collins would surely inquire after her health when they returned from Rosings Park, but she could give no favorable answer. Mr. Darcy's surprise visit had only added to her distress.

Elizabeth paced her tiny room, agitation giving force to her steps. *I cannot speak of his proposal to Charlotte.* She knew what her friend's advice would be. After all, had Charlotte not declared happiness in marriage to be entirely a matter of chance? Charlotte had even insisted a woman should know as little as possible of the defects of her future husband! She had followed word with deed, too; in marrying Mr. Collins, Charlotte had secured a comfortable home but was now irrevocably connected to the stupidest man Elizabeth had ever met.

Charlotte contrives to see Mr. Collins but rarely. Could I do such a thing? Elizabeth laughed aloud at her own foolishness. *Nay, that would be impossible. Mr. Darcy does as he desires, irrespective of the advice or wishes of others. I should have no power to keep him away.*

Elizabeth stopped before the window. Rosings Park stood across the lane, stately and forbidding in its grandeur. *Not unlike Mr. Darcy,* she thought. She could not be insensible of the compliment, that such a wealthy and powerful man should be attached to her, but neither could she be serene.

How can a man who declared me "not handsome enough to tempt him," and behaved abominably to me and all my family, now profess to admire me?

She was not ill-favored, with her thick chestnut hair, clear skin and brown eyes made lively by her merry temper; but neither was she her sister Jane, whose blond ringlets and blue doe-eyed gaze were the epitome of female beauty.

How did I not notice his regard? Reviewing the course of their acquaintance, she reluctantly discovered signs she had missed. *Charlotte often observed that he looked at me a great deal, and that he sought my company and conversation. He even asked me to dance three times, though he never dances if he can avoid it!*

Elizabeth had consented to dance with Mr. Darcy only once, at Mr. Bingley's ball at Netherfield. *What an unpleasant half hour that was!* Mr. Darcy had become agitated when she spoke warmly of Mr. Wickham.

Could he have been jealous?

The two men had not been on speaking terms for many years. Elizabeth could not imagine them as the childhood playmates Mr. Wickham described; they were so dissimilar! George Wickham was greatly the superior in manners and conversation. He had immediately charmed the entire neighborhood, whereas Mr. Darcy's disdainful silences had ensured his unpopularity, despite his great wealth.

Elizabeth had always particularly enjoyed Mr. Wickham's company. He shared her love of laughing at the follies of others, particularly those of Mr. Darcy. And Mr. Wickham had made no secret of his admiration for her. Had she any dowry to speak of, his interest would likely have been even more enthusiastically displayed, but a military man could not afford to marry without regard to fortune.

Perhaps Mr. Darcy's rudeness at the Netherfield ball was founded in jealousy of my friendship with Mr. Wickham. I suppose I must forgive such feelings, if he truly admired me then. But can I marry a man who holds my family in such disdain? He never said more than civility required to any of them — not even Jane!

She again recalled her conversation with Colonel Fitz-william. *Can I marry the man responsible for Jane's heart-break?* Dear Jane had been so in love with the obviously-besotted Mr. Bingley, and so wretched when Mr. Bingley departed to London just after the Netherfield ball, never to return. Naturally, Jane insisted she was well — Jane had never been one for displays of emotion — but Lizzy knew her too well to doubt her suffering.

Mr. Darcy overcame all his objections in his own case, but saw fit to impose them on his friend! It was true that Mr. Darcy's condition in life was so far above the Bennets' that for him to marry Elizabeth must draw censure from the *ton*, but the same could not be said of Mr. Bingley and Jane! The hypocrisy was galling. *Presumptuous man!*

These thoughts reminded her of Jane's letter, which had earlier so disturbed her. She snatched it up again.

Longbourn, 10th April 1812

Dearest Lizzy,

I so enjoyed your long letter with all the news of Hunsford Parsonage and Rosings Park. You are such an eager traveler, I fancy it shall not be long before you have seen the whole of

England! And what an extraordinary coincidence, that Mr. Darcy should arrive just when you were visiting in Kent! If his cousin the colonel is even half as charming as you describe, he must be a delightful acquaintance.

I confess we have been uneasy here at Longbourn. Two days past, Papa began coughing and complained of a touch of fever. By evening he had taken to his bed, and the apothecary has declared it an infectious pneumonia. We are told the next day or two shall determine his likelihood of recovery. In the meantime, we apply cool cloths and give him draughts to combat the fever.

When I say "we," you must know I mean Mrs. Hill and myself. Our mother is overcome at the prospect of Papa's death and has not left her room for two days. Our sisters are hardly more helpful. Mary chiefly sits with Mamma, though I can occasionally persuade Kitty or Lydia to take on that duty. I do not ask them to join me in the sick-room for fear of exposing them, though they have not the temperament for it in any event.

I long for your presence, though it seems selfish to ask it. Papa would not wish to expose you to illness, and by the time you might return home I hope he shall be out of danger. Therefore stay where you are, and I shall write again as soon as I have news.

Your loving sister,
Jane

Elizabeth slumped onto the bed. Their father was not elderly, and she had never known him to be truly ill. Therefore she had not taken seriously her mother's hysterics about being "turned out by the Collinses to starve in the hedgerows" upon her father's death, at which point Mr. Collins — her father's closest male relative — would become master of Longbourn. Nor did she truly believe Charlotte and her husband would do so, but if Papa died her family could hardly remain at Longbourn.

What are we to do if it comes to that? How can six women support themselves? Our mother has no fortune. Our uncles would do all they can, but if none of us has married well, our options will be few. Some of us, at least, would be required to seek a position.

Most likely Jane and me, she realized. Mary's disinterest in society would make her a poor companion — not even a worthy governess — and Kitty and Lydia were too silly for any sort of serious work.

Oh, if only Mr. Darcy had not interfered in his friend's courtship! Left to himself, Mr. Bingley must certainly have proposed to Jane by now. They might even be married! And I would not be forced to contemplate marriage to a man whose company I have always avoided.

Elizabeth paced and fretted for hours. She did not want to marry Mr. Darcy. But no matter how many times she turned it over in her mind, she could find no other recourse. For all his faults, Elizabeth did not doubt Mr. Darcy would take on the responsibility of providing for her mother and sisters in the event of her father's untimely death.

Can I refuse him? No, of course not. I cannot possibly hope to receive another proposal from a wealthy man. Jane might, but only if Papa lives. Were her father to die with none of his daughters advantageously married, their respectability — and thus their access to good society — must naturally fade.

Exhausted and disheartened, she slept fitfully and woke with the dawn, head still pounding. Eager to escape the parsonage and avoid Charlotte's scrutiny, Elizabeth struck out before breakfast toward her favorite wooded path. With luck, she might enjoy some time to sit in solitude in her favorite grove. She walked slowly, inhaling deeply, soothed as always by the rustling of leaves and the smell of earth.

Her wish was not to be granted, however; Mr. Darcy awaited her in the grove. He turned at the sound of her approach, smile faltering when he caught sight of her. "Good morning, Miss Bennet. Are you well? Please forgive me if our agreement to meet here induced you to be out of doors when you should rightly have remained in bed."

"Nay, Mr. Darcy. It is merely that sleep did not relieve my headache. I hoped a walk might achieve what rest did not."

"I am sorry to hear it. Shall we walk together?" He spoke gently, his countenance radiating concern. "There is a spot perhaps a half-mile from here, through these trees, which affords a delightful view of the surrounding countryside."

At her nod, he led the way. The path was hardly more than a game track, but Mr. Darcy was attentive and solicitous, holding aside branches and lending his hand to assist her over the difficult spots. Eventually they reached the edge of the trees where they stood upon a little rise, farms and fields sprawled out below them. He spread his greatcoat out across a convenient fallen log, and she sank down gratefully.

He towered above her, only his handsome profile visible. Elizabeth knew not what to make of him. Had he ever shown her such consideration? If so, she could not recall it. She had heard it said of him that he was devoted to his sister Georgiana; that he could be generous and liberal-minded, even amiable, when among his equals. She had never believed it — his behavior had always been so pompous and unyielding — but perhaps it was true after all?

"You must surely be awaiting my answer, Mr. Darcy."

He turned instantly to face her. "Nay, madam. While I am anxious to know my fate, I cannot in good conscience importune you when you are ill."

"I believe you overestimate my infirmity. A headache is never comfortable, but it does not render me incapable of rational thought. And there is a question I must ask before I may give you my decision."

It had occurred to Elizabeth, sometime late in the night, that she could hardly tell Mr. Darcy the truth about her reticence to marry him. Even so confident a man would never have proposed if he knew her feelings! But she must have some plausible reason for her reluctance.

"You mentioned your relations could not but disapprove your choice. I certainly never dreamt I might join the ranks of such elevated society. How fierce shall be the opposition? Shall I have any allies at all?"

She had taken him by surprise, she saw. *I imagine he thinks of such things as minor impediments.* He sat next to her, appearing to give her question due consideration.

"The fiercest opposition is likely to come from Lady Catherine. You must surely have noticed that she intends for me to marry her daughter Anne. While I have the greatest respect for my cousin, we have no desire to marry. Even so, my aunt is unlikely to be gracious when she learns I am engaged elsewhere."

"I confess, Lady Catherine's reaction has been a concern. But what of your uncle? An earl cannot be satisfied to see his nephew wed the daughter of a country squire, to say nothing of society's opinion."

"Uncle Henry shall come around. My cousin Richard — Colonel Fitzwilliam, that is — likes you immensely. Since he approves of you it is likely his mother shall as well, and Aunt Eleanor typically succeeds in convincing my uncle to view things as she does. She is also a powerful ally amongst the *ton.*" He smiled. "One person, I know, shall be delighted. Georgiana has been eager to meet you, ever since I told her of you in my letters from Hertfordshire. She is shy, and it must do her good to have a sister with your lively disposition."

"Indeed? I had not heard that about her, but you must know my information comes almost entirely from Caroline Bingley and Mr. Wickham. You have said very little."

"An oversight I shall immediately rectify, whether you accept my hand or not." His gaze was warm and serious. "If you do accept me, you must know I shall always stand against any who might look down upon you. I shall tolerate no disrespect of my wife, even from my relations."

Elizabeth swallowed hard. "And you understand my feelings are... not the equal of yours?"

His expression became wry. "How can it be otherwise? Even those closest to me agree I am a difficult man to know. I must be patient and have faith that, in time, you shall look upon me with equal affection."

"In that case, Mr. Darcy, I accept."

Two

Disapproval at Home

ELIZABETH PREPARED HERSELF to enter Rosings Park on Mr. Darcy's arm. After she had given him her decision yesterday, he had grimly declared himself honor-bound to present her to Lady Catherine before leaving Kent. Elizabeth had tried to dissuade him. After all, they had not yet obtained her father's approval.

He had smiled sympathetically. "You tell me your father shall certainly give his consent when we apply to him."

"I believe he shall," Elizabeth had said. What she did not say aloud was that Papa would need convincing. She did not doubt he would give way if she held firm, but Papa would not wish to see her wed a man she did not like.

"I want there to be no question of my marrying Anne," Mr. Darcy said. "Nor do I wish to see Lady Catherine descend upon you at Longbourn if she learns of our engagement after you depart. It is the sort of thing she would do, to convince you to give up the engagement entirely."

"I see." Elizabeth's chin had lifted. "If I am to disappoint her, I suppose I might as well do it now. There is no need to expose my family to such a scene."

He had taken her hand with a grin. "We shall disappoint her together."

Elizabeth dressed with care for this visit to Rosings Park. She wore her finest day dress, a russet-colored muslin with subtle embroidery about the square neckline that brought out hints of gold in her chestnut curls. The skin around her dark eyes no longer looked sallow and her cheeks were once again a healthy pink; her decision made, she had fallen last night into a deep, dreamless sleep.

Mr. Darcy looked as he always did, though he was also somehow different. His dark brown hair fell in tidy waves around his forehead and collar, and his clothing was simple but impeccably tailored. He was impossibly tall — the top of Elizabeth's head just reached his cravat — and the rigid set of his shoulders was familiar.

He looks as though he were girding himself for battle, she thought. Then he flashed her an encouraging smile, and she realized what was different. *He looks happy, too.*

They were met in the hall by Colonel Fitzwilliam, who shook her hand with a wide grin. "What a delight it is to see you here today, Miss Bennet," he said. "I hope you do not object to my joining you."

"Not at all, Colonel. I am glad for any reinforcements."

"I regret to say you may need them. And please call me Richard. We are to be family, you know."

"Then you must call me Elizabeth. Or Lizzy, which is what my family calls me."

"Of course." He looked at her seriously. "As Darcy may have mentioned, my aunt is not expecting you. We felt surprise was the wisest strategy. If you are ready, I shall lead the way." At Elizabeth's nod he flung open the drawing-room door. "Good morning, Aunt Catherine! Darcy has brought us a delightful visitor."

Lady Catherine was perched upon her throne-like chair, a deep suspicion overtaking her countenance as she perceived Elizabeth on Mr. Darcy's arm. Anne de Bourgh sat nearby, listlessly permitting her companion to fuss with the shawl about her shoulders.

Mr. Darcy placed his hand protectively over Elizabeth's. "Lady Catherine, Anne, I am pleased to share with you the happy news that Miss Elizabeth Bennet has consented to be my wife. I am certain you shall welcome her to the family with all the gracious condescension of your rank."

For several seconds, the room was utterly silent. *Cleverly done, Mr. Darcy,* Elizabeth thought. *Your aunt cannot now make a scene without reflecting poorly on herself.*

Lady Catherine was the first to respond. Her tone was icy. "This is momentous news, nephew. Do I assume correctly that you have very recently entered into this engagement?"

"Yes ma'am."

"I see. Leave us, all of you." Lady Catherine waved away servants and family alike. "You too, Darcy. I would speak to Miss Bennet alone."

Everyone departed but Mr. Darcy, who gave Elizabeth a look of concern. She answered with a determined smile and a nod, removing her hand from his arm. When the door had closed behind him, Lady Catherine fixed Elizabeth with a stern glare. "Sit down, girl."

Elizabeth sat, keeping her face carefully neutral. *Now it begins*, she thought.

"I know not what my nephew has told you, but he is not free to marry."

"Oh? Why not?"

"He has been engaged for many years to my daughter Anne."

"The banns have been read? I saw no announcement in any of the papers."

"It matters not. The pertinent fact is that he cannot marry you."

Can she truly think I would believe such a thing? Elizabeth deliberately lifted her brows. "I am astonished by this claim! I have never believed Mr. Darcy so lost to honor that he would make me an offer neither legal nor moral. Nor can I believe you would wish him to marry your daughter, were he truly so reprehensible."

"Miss Bennet," Lady Catherine said, her frown deepening, "I had hoped you might be innocent in all this. Clearly, that is not the case. Darcy knows his duty. You must have drawn him in."

If only she knew. "I have done no such thing."

Lady Catherine continued as though Elizabeth had not spoken. "You cannot have your father's consent, and as you are not one and twenty, you are therefore not engaged. I insist you give up this fraudulent arrangement now. You have my word I shall never speak of it to another soul."

It took some effort not to laugh. *I suppose she imagines herself gracious.* "Your nephew did inform me you have long desired a union between himself and his cousin. Under the present circumstance your frustration is understandable, and you have my pity. But neither he nor you have said he is legally obligated to his cousin. If he is free to make his own choice, then I am free to accept him."

"Impudent child! If you were sensible of your own good, you would not wish to quit the sphere in which you have been brought up." Lady Catherine's face filled Elizabeth's vision. "Your father is a nobody, your mother is a vulgar, common woman, and your younger sisters are undisciplined and uneducated. The youngest not sixteen and already a hoyden! Oh yes, I know the truth. Is my nephew to suffer such relations? No! It cannot be."

Elizabeth took a deep breath. "If Mr. Darcy does not object to my connections, then they can be nothing to you."

"On the contrary. I am one of his nearest relations, and I cannot permit him to be taken in by the upstart pretensions of a shameless Jezebel!"

Elizabeth surged to her feet. "Lady Catherine, I cannot know how Mr. Darcy will respond to this attempt to interfere in his affairs, but I am under no obligation to tolerate your insults. I bid you good day."

She stalked out of the room and past the two gentlemen waiting in the hall, ignoring Lady Catherine's imperious commands. Plucking her bonnet and pelisse from the hands of the waiting footman, she continued directly through the front door.

Mr. Darcy was close behind her. "Elizabeth, wait! What did my aunt say?" He looked at her intently, his expression a mixture of concern and simmering anger.

"About my family? Nothing you did not also say."

His eyes widened. "Wait, please. Allow me to accompany you."

From inside the house came Lady Catherine's bellow: "Darcy! I wish to speak to you this instant!"

"Perhaps you should hear it for yourself," said Elizabeth. "You may call upon me later, when my temper has cooled." She set off without a backward glance, making for her favorite walk and the shaded grove.

An hour later Mr. Darcy entered the grove, the stallion beneath him blowing hard. His ferocious scowl eased when he caught sight of her. *His interview was equally pleasant, then.*

"Elizabeth. I hoped to find you here." He dismounted. "Will you walk to the stream? Caesar needs a drink."

She fell in beside him; neither spoke. To her surprise, when they reached the stream Mr. Darcy crouched beside the water and doffed his hat, splashing his face and hair.

"I must apologize for my ungenerous words about your family last evening," he said at length. "Not until I heard the same sentiments from Lady Catherine's lips did I understand how offensive they must have been to you. What she said of *you* is unpardonable." He scowled again, then sighed. "Your generosity in accepting me, despite the appalling nature of my proposal, is unparalleled. That you did not throw off the engagement in the face of my aunt's rudeness is even more extraordinary."

She could hardly meet his eyes. "I was angry with you last evening, to be sure. On further reflection, however, I was forced to admit the justice of what you said, and not only about the inferiority of my connections. My family's behavior is often mortifying. At Mr. Bingley's ball at Netherfield, I believe every one of them managed to expose themselves to ridicule."

"Nay. If it brings you any comfort, you and your sister Jane have always conducted yourselves in a most ladylike manner. And as you have witnessed, I also have relations of whom I must be ashamed."

"Dearest Jane! She has always been the best of us, though she is not herself since you all quitted Netherfield last November. In her last letter she nearly asked me outright to come home. Being Jane, she naturally declared it a selfish impulse and told me to stay where I am."

His brows knitted. "Why does she desire you to return home?"

"My father is ill. Pneumonia. Her letter did not suggest he was in grave danger, but she bears the burden of caring for him and all the family alone. I would help her, but I have not the means to return early."

He snorted. "You most certainly do. I shall be happy to convey you home with all possible speed."

* * *

They were gone from Rosings before two hours had passed. Elizabeth was doubly grateful for Mr. Darcy's alacrity, as it saved her from the misery of Mr. Collins's company.

Having heard all his patroness had to say on the subject of the engagement, Mr. Collins hurried back to the parsonage to forcefully represent to Elizabeth the inadvisability of marrying against Lady Catherine's wishes. He evidently assumed any degree of notice and condescension from such a great lady must cause Elizabeth to feel a sense of gratitude and obligation.

She rolled her eyes. *What a preposterous notion!*

Elizabeth allowed Mr. Collins's words to flow past her as she packed her trunks. He followed her through the house, scarcely pausing for breath; his entreaties for Charlotte's agreement were met only with noncommittal replies.

When Mr. Darcy's carriage was at the door, Elizabeth finally interrupted her cousin's exhortations to inquire if he had a message for her parents, given the worrisome state of her father's health. Red-faced, he stammered out his best wishes for a speedy recovery. She was spared a return to the subject of Mr. Darcy by the presence of the man himself; judging by his countenance, he had overheard some of Mr. Collins's pronouncements.

Elizabeth embraced Charlotte and bade farewell to Mr. Collins with as much cordiality as she could muster before escaping into the carriage. After her cousin's uninterrupted sermonizing, Mr. Darcy's awkward silence was a blessed relief.

They arrived at Longbourn before noon the following day. Elizabeth had scarcely alighted when her youngest sisters Kitty and Lydia came out to meet them.

"Why Lizzy, what do you do here?" asked Lydia. "And with Mr. Darcy, too?"

"Mr. Darcy was kind enough to convey me home. You did not expect me to stay away with Papa ill, surely."

Kitty embraced her. "Jane shall be glad of your help. With Papa sick and Mamma keeping to her room, Jane has hardly slept or eaten."

"Then I am pleased to have been of service," said Mr. Darcy. "I shall leave you to see to your family, Miss Bennet. May I call tomorrow?"

"Yes, thank you, Mr. Darcy. I am excessively grateful to you."

Lydia watched him go. "La, how strange! I suppose it was kind of him to bring you, but what cause has he to stay with Mr. Bingley still gone out of the country?"

"Perhaps he is violently in love with Lizzy!" Kitty giggled.

"What a laugh that would be! As though a stick in the mud could be violently in love with anyone!"

Elizabeth's reply was forestalled by Jane, who flew down the stairs and threw her arms around Elizabeth. "Oh, Lizzy! I am so happy you are home! I feared we should not see you for weeks yet!"

Kitty had spoken true; their beautiful elder sister looked exhausted and thin. Elizabeth knew it would do no good to insist that Jane eat, so she did the next best thing. "I came as soon as I could," she said. "You must tell me how Papa is doing, but let us talk over luncheon. I am famished!"

Jane was eager to share the good news. "Papa's fever finally broke overnight," she said. "Dr. Burke examined Papa this morning and declared him out of danger, though he remains weak and short of breath. Dr. Burke says his lungs may never fully recover." Jane's countenance shifted from relief to worried exasperation. "Mrs. Hill is giving him some broth now, and he insists on getting out of bed afterward."

"It has been excessively dull to be always stuck indoors with a sick person, though Mamma is not half so ill as she would have us believe," said Lydia. "Now you are home, Lizzy, perhaps Kitty and I might go to Meryton."

"Perhaps tomorrow, Lydia." It would not do to have her bored younger sisters around when Mr. Darcy called. *Though how am I to explain his continued presence with Papa too ill to receive him?*

After luncheon, Elizabeth and Jane found their father seated next to the window in his bedchamber. Elizabeth sat next to him, unable to tear her eyes away.

Papa looked up from the letter in his hands. "Well, Lizzy! I am glad you are come back, though I fear you have made the journey to no purpose. Burke tells me I am on the mend." His brow lifted as he took in Elizabeth's expression. "I look that bad, do I? Yes, well, I suppose I must."

"Are you certain you are well enough to be out of bed?"

"I am certain I cannot tolerate laying there another moment. Besides," he said with a meaningful glance at Jane, "your sister shall never allow me to read in peace unless I make some effort at improvement."

Jane smiled. "If you can tease me then you are certainly improved."

"I have no wish to dwell on my own infirmity," Papa said. "What of you, Lizzy? How was your time in Kent? Were Lady Catherine and Rosings everything you hoped after hearing my cousin's description?"

"Mr. Collins certainly did justice to the sixty-four windows and grand chimney-pieces at Rosings, but he failed to mention how beautiful the grounds are! There are some lovely woods nearby. I became quite fond of a snug little grove near the parsonage."

"And Lady Catherine?"

"She is as attentive to the details of everybody's lives as our cousin led me to expect, and she never withholds her advice."

"Indeed! Mr. Collins has proven to be a valuable correspondent. His letters always seem to contain something to interest or amuse. In fact, this letter just arrived express." He indicated the pages still in his hand. "I find it exceedingly interesting. Perhaps you may guess the subject."

Likely a repetition of everything he said to me yesterday, Elizabeth thought. It appeared there was nothing for it but to tell her father now about her engagement. She nodded reluctantly.

"Jane, please allow me to speak with Lizzy alone," Papa said.

Elizabeth took her sister's hand. "No, please stay. I prefer to discuss this only once."

"As you will." Papa fixed her with a stern look. "Tell us, then, is Mr. Collins's information to be trusted? Are you truly engaged to Mr. Darcy?"

Jane gasped. "What? No, Lizzy, it cannot be!"

"It is true," Elizabeth sighed. "He asked three nights ago. After careful consideration, I accepted him the following day. Lady Catherine was not pleased."

"But why? Have you not always hated him?"

It was easier to answer Jane than to look into her father's forbidding countenance. "Indeed, and I was certain he hated me. When he told me he loved me, you could have knocked me over with a feather! It forced me to reconsider everything I believed of him."

"You do not love him, surely!"

"No. He knows I do not love him. But his friends have always spoken well of him, and he has been exceedingly kind and attentive these last few days. Apologetic, even! Lady Catherine must have shared with him what she said to me about the inferiority of my connections. I have never seen him look so angry. He apologized very handsomely for his own words on that subject."

"What of his foul treatment of Mr. Wickham?" Papa asked. "Your opinion on that topic was decided, I recall."

Elizabeth's face heated. "I thought of what you said, Papa, that Mr. Darcy might prove no more of a villain than any rich man who is used to his own way. And you, Jane. You always insisted his friends could not be so deceived in him. Perhaps there is more to the story of what happened between them than we know."

"It was very wrong of Mr. Wickham to go about blackening Mr. Darcy's name when he could not defend himself," said Jane.

"He did, didn't he?" Elizabeth started. *Did not Mr. Wickham tell me he would never expose the son because of the love he bore the father?* Yet Mr. Wickham had told his tale of woe to her, an acquaintance of only half an hour, after she boldly declared Mr. Darcy disagreeable. Then, within just days after Mr. Darcy's departure, the entire neighborhood seemed to know the story of how he spitefully refused to honor his late father's will to provide for his father's godson.

Her blush deepened. "The more I think on Mr. Darcy, the more I believe I judged him too harshly."

"That is hardly sufficient foundation for a marriage." Papa's voice was hard. Elizabeth avoided his gaze.

"Lizzy, you have always said only the deepest love could induce you into matrimony," Jane said gently. "We all understood when you refused Mr. Collins — well, Mamma did not, but Mamma wishes more for security than affection for us. I never expected you to marry a wealthy man you do not like."

Elizabeth shrugged. "I did say that. But I also said at least one of us must marry very well, with Longbourn entailed to Mr. Collins." *It should have been you, Jane,* she thought, but she would not injure her sister by speaking of Mr. Bingley. "For a man of Mr. Darcy's stature to propose... Jane, no inducement but love could have made him do it! I cannot now say I hate Mr. Darcy, and I believe I may come to truly esteem him."

"Elizabeth, I beg you to reconsider," Papa said. "Let me not have the grief of seeing you unable to respect your partner in life."

Elizabeth silently examined her father. *He looks old,* she realized. He was thin and pallid, his breathing raspy and short. A frown carved deep lines into his face and his hair was entirely gray. *When did the brown disappear?* His clothing hung loosely, as though he had lost considerable weight in the weeks she had been gone. *His lungs may never recover,* Jane had said.

"Speak to him, Papa," she said. "I have endeavored to look beyond my initial opinion of him. I ask only that you do the same. If you can be satisfied by what he says, then I am content to accept him."

Her father's mouth pressed into a thin line. "He is to call tomorrow, I presume?" At her nod he sighed. "I shall see what he has to say for himself. If you are determined to do this, I shall not deny you, so long as I am convinced he will treat you with the care and respect you deserve."

"Thank you, Papa."

Three

Courtship

$\mathcal{A}$FTER BREAKFAST the next morning, Jane sent Kitty and Lydia to Meryton with instructions to purchase items from at least three separate shops. Mary sat with their mother, who had not yet left her room. Elizabeth was grateful: when Mr. Darcy called he need speak only to herself, Jane, and her father.

Lizzy had importuned Jane to say nothing of her engagement for now. She could not bear the thought of her mother's voluble delight over Mr. Darcy's income of ten thousand a year, particularly before her father had given his consent. Faced with such a prospect, Jane readily agreed.

Mr. Darcy called early, as expected. Jane greeted him warmly and he asked after her health with kind solicitude, his manners relaxing immediately when he learned he should not encounter Elizabeth's mother or her other sisters this morning. After ten minutes of easy conversation, he sought out her father in his book-room.

Jane stared after him for several moments. "Do you know, Lizzy, even I doubted you last evening. But Mr. Darcy was so friendly just now, I begin to be of your opinion."

"I am as astonished as you are, Jane. Colonel Fitzwilliam did say he could be lively in other places, but I did not truly believe it. I hope we shall see more of this Mr. Darcy!"

"Was he not lively at Rosings, then?" Jane's smile was impish.

Elizabeth laughed. "Nobody is lively at Rosings!"

They sat together with the mending basket while they waited. Jane prodded Elizabeth to say more about her time in Kent. Elizabeth filled the next twenty minutes with tales of Lady Catherine and Rosings, the Collinses and Hunsford parsonage. She had not expected the gentlemen's conference to be brief, but when more than half an hour passed with no sign of Mr. Darcy, she began to be concerned.

Mr. Darcy emerged twenty minutes later, his countenance shuttered. He must have read anxiety in her face, however, for he seemed to give himself a little shake and smiled. "I am sorry to have kept you waiting, Elizabeth. I thought perhaps we might walk to Oakham Mount this morning. The day is very fine."

"Should I not go to my father?"

"Your father asked me to tell you he wishes to rest now and shall see you after luncheon."

"Then I shall be pleased to walk with you. Jane, will you not join us?"

"Nay, Lizzy, Oakham Mount is too far for me. Please go and enjoy yourself. I am very well here."

Mr. Darcy was silent and thoughtful as they set out. Elizabeth's curiosity was intense, but she knew not how to inquire what had passed between him and her father. He caught her looking, however, and chuckled.

"You are clearly bursting to ask me what your father said. Very well, I shall tell you, though in truth it was I who did most of the talking." He shook his head. "I was not prepared for such a thorough interrogation, I confess. He asked about my parents' marriage, and why I wished to marry you. He inquired minutely about the likely reactions of my family and society, and what plans I had made to ensure your successful introduction. We also discussed the settlement, of course."

"I should have warned you, I suppose."

"Nay, you are obviously dear to him. Naturally he wishes to know you shall be well cared for." He smiled. "I intend to be equally rigorous whenever a young man comes to me about Georgiana."

Elizabeth laughed. "I have no doubt you shall do all in your power to frighten the poor man out of his wits."

"Certainly. If he loves her enough to face me, he might be worthy of her. Heaven help him if Richard gets his hands on him."

"Is the colonel truly so ferocious?"

"Yes. Richard and I were appointed Georgiana's guardians upon my father's death. I may be fearsome, but he can be truly terrifying."

"I must take you at your word. I have seen nothing of it."

There was a brief silence. "I must say I am surprised your father agreed to see me today," Mr. Darcy said suddenly. "You mentioned he has been ill. He does not yet look fully recovered."

"You are too polite to say he appears very ill. He is on the mend, however. As you said, I am dear to him, and he does not know you well enough to give his consent solely on the strength of my recommendation."

"We should marry quickly if it will set his mind at ease. I could procure a special license."

Papa must have given his consent, then. She smiled. "I do not think he would forgive you for taking me out of the country before he has recovered. By all means, procure the license if you think it best, but I should prefer to wait until Papa can walk me down the aisle."

"Very well. I shall go to London this afternoon; then we need not wait if your father takes a turn for the worse. If he continues to recover, so much the better — your mother shall have the pleasure of planning an extravagant wedding-breakfast with too many guests. Every mother I know seems to delight in such things."

"I shall wait to tell her of our engagement until you have gone, so you need not hear her effusions."

His smile was pained. "I thank you."

After Mr. Darcy's departure, Elizabeth sought out her father. Papa was in his chair by the window when she entered his room. She was pleased to see he was reading, and his color was improved.

"Well, Lizzy, I have done as you asked," he said as she kissed his cheek. "I cannot say I am satisfied by a union that begins with such unequal affection, but his attachment to you appears genuine, and he is not a reprobate. I have given him my consent."

"How do you know he is not a reprobate?"

He lifted a brow. "I made some inquiries that are not suitable for a young lady's ears. He would like to marry immediately, of course, but I would encourage you to press for a long engagement. You would do well to learn if you can feel anything more for him than you do at present. If you cannot, I would strongly advise you not to go through with it. Better a broken engagement than a miserable marriage."

"Thank you, Papa. I will do my best."

* * *

Mr. Darcy remained in London for several days. On the third morning of his absence, Elizabeth sat with her father in his bedchamber; Papa's strength had been slow to return and he frequently did not venture downstairs until the afternoon. Looking up from his paper he wryly remarked, "Mr. Darcy has anticipated me, I see. Not only is your engagement prominently announced, Lizzy, but the society editor filled an entire column bemoaning the loss of such a fine prospect from the marriage market."

Elizabeth read over his shoulder, rolling her eyes as she finished. "From this description I appear to be a mysterious foreign bidder who carried away the prize steer at auction. I cannot imagine Mr. Darcy enjoys being described in such a way."

"For a man in his position it is an inevitability, I fear. What concerns me is the publicity."

Of course, Elizabeth thought. *I cannot now break the engagement without the sort of public censure that will reflect poorly on my sisters as well as myself.* But her determination to marry Mr. Darcy increased every time Papa suggested she should not, so she made no reply.

Following his return to Hertfordshire, Mr. Darcy was received graciously at Longbourn. To Elizabeth's great relief, her mother was too much in awe of her future son-in-law to say much in his presence, and her younger sisters often found occupation elsewhere.

Over the next few weeks his visits fell into a pleasant pattern. In the mornings he usually sat with Elizabeth and Jane, sometimes making an effort at conversation and sometimes reading as the ladies sewed, though during such times Elizabeth often felt his eyes on her. Occasionally he would spend an hour with Papa in his book-room; he generally emerged from these discussions looking thoughtful.

In the afternoons he would accompany Elizabeth on a long ramble, and she was astonished to discover he could be easy — even playful! — when it was just the two of them. He told her in great detail of Pemberley, his family's estate for generations; his pride and care for the place and its people were readily evident as he described its beauties.

"Richard and I spent many a summer running through the woods and swimming in the lake as boys," he said on one of these afternoons. "We even built a tree-fort one year, with old Wickham's help. Mr. Wickham's father was Pemberley's steward then. He was an excellent man. He declared himself exceedingly pleased to assist us in any endeavor that would confine our antics to the trees." Mr. Darcy laughed. "We got into some particularly fine scrapes that summer, as I recall."

Elizabeth waited, but he did not elaborate. "Will you not tell me what they were?"

"Nay, I do not think I shall. Not yet, at any rate. I believe you should hear Mrs. Reynolds's version first, and then I shall tell you the rest."

"Mrs. Reynolds is —?"

"Pemberley's housekeeper. She and her husband came to Pemberley when I was four." He grinned. "Whenever Richard and I returned home covered in mud and brambles Mrs. Reynolds always caught us, no matter how careful we were to evade detection."

"Did you suffer many lectures about smudging her clean floors?"

He shook his head, his expression fond. "She tried, but her heart was never in it."

Elizabeth studied him. "I confess, I have great difficulty picturing you as a rambunctious, mud-covered boy. You are always so serious."

"I can well believe it." His smile was self-deprecating. "I am never easy among strangers. Bingley says I am overfond of brooding silences, but it is only that I find it difficult to catch the flow of others' conversation. At Pemberley it is different. Only there am I entirely comfortable."

"I shall never know you until I have seen you there, I suppose."

"One of the many reasons I look forward to returning with you at my side."

Elizabeth blushed, but made no response. He had lately made many such statements, which served only to remind her how unequal were her own feelings. She cast about for another topic. "You mentioned your sister is also shy."

"Yes, I fear Georgiana has little need or opportunity to exert herself. She is happiest seated before her pianoforte, playing to an empty room. Aunt Eleanor insisted Georgiana must learn to ride — if for no other reason than it requires her to interact with other people, I believe — and she has surprised us all by taking to it like a duck to water."

"Aunt Eleanor is your cousin Richard's mother, correct?"

"Yes. My cousin Arthur is Uncle Henry's heir and Richard is the second son. I fancy Aunt Eleanor must have wished for a daughter, for she dotes on Arthur's wife and has been of invaluable help with Georgiana since my father died. It cannot surprise you to hear I had no notion what to do with a girl of only eleven years."

Elizabeth laughed. "What, do they teach the young men nothing of child-rearing at university? What a shameful oversight in your education!"

"I am in complete agreement," he said without hesitation. "I shall send a strongly-worded letter to the president of the college this very day."

Is this the man his friends and cousin described? Elizabeth wondered. *I could almost call him amiable!* "How old is Georgiana now?" she asked.

"She is but fifteen. I have ordered a Broadwood grand pianoforte for her birthday in July; Georgiana's London music-master has been hinting about the superiority of the new six-octave instruments for some time." He smiled. "I shall hope to hear you play as well, naturally."

"You are too kind. My meager skill is no match for such a fine instrument."

"Nonsense. It always gives me great pleasure to hear you. I shall certainly entreat you to favor us with a song after dinner this evening. Several, in fact."

Elizabeth's mother had insisted on giving a dinner party to celebrate their engagement; Longbourn would be filled to bursting with members of every prominent local family.

Elizabeth lifted a knowing brow at Mr. Darcy. "I suppose it is merely coincidence that such a display on my part shall make it unnecessary for you to engage in conversation with my neighbors?"

"Entirely so," he said with only the tiniest twitch at the corners of his mouth. "Though if Sir William Lucas seeks to engage me on the subject of St. James's court, I shall be driven to beg your sister Mary to play a jig, that I might dance with you."

"Dancing, Mr. Darcy? That would indeed be extreme!"

"Desperate times call for desperate measures, my dear."

* * *

"Well, Lizzy," said her mother that evening after their guests departed, "I believe we had a very successful dinner. The lamb was cooked to a turn — everybody said so. And your Mr. Darcy was so gallant!"

"Indeed, he did not openly ignore even one of your guests, Mrs. Bennet," said Papa. "One might be forgiven for forgetting what a proud, disagreeable man he was last year."

"How can you be so tiresome? He is merely reserved. Besides, what cause had he then to give consequence to those so far beneath him in society? None at all."

Elizabeth stared at her mother. Apparently, it required only an engagement to her daughter for Mamma to overthrow all her former dislike of Mr. Darcy. *His ten thousand pounds a year must positively endear him to her*, Elizabeth thought.

Her own feelings were far murkier. When they were alone his behavior was everything she could wish: warm, attentive, and respectful. She was particularly grateful for his restraint in displays of affection. He never intruded upon her or pressed her to show more than she felt, though his regard was evident.

In company, however, he remained stiff and silent. This evening he had spoken with ease only to herself, her father, and Jane. During dinner Papa had broached the subject of Pemberley's library; Mr. Darcy spoke with enthusiasm about a German treatise on ancient Rome he hoped to purchase when it was published, impervious to the general disinterest of his dinner companions about such an arcane subject.

Hoping to turn the conversation, Elizabeth had laughed. "Pemberley shall never succeed in properly wooing me if its library contains only dusty tomes about dead civilizations."

"Aha! Finally she gives me some encouragement!" he had said. "Tell me which dusty tomes you would prefer to see on my shelves and it shall be done."

To everyone else he was perfectly cordial, but made no attempt at conversation — indeed, he said as little as civility allowed. He kept his promise to entreat several songs from her, remaining near the pianoforte to hear her performance, and otherwise stationed himself at her side or Jane's. It pleased her to see him unbend in Jane's company, but Elizabeth still saw wistfulness in Jane's countenance and could not entirely forgive his brotherly cordiality to the sister whose prospects he had blasted.

Even more disconcerting was his behavior as he departed tonight. By Mamma's contrivance Mr. Darcy was the last to go, and there was nobody in the hall when Elizabeth escorted him to the door. He bowed low over her hand, wordlessly pressing his lips to her fingers for a very long moment before taking his leave. She wished him a breathless good-night, a flush suffusing her body, the sensation of his kiss lingering on her skin long after he was gone.

The following day he was not expected until the afternoon. Elizabeth spent an exhausting morning battling her mother, whose plans for the wedding-breakfast grew more elaborate by the day. Mary, Kitty and Lydia had walked into Meryton to escape the argument, but Jane had stayed, attempting to soften Elizabeth's complaints of pretension and Mamma's accusations of ingratitude.

When she spied Mr. Darcy approaching on horseback, Elizabeth fled the house, eager to keep him out of doors and away from her mother. Her step faltered as she caught sight of his countenance. He had not looked at her with such agitated hauteur since the ball at Netherfield last November, when she had prodded him to speak of Mr. Wickham.

Mr. Darcy dismounted, shaking his head as the man-servant began to lead his mount to the stable. "No. Keep him here. I shall not remain long. Miss Bennet," he said, glancing at her, "perhaps you will take a turn with me." He strode off toward the wide expanse of lawn bordered by trees without waiting for her reply.

'Miss Bennet?' Elizabeth hurried after him. *What on earth could have happened?*

She was not kept long in suspense.

"Why did you consent to marry me?" he demanded, rounding on her as she reached the little copse of trees.

"What? I — Why do you ask?"

"As you know, I spent the morning attending to business correspondence. My room at the inn overlooks the street, and I opened the window to enjoy the breeze. Your younger sisters were talking in the street below. Lydia spoke of us freely, though I doubt she knew I overheard. Do tell me, Miss Bennet: did you choose to sacrifice your future happiness, to marry a man you despise?"

She stared at him, unable to form words.

"Well? Did you?"

"Please, Mr. Darcy, I do not understand."

"'Mr. Darcy.' I should have known! Never once have you called me by my name." He turned, speaking to the trees. "I did not wish to believe it when I heard Lydia this morning, laughing that you were to marry a man you always hated. I know how little she heeds the dictates of propriety. I thought she was joking until your aunt Mrs. Phillips said you have never been shy with your opinion." His hands clenched into fists. "Is it true? Did you tell all of Meryton you hate me?"

How could she deny it? "I did, but that was when —"

He whirled to face her again, his expression scornful. "You are a remarkable actress, madam. I never suspected. When you said your feelings were not the equal of mine, I was fool enough to believe you held me in some affection, at least."

Elizabeth's face was aflame. "I do not hate you." Her eyes fell. "Not anymore." She opened her mouth to elaborate, but her voice died. What could she say? '*I have come to enjoy your company, and I believe I might truly like you?*' *That would only add insult to injury.* She certainly did not love him.

He let out a bark of contemptuous laughter. "A fine concession! You hated me when we met two months ago in Kent, if your sister speaks truly." A thought struck him. "Was that why you could not give me an answer at once? Did you spend the night convincing yourself to accept me?"

Elizabeth would not have believed it possible, but her cheeks burned even redder. "Yes. I —" She took a deep breath and plowed on. "I was surprised by your proposal, as I told you. I was angry, too. It was... some time before I could think on it rationally. Surely you must see how foolish I would have been to refuse."

"Then it is as your sister Mary said? You sacrificed yourself, that one of you might marry a wealthy man?"

Elizabeth stared down at her hands, clasped so tightly the knuckles were white. "Yes," she whispered. In the furious silence that followed she brought her eyes to his. "Please, allow me to explain."

"No explanation is necessary, Miss Bennet. It seems Lady Catherine was correct after all." His voice carried a flat, distant note. "I vowed long ago never to marry a woman who desired only my money. I have spent half my life evading the mercenary wiles of fortune-hunters. Fool that I am, I threw myself in your path because you were clever enough never to seem as though you were throwing yourself in mine."

"Nay, Mr. Darcy, I never —"

"I cannot now throw you off without injuring my own honor." He drew himself up. His face bore the contemptuous expression he had worn the first time she saw him, when he had called her *not handsome enough to tempt him* at the Meryton assembly. "I keep my commitments, though I might wish it otherwise. I shall return on the appointed day and make arrangements that we might see as little of each other as possible after we marry. Until then, madam." He gave her a perfunctory bow and stalked away, ignoring her attempts to call out to him. Moments later he was astride his horse and racing out of the courtyard.

Elizabeth sank to the ground, heedless of her skirts. *What am I to do now?*

Four

Wedding Preparations

*F*OLLOWING Mr. Darcy's furious departure Elizabeth set out for Oakham Mount; the walk was long and she needed solitude.

On reflection, she could not be surprised by Mr. Darcy's reaction to learning of her very public dislike. *Mr. Wickham was right about him after all — his wretched pride dictates all his actions! And what could be a greater blow to his pride than this?*

Elizabeth could not even fault her family for believing she still hated Mr. Darcy. She had told nobody of her increasingly unsettled feelings.

She picked up a long branch and wielded it against the bushes she passed, lopping off green leaves with every broad sweep. *If only he had permitted me to explain! How could he believe Lady Catherine? Should not a man who loves me wish to hear me?*

He had accused her of being an actress. *An actress! I never once feigned affection I did not feel! Am I to blame if he cannot perceive how his own behavior offends others? Would he have preferred I tell him to his face how little disposed I was to like him after his rudeness to me and all my family?* She swung her stick with all her might against a tree, breaking it in two.

Yes, said the small voice in the back of her mind. *He would have preferred the truth. Why should he wish to tie himself forever to someone who despises him? Why should anyone?*

She should be grateful, she supposed, that he had not chosen to break their engagement. Had he done so, her reputation would have been irrevocably ruined.

She sighed. *Should I release him?* It might be better for them both, given his vow to ensure they saw nothing of one another.

Surely he would not banish me! He needs an heir. Besides, how could I release him? Though she knew it to be selfish and mercenary, the simple fact was they had spent a great deal of time alone, and people would make certain assumptions. If their engagement ended — no matter which of them broke it off — neither her reputation nor her family's fortunes would survive.

Perhaps, once the fury of the moment was past, she might persuade him that they could still enjoy an amicable union. *Surely that must be superior to a lifetime of estrangement? I do not truly hate him.*

By the time Elizabeth returned to Longbourn the sun was nearly down and she had made her decision: she would play for time. She informed her family that Mr. Darcy was obliged to go to town on a matter of business, avoiding Jane's too-discerning gaze, and retired early. *I must give his temper time to cool before I write to him,* she decided.

Unbidden, a memory came to her mind: Mr. Darcy, in the drawing-room at Netherfield last autumn, confessing to a resentful temper that rarely forgave. She shuddered, stomach coiling into knots as she crawled into bed.

In the following days Elizabeth attempted to behave as though nothing was amiss. Jane suspected something, she knew; her sister watched her with a thoughtful expression, though she did not press Elizabeth for details.

Jane never spoke of her own disappointed hopes, but Elizabeth could see her quiet suffering whenever Mamma declared Mr. Bingley would surely return with Mr. Darcy to throw himself at Jane's feet. Elizabeth thought this highly unlikely, but her mother clearly hoped to best their neighbor Lady Lucas, Charlotte's mother, by having two daughters advantageously married.

When Mr. Darcy had been gone four days Elizabeth wrote her letter. She pitched it into the fire, however, after attempting to read it from Mr. Darcy's perspective; she could not abide what now seemed a wheedling, insincere tone. It took three more tries before she did not instantly wish to consign her own words to the flames; by that time six days had passed since his departure. She set the letter aside, vowing to send it in the morning if she did not burn it.

The following morning Elizabeth imagined herself a wealthy but reticent man who had recently discovered the woman he loved enough to marry, despite her lack of fortune and connections, did not even like him. In this frame of mind she read her letter again.

Longbourn, 22nd May 1812

Dear Mr. Darcy,

You may wonder what I might possibly have to say after our last meeting. To own the truth, it has taken me some time to write this, but write I must — you lay a serious charge at my door. I shall hope my faith in your honor is not misplaced and that you shall hear my defense.

I stand accused of using feminine wiles to entrap you — specifically the ploy of making no apparent attempt to endear myself to you. A fine accusation, as I appear equally guilty whether or not my aim was marriage. My only defense is to reveal the truth I previously withheld, which you may choose to reject as falsehood. I pray you consider that I have no cause to lie about what I am about to disclose.

It was very evident, when we were introduced at the Meryton assembly last September, that you thought little of the company in which you found yourself. In subsequent months I saw nothing to suggest you had any desire for my good opinion. You were generally civil but took pains to ensure I knew where I stood — inescapably far beneath you.

I now know your feelings were far warmer than I believed them to be at the time, but given what I observed, I could not be disposed to like you and believed the sentiment was mutual. I was therefore, as I said, greatly surprised by your proposal. I had no idea of your having any such affections, and I certainly did not seek them.

Indeed, had I sought only security, I should not have pinned my hopes on such an unlikely occurrence as receiving an offer of marriage from a man in your position. I would, instead, have accepted my cousin Mr. Collins when he applied for my hand last November, on the very day Mr. Bingley departed Netherfield.

I hardly need tell you how ill-suited I am to be Mr. Collins's wife — whatever you might think of me, I should hope you know enough of my temper to see that for yourself. I therefore refused him, over my mother's strenuous objection. With that decision it was assured that Longbourn will pass out of the Bennet family upon my father's death. I fully expected I would end a spinster aunt or governess or some such, but it was nevertheless the best choice. Mr. Collins is much happier with my dearest friend Charlotte than he could ever have been with me.

With you — once I recovered from my astonishment — I was willing to hope for better. When I decided to accept you I knew I must give over my dislike, and then you were so altered I felt as though I were meeting an entirely different man.

Naturally I did not share any of this with you. How was I to say, "I was certain we hated each other before, and I hardly know what to think now" without being needlessly hurtful?

I am sorry I was so free with my uncharitable opinion last autumn. That it has become hurtful now, when I no longer feel the same way, is mortifying. I have no wish to hurt you. Nor do I desire an estranged marriage. If you can give any credence to what I have written, perhaps we may begin again.

I travel to London next week and shall stay a month with my aunt and uncle Gardiner in Gracechurch Street. I cannot imagine you have plans to be in London at this time of year, but if you are, I hope you will call on me there.

Yours ever,

Elizabeth Bennet

* * *

Elizabeth's stomach churned as her uncle's coach made its way to one of the best addresses in London's fashionable Mayfair district. She was not at all prepared for this evening.

Mr. Darcy's reply to her letter had given her no indication of anything — she could not tell if he believed a word she said, nor if he ever expected to see her again after the wedding — and he had not called in Gracechurch Street. So the invitation to dinner at Darcy House, coming as it did with gracious sentiments about meeting her aunt and uncle and introducing her to his sister, was wholly unexpected.

I suppose he has simply decided to maintain appearances, she told herself. *Surely if he desired more he would have said something before now.* But her rebellious stomach declared she had not succeeded in fooling herself. She had no idea what he desired. Elizabeth knew not how she would manage even a single bite this evening.

Elizabeth had been in London for nearly a month already. Mamma had sent her here ostensibly to buy wedding clothes with her aunt's assistance; Elizabeth expected Mamma's primary desire was to arrange the wedding-breakfast without interference from the bride. Despite her trepidation on that score, Elizabeth was grateful for the respite from home. She had spent many happy days playing with her young cousins, shopping with her aunt, and taking in the sights at Hyde Park and Kensington Gardens, but she had never ventured to Mayfair.

The coach stopped before a large and stately home. As Elizabeth alighted and took in her surroundings — the fine carriages, clean streets, elegant stone façades, and of course the graceful lawns and plantings of the park at Grosvenor Square — she was struck with gratitude for her aunt's insistence that she choose silk instead of muslin for her evening gowns. Never had she been so aware of her social inferiority. She had to force herself not to smooth imaginary wrinkles from her ivory skirts, but she refused to quaver. She lifted her chin and pasted a smile on her features as they were ushered inside.

Mr. Darcy waited in a tastefully appointed drawing-room with a girl about Lydia's age and an older woman: his sister Georgiana and her companion, a Mrs. Annesley. Georgiana was as fair as Mr. Darcy was dark, with pale blond curls and translucent skin. Had Elizabeth not seen them together she would not have known them for siblings, but they shared the same straight nose and deep-set eyes — his brown, hers gray. Mr. Darcy greeted them cordially and smiled encouragingly at his sister to do the same; her voice, when she finally spoke, was almost inaudible.

During the meal her Aunt and Uncle Gardiner and Mrs. Annesley carried the conversation. Mr. Darcy said little, and Elizabeth could hardly get more than a monosyllable from Georgiana, even on the topic of music. Mrs. Annesley proved to be a well-bred and well-traveled woman, which delighted Elizabeth's aunt and uncle; tales of Scotland and Portugal filled the largest part of the evening.

Elizabeth did her best to eat. Her stomach still threatened to rebel, so she took tiny bites of the blandest dishes and hoped her lack of appetite would go unnoticed. Eventually the last dishes were cleared away. It was only owing to Mrs. Annesley's gentle prodding that Georgiana recalled her duty to signal the ladies' departure from the table, and the girl appeared paralyzed by indecision once they returned to the drawing-room.

Mr. Wickham was mistaken, Elizabeth thought. *Mr. Darcy spoke truly — this girl is not proud, only terribly shy.*

Determined to draw her out, Elizabeth inquired gently about riding, a subject about which she knew nothing. By the time the gentlemen joined them, Georgiana was telling Elizabeth about Willow, the sweet-tempered mare Mr. Darcy had given her for her fifteenth birthday.

"An ideal elder brother, then," said Elizabeth, smiling, as Mr. Darcy approached with an inscrutable expression.

Georgiana smiled in return. "Oh, yes! I could not imagine a better or a kinder one."

"You make me feel quite envious. I have no brothers, only four sisters."

"I cannot imagine so many sisters! Was Longbourn very loud when you were children?"

Elizabeth laughed. "Yes, especially after my youngest sister Lydia was born. It still is, in truth. Your brother has been very forbearing."

Mr. Darcy finally spoke. "Are all your sisters still at Longbourn?"

"My youngest sister is at Brighton for the summer," Elizabeth said, wondering at the question. "As a guest of Colonel and Mrs. Forster."

Lydia's letter, gleefully announcing her plans and blithely assuring Elizabeth that missing the wedding was a necessary sacrifice so Lydia might find a husband, had arrived shortly after Elizabeth's arrival in London. Elizabeth had written her father immediately, urging him to reconsider — her sister's impulsive, flirtatious behavior was sure to lead her astray and bring shame upon their family.

Papa did not share her concern. Colonel Forster was a sensible man, he had replied, and Lydia was luckily too poor to be an object of prey to a fortune-hunter. Elizabeth was not reassured but told herself she could do no more. She scarcely acknowledged feeling relief that her wild and willful youngest sister would not be present on her wedding-day.

Mr. Darcy's countenance did not alter at the news of Lydia's removal to Brighton. "Her absence must be keenly felt," he said.

What can he mean? Elizabeth wondered. It must be a slight — she knew too well his opinion of her sister — but his tone was bland. "My sister Kitty misses her greatly. Mamma would be quite beside herself, I believe, were I not so vexing."

"Vexing? That cannot be!" Georgiana said.

Elizabeth flashed a mischievous grin. "I fear it is. Were it only up to my mother, the wedding guests would be so numerous as to spill out of the windows, but I cannot bear the thought of being stared at by so many! We have bickered over it endlessly. I am fortunate to have reinforcements; while I have been in London my sister Jane has been the one to prevent Mamma from inviting half a hundred people I never met."

Elizabeth was certain Mr. Darcy would not wish the church to be packed with strangers either. This must have occurred to him, for he lapsed into silence. She was spared the effort of further conversation when Georgiana applied to her for some music. Though Elizabeth's skill at the pianoforte was limited and her voice unexceptional, she was happy to oblige.

As she finished her first song, she saw nearly identical expressions of thoughtful curiosity on the faces of Mr. Darcy and his sister. *How much does Georgiana know?* Elizabeth wondered. Mr. Darcy's expression remained inscrutable. *I suppose it does not matter. If he no longer likes me, he cannot wish his sister to spend time with me.* She sighed. Returning her attention to the music, she began another song.

The remainder of the evening was equally awkward. Elizabeth had no opportunity for a moment alone with Mr. Darcy, and could not decide if she felt more irritation or relief. He talked of Derbyshire with her aunt, who had grown up there, and of fishing with her uncle. He hovered protectively near Georgiana, who could be enticed to speak about only three topics — music, riding, and Pemberley — and thus Elizabeth's conversation with the man she was to marry strayed no further.

As they returned to Gracechurch street that evening her aunt and uncle praised Mr. Darcy's taste and declared his sister to be sweet, if timid, but said hardly a word about the man himself. She could not wonder at their silence. They knew Elizabeth had not been compromised by Mr. Darcy and the only other plausible reason for the engagement was great affection, of which they had seen no sign. His behavior had been gentlemanly but certainly not that of a lover.

They condemn him with faint praise, Elizabeth thought. *Am I making a terrible mistake?*

* * *

Elizabeth felt a rush of affectionate gratitude the next morning when Aunt Gardiner contrived for the two of them to be alone for part of the morning. The older woman asked no questions, but the invitation for Elizabeth to unburden her heart was obvious. Indeed, Elizabeth nearly did so, but shame and confusion silenced her. Aunt Gardiner could no more easily guess Mr. Darcy's motives than Elizabeth.

And in any event, Elizabeth thought, *it is unthinkable to break the engagement now that I have been introduced to Georgiana and the Darcy House staff.*

After luncheon Elizabeth accompanied her aunt and the children on an outing to Hyde Park, though her mind wandered. *Mr. Darcy did not seem to be keeping Georgiana away from me,* she thought, *but neither did he make any obvious effort to further our acquaintance. He certainly never singled me out, though he stared at me almost as much as he used to.* It was baffling. She knew no more than she had a month ago about his opinion of her, nor even where she was to live after they married.

She was roused from her thoughts when they arrived at the lake and her aunt handed her several large pieces of stale bread. Stammering an apology for her inattentiveness, Elizabeth determined to put Mr. Darcy out of her mind and gave herself over to the cheer of the afternoon's adventure. Standing before the water, breaking off hard crusts of bread for her cousins to throw to the ducks, she tilted her head back to enjoy the sensation of warm sun on her face.

"I say, is that Miss Elizabeth Bennet? I cannot believe my good luck!"

Starting, she found a grinning Charles Bingley standing not ten paces away. "Good day, Mr. Bingley. This is indeed a surprise."

He took in her aunt and cousins. "Good afternoon, Mrs. Gardiner. It is a great pleasure to see you again, but I do not mean to interrupt your outing. Miss Bennet, might I call upon you tomorrow?"

"I shall be returning to Hertfordshire early tomorrow morning, sir." At a slight nod from her aunt she added, "But I should like to explore the rose garden just over there, if you care to join me."

"Delighted!" He fell in beside her. "It seems an age since we last met. Indeed, it must be above seven months! I do not believe I have seen you since we were dancing together at Netherfield last November."

"I believe you must be correct. I hope you and your sisters are well."

"Very well, thank you. And your parents, and all your sisters?"

"Very well, sir."

"You must wonder that I should think myself lucky to find you here. I was just with Darcy, you see. I understand the wedding is but three weeks hence."

"Yes, the ninth of July. Are we to see you there?"

He looked away, clearly discomfited. "I cannot say, Miss Bennet. My plans are not yet firmly settled."

So this is why Mr. Darcy asked after my sisters. He means to keep Mr. Bingley away from Jane. "I see."

They walked in tense silence for several moments. Mr. Bingley halted beneath a large tree with spreading branches, well away from the half-dozen people in the rose garden. "Miss Bennet, I know it is none of my affair, but I must speak. Darcy has been my friend for years, and in all that time I have never seen him display a preference for any lady. That he proposed to you is evidence of his strong attachment. He would never ask this, but if you do not return his regard, I beg you, do not sport with his affections. Free him from this obligation. I shall do all I can to ensure no blame is attached to you."

Elizabeth examined him closely. *'Do not sport with his affections?' How can he justify such hypocrisy?* His expression appeared open and artless. *Nay, he cannot possibly be so ignorant of what he did to her!* Rage boiled up in seconds, born of witnessing Jane's long months of suffering combined with her own frustration and doubt.

"Mr. Bingley," she said without thinking, *"you* are hardly in a position to lecture me on the subject of making sport of another's heart! But I suppose, for young men, it *is* sport. When you go to a new place, do you always seek to attach yourself to the most eligible young lady? Are extra points awarded if she falls in love with you? I cannot suppose you give any thought to the injury you cause when you abandon her. What do young men care for the misery of ladies, or the blame and suspicion they must endure? You have already scored your victory!"

His eyes were round as saucers and the color had fled from his face. "Miss Bennet—" he croaked. "You cannot truly believe I would be so cruel."

"Can I not? I know nothing of the games fashionable people play. I only know you had not been acquainted with my sister three months and your preference for each other's company was obvious to anyone with eyes to see. Then you left Hertfordshire with nary a word and did not return. She is too generous to blame you, but I am not so trusting."

"Do you mean to say — Jane was *not* indifferent to me?"

"*Indifferent?* Was that why you left Hertfordshire? Why you never called in all the time she was in London? Why you have not returned for the summer to a house you have legally rented, and will not stand up with your friend at his own wedding? Because you believe my sister to be *indifferent?*"

Mr. Bingley appeared to collapse. Only the broad trunk of the tree kept him upright. "She was in London?"

Elizabeth gave an unladylike snort. "Yes, for three months after Christmas, but you knew that. Your sister Caroline told Jane you were too much engaged with Mr. Darcy — and his sister — to call."

He surged upright with a vehement shake of his head. "No. No, you must believe me, Miss Bennet. I did not know! If I had known, I would never..." He trailed off as realization dawned on his face.

Elizabeth lifted a brow. "Never dropped her like a hot coal, without taking the trouble to learn for yourself what her feelings were? But you did, Mr. Bingley. Last November."

He looked about to speak again, but she forestalled him. "You need say nothing more. I cannot find I have much sympathy for you. Jane deserves far better than an amiable young man who *makes sport of her affections.* As for your friend's heart, I am certainly not going to explain myself to you. Good day, sir."

Five

For Better For Worse

DAWN BROKE clear and cool on Thursday, the ninth of July. Elizabeth was awake to see the sunrise, tucked into her favorite window-seat with knees drawn up to her chin. Her trunks, stacked neatly by the door, became visible as the night's darkness gave way to the dim light of dawn. The room no longer felt like her own; every book and keepsake was packed with everything else, waiting to go to Pemberley.

There was a soft knock at the door and Jane entered. "I thought you might be awake."

"I have hardly slept, I confess." Elizabeth smiled tiredly.

Jane sat beside her. "Are you certain you are doing the right thing, Lizzy?"

"Of course not." Elizabeth sighed. "I have no notion how to manage a house so large as Pemberley. I cannot say if I shall ever truly be a sister to Georgiana, or if Mr. Darcy and I may ever have an amicable union. I dare not hope for friendship — certainly not love. I do not even know if I shall be permitted to see you again. I am only certain Papa has not recovered his strength, and he is too thin. Mamma and our sisters must not be destitute if he dies."

It was a relief to be entirely honest with someone. Jane had come to Elizabeth's room the evening after her return from London, bearing a letter from their aunt Gardiner. Armed with their aunt's intelligence and her own suspicions, Jane had begged Elizabeth to confide in her, and Elizabeth had been too exhausted to keep silent.

She had told Jane everything: Mr. Darcy's fury, her own shame and fear, his inexplicable behavior since. She would not have mentioned Mr. Bingley but her aunt had disclosed their confrontation, so Elizabeth had even admitted her own harsh words. She had wept in her sister's arms that night and Jane had lain beside her, soothing her hair and assuring her all would be well.

But all was not well, and they both knew it. They had only to observe their father, who could neither ascend a single flight of stairs nor make the short walk to the church without pausing to catch his breath.

"We may not need to rely on Mr. Darcy's kindness, you know," Jane said quietly.

Elizabeth caught Jane's hand and squeezed it. Mr. Bingley had returned to Netherfield only a few days after her own return to Hertfordshire, and proved Mamma correct after all: he had immediately thrown himself at Jane's feet. He had abased himself as a too-trusting imbecile, asking only for the chance to prove himself worthy of her regard. Since then, he had been a daily visitor at Longbourn.

He had found Elizabeth alone one morning about a week ago. "I must thank you, Miss Elizabeth," he had said, "for being a better friend to me — a better sister, I dare hope — than my own sisters have been. Had you not taken me to task I might never have known how I was duped, nor faced the depths of my own cowardice in not returning to Hertfordshire last December."

"You are welcome, I suppose. I certainly did not say it to be thanked."

"Nay, and you had every right to be angry. I thank you in any case. And I apologize for my unjust words regarding Darcy. Do you truly hate him?"

"Nay, though I confess I did not think well of him when he publicly insulted me at that first assembly in Meryton. I was unguarded in my speech afterward. Until we met in Kent this spring he took no pains to improve my opinion, but it did improve."

Mr. Bingley had paled. "You heard him? No wonder, then, you thought so little of us both. But seeing your father now... I think, perhaps, I understand better why you accepted him despite all that. I beg you to be patient. He is a good man at heart, for all his resentful temper. He shall come around in time."

Elizabeth had not been reassured; Mr. Bingley was nearly as blind to the faults of others as was Jane. He had been diligent in making his amends, however.

Now Elizabeth smiled at her sister. "If Mr. Bingley is truly the good and faithful man he aspires to be, you shall be happy, and I shall be well satisfied."

Jane stayed with Elizabeth all morning, arranging her hair and helping her on with her gown. Several times Jane was obliged to shoo their mother away with repeated assurances that Elizabeth would not keep Mr. Darcy waiting. Just as Jane was placing Elizabeth's new bonnet atop her curls, the door opened, and a breathless Kitty rushed in.

"This just arrived from Netherfield. I am to put it into your hands directly, Lizzy." She held a long, narrow box and a note in Mr. Darcy's bold hand.

Elizabeth opened the note with trembling fingers.

Netherfield, 9th July

Madam,

The enclosed belonged to my mother, Lady Anne Darcy. She wore it on her wedding-day. I would be honored if you would wear it today in her memory. — F.D.

Inside the box was a large oval sapphire framed by tiny diamonds, on a delicate silver chain. Tears sprang to Elizabeth's eyes and her hands shook so badly Jane took the box from her, removing her garnet cross and fastening the sapphire around her throat.

"It looks beautiful with the yellow silk of your gown," Kitty sighed. "Mr. Darcy must care about you a great deal!"

Elizabeth could only nod.

"Thank you, Kitty," said Jane. "Tell Mamma we shall be down directly."

When the door had closed behind her, Elizabeth gripped Jane's hands. "What can he mean by it, Jane? He said he shall see me as little as possible after the wedding. He as good as called me a fortune-hunting Jezebel! For him to send such a gift — can it be a test?"

"I cannot be sure, but I do not think so. Lizzy, today you become Mrs. Darcy. You will be his wife and the mother of his children. He cannot mean to shame you before all his family."

Elizabeth nodded again, taking deep breaths in an attempt to stop her trembling. She gave Jane a watery smile as her sister tied the bonnet at a jaunty angle under her chin, leaving the enormous gem clearly visible.

At the foot of the stairs Kitty eagerly thrust her bouquet at her. Mamma clasped her hands together, exclaiming loudly over the extravagance of Mr. Darcy's gift. "The first of many, I am sure," she said, "if only you behave with all the dignity and gratitude he expects. Mrs. Darcy cannot be so quarrelsome or teasing as Miss Elizabeth Bennet, you know."

Elizabeth had heard this lecture many times. It was her father's wry smile that steadied her. He stood next to Mamma in a new jacket and waistcoat, his face still hollow beneath prominent cheekbones, but his eyes held the same amusement they always had — a private joke between the two of them.

They made their slow way to the church. Elizabeth clung to her father's arm, quailing a bit as her mother and sisters preceded them inside and she caught sight of the full pews. It seemed every family in the neighborhood, and many more besides, were in attendance.

"Courage, my dear," Papa murmured.

A moment later the doors were thrown open and the congregation stood, but she took no notice of the faces they passed as her father led her forward — her eyes were fixed on Mr. Darcy.

He stood tall and straight, dark hair falling across his brow. His coat was the exact color of the sapphire at her throat, his waistcoat a paler blue with yellow stripes. Her eyes widened; Georgiana had asked the color of her wedding-dress, but she had thought it an idle inquiry. Mr. Darcy took in Elizabeth's appearance in turn, expression softening as he caught sight of the necklace.

She heard the parson's voice and then her father's, and then her hand was placed in Mr. Darcy's. His grip was firm as she stepped forward to stand next to him.

"Thank you for wearing it," he whispered.

She nodded, tears threatening again, hoping he would see gratitude in her smile.

Afterward Elizabeth remembered almost nothing of the ceremony. She followed along like a puppet, speaking and moving when prompted; all that really penetrated the fog was the expression in Mr. Darcy's eyes as he spoke his vows. She saw there the same fear and hope that lived in her own heart, and his voice was solemn as he promised "to have and to hold from this day forward, for better for worse, for richer for poorer, in sickness and in health, to love and to cherish, till death do us part, according to God's holy ordinance."

He kept hold of her hand after placing a ring on her finger: an oval sapphire ringed in diamonds, she saw with fresh tears. She could not have said why she was crying — her emotions were too jumbled and disorienting — only that she could not have prevented herself. When at last the parson gave Mr. Darcy permission to kiss his bride he bent slowly, a question in his eyes.

He is giving me the choice, she realized. She lifted her face. His lips were feather-light on hers and a sad smile ghosted across his face at the tears spilling down her cheeks. She hastily patted them away with his proffered handkerchief.

Only then did she notice Mr. Bingley grinning at them both. His brow lifted as though to say, '*Did I not tell you he would come around?*'

The wedding-breakfast was a sea of well-wishers. Elizabeth soon found it necessary to exert herself, for Mr. Darcy had fallen back into the cold civility he always displayed in company.

"Poor Fitzwilliam," Georgiana said, regarding him across the expanse of lawn. "He is never easy in large gatherings. Nor I, but hardly anybody is paying me any attention today." She impulsively took Elizabeth's hand. "I know not how you smile and laugh so! But I am grateful, for his sake. He shall be easier in company with you to help him."

Elizabeth observed her new husband carefully. *Does he truly mask unease with disdain?* He bowed stiffly to Sir William and Lady Lucas. *Perhaps he does.* She crossed to his side, accepting the boisterous compliments and felicitations of her neighbors, and felt Mr. Darcy gradually relax.

When Georgiana approached them accompanied by an elegantly dressed and still handsome woman in her middle fifties, Elizabeth required all her courage to keep the smile on her face. This could only be Eleanor Fitzwilliam, Countess of Matlock and Mr. Darcy's aunt.

Lady Matlock smiled affectionately. "Congratulations, my dears. Henry and I are delighted for you both."

"I am very happy to see you, Aunt." Mr. Darcy embraced her, and Elizabeth was clearly expected to follow suit.

The countess clasped Elizabeth's hands warmly. "I am so sorry my husband could not be here today. His business in Scotland has taken far longer than any of us expected." She smiled wryly and lowered her voice. "And you need not look so terrified, my dear. I am not Catherine. Your success can only benefit the family, and I shall do all I can to assist you."

"I am excessively grateful to you, my lady," Elizabeth said. "Your son Colonel Fitzwilliam is well, I hope? I have not seen him these many months."

"He is, or so he says in his latest letter. Richard's regiment is now stationed in Portugal. He sounded as well as ever, but of course he can say nothing of consequence."

"How difficult it must be, not to know if he is in danger!"

"Indeed. I shall not be easy until he is returned to us safe and whole."

Elizabeth glanced up to see her mother approaching and silently said a prayer. She had no wish to be mortified before her new family by Mamma's unguarded speech.

"Forgive my interruption, Mr. Darcy," Mamma said, "but I beg you and Lizzy would sit and enjoy some breakfast. Lizzy has eaten nothing since supper! What kind of mother would I be if I sent her off with an empty stomach?"

There were exclamations all around. Mr. Darcy politely introduced his aunt and sister, and Elizabeth watched in astonishment as her mother graciously welcomed them both without the slightest hint of excessive deference.

Lady Matlock thanked Mamma for her hospitality and praised the breakfast, waving Elizabeth and Mr. Darcy away. "If I had known you had not yet eaten, child, I should never have permitted you to tarry here so long!"

Once Elizabeth was seated, she realized she was famished. Mr. Darcy filled a plate for each of them. "Your mother sets an excellent table," he said. "Why did you say nothing about it before?"

"I was too nervous to eat until now."

"I see. Is that why you hardly touched your food when you dined at Darcy House?"

She flushed. "I had hoped you would not notice."

"Even if I had not, my cook certainly did." The corner of his mouth lifted in a half-smile. "I was forced to pay her some very extravagant compliments before she believed me that there was nothing wrong with the meal."

Elizabeth sighed. "Of course. She wished to impress her future mistress, and I insulted her. Pray forgive me."

"There is nothing to forgive." Mr. Darcy appeared to be studying her parents. "How does your father now?" he asked quietly. "Is he recovered from his illness?"

"Not entirely. The physician warned us his lungs might suffer permanent damage, and it appears to be so."

"I am sorry to hear it. I suppose it is fortunate, then, he is so fond of reading."

Their quiet conversation was interrupted by the sound of pounding hoofbeats. All heads turned as an express rider leapt off his horse and looked around at the assembled company. "Is one of you gentlemen Mr. Bennet?"

Papa stood. "I am." He opened the missive with a frown as he went around to the front of the house, disappearing inside as the rider cantered away.

A few minutes later Mrs. Hill emerged and spoke quietly to Uncle Gardiner, who instantly went into the house. The housekeeper then approached the table where Elizabeth and

Mr. Darcy sat. "Beggin' your pardon, sir," she said, "but the master wishes you to join him in his book-room as soon as possible."

Mr. Darcy's lips pressed briefly into a line. "I shall come directly." He looked apologetically at Elizabeth. "Pray, excuse me."

"It's not right, callin' a man away from his own wedding-breakfast," said Mrs. Hill. "I'm mighty sorry for it, Miss Lizzy. Er, beg your pardon, Mrs. Darcy." She bobbed a curtsey and hurried back to the house.

Elizabeth had hardly enough time to feel surprised before Aunt Gardiner was claiming Mr. Darcy's vacated chair. "Sit up straight, Lizzy. Now smile. You must go on as though nothing is amiss."

"What could have happened?" Jane asked, approaching from the other direction.

"We must not be seen to speculate, Jane," said their aunt. "Our responsibility is to ensure the guests keep their attention on the innocent diversions of the day. Come, Lizzy, we must mingle."

Aunt Gardiner pulled Elizabeth to her feet and paraded her around the lawn, making pleasant conversation with nearly every member of the party. When a quarter of an hour had passed with no sign of the gentlemen, she turned to Elizabeth and said loudly, "Well, my dear, it is nearly time to bundle you into the carriage! Come, we must help you into your travelling gown."

They passed Mamma as they made their way toward the house. "I am sure I do not know where Mr. Bennet has gone off to," she was saying. "Like as not, he sat down in his book-room and fell asleep in his pages! If not, he shall certainly be along directly. Have you taken a slice of cake?"

Elizabeth rolled her eyes with exasperated fondness. *It is probably best Mamma remains unaware of any difficulty,* she thought. Her mother could be relied upon to shriek the news, whether good or bad, so all could hear. And what of good news could be expected, that would keep the men inside the house so long?

As soon as Elizabeth entered the hallway, she broke from her aunt's grasp and rushed toward her father's book-room. She pulled up short as Mr. Darcy stepped into the hall, letter in hand, his expression grimmer than ever.

"I am glad you are here. I was going to look for you," he said without preamble. "Come, you must see this as well." He steered Elizabeth into the family sitting room and closed the door, wordlessly holding out the letter.

Brighton, 8th July 1812, 5:00 pm

Dear Mr. Bennet,

I am profoundly sorry to inform you that your daughter Lydia was discovered missing this morning at breakfast. One of my officers, Wickham, has vanished as well. Miss Lydia left a note for Mrs. Forster, suggesting they departed together, with the intent of eloping to Scotland. I sent men to trace them, but the pair disappeared into a hackney-coach in Clapham and my men cannot find out that they have gone any further than London. Lt. Denny, who was Wickham's close companion, is not disposed to believe his friend intent on marrying your daughter.

We shall make a thorough search of the London area and the northern roads. If you have any knowledge which might

direct our search, I should be glad of it. I shall call tomorrow
evening to provide you whatever information I may.

Your most humble servant,

Wm. Forster

Elizabeth sat heavily, nearly missing the chair. "How could this be? How...? *Why* would Mr. Wickham do such a thing?"

"I am sorry to pain you," Mr. Darcy said, "but in this he has revealed his true nature. Your sister is... well, let us say she is not the first young lady he has charmed away from her family."

Elizabeth's hands closed into fists. "Oh, Lydia, you stupid, *stupid* girl!" Unable to remain seated, she propelled herself across the room. "Papa should never have permitted her to go to Brighton! I cannot suppose Mr. Wickham truly means to marry her."

"It would be contrary to his character. He means to marry for money."

"And she has nothing." Elizabeth thought of Miss King, who had first caught Mr. Wickham's eye after inheriting ten thousand pounds. At the time Elizabeth had seen it as quite sensible — young men must have something to live on, after all — but now it appeared wholly mercenary.

A thought came unbidden to Elizabeth's mind. *Nearly as mercenary as Mr. Darcy believes me to be.* She could not meet his eye. *He must want nothing more than to be rid of me and my whole sorry family.* She fidgeted as the silence stretched.

Finally, she decided she could wait no longer for him to speak. "Mr. Darcy, I—" She choked back the sudden tears. "I expect you are now wishing this day might be undone. I could never blame you for throwing me off, not with such a sister. Not with… all that has come before."

He sighed. "What I do or do not wish is immaterial. The words have been spoken. For better or worse, you are Mrs. Darcy, and Lydia Bennet is my sister. I must go to London. Today."

"What?" Her head snapped up. "Why?"

"I have an idea where they might be found, but your uncle could not succeed in discovering them alone and your father is in no condition to travel. You shall go on to Pemberley, as planned, with Georgiana. I shall ask my aunt to accompany you."

"I cannot go to Pemberley! I must remain with my family. Jane will need me."

"No. Georgiana needs you. Pemberley needs you. You are Mrs. Darcy now." He loomed over her. "Were you to remain here, the gossip would begin immediately. If we are to have any hope of keeping this quiet and prevent it from covering your family — *and mine* — in dishonor, you must be seen to act as Mrs. Darcy. Not Miss Elizabeth Bennet."

She lowered her eyes again. "Very well." He was correct, she knew, but the prospect of entering Pemberley as its mistress, without him, was terrifying. "I shall go and change my gown."

$\mathcal{S}ix$

Mistress of Pemberley

"WELCOME TO PEMBERLEY, Mrs. Darcy."

Elizabeth heard the words everywhere — in the house, on the grounds, anywhere she encountered one of the seemingly endless parade of servants. They were all polite and deferential, but she dearly missed Mrs. Hill. Longbourn's housekeeper had been there longer than any of the girls had been alive, and she treated them with all the intimacy and impertinent frankness such long service granted her.

Mrs. Reynolds, Pemberley's housekeeper, spoke with the same affection (though nothing like the same impertinence) to Georgiana. She was an older woman, nearing sixty, still full of cheerful energy. She was even more lavish in her praise of Mr. Darcy than she was of Georgiana, which was a feat, for Georgiana seemed to have no flaw in Mrs. Reynolds's estimation.

"I never had a cross word from him in my life, and I've known him since he was four years old," Mrs. Reynolds said, standing with Elizabeth before Mr. Darcy's portrait in the gallery. "But then, I have always observed that good-natured children are good-natured when they grow up."

I do not believe I have met the man she describes, Elizabeth thought. He certainly had not been so genial when last they spoke. He had pulled her aside as the other ladies were being handed into the carriage, just before they all departed Longbourn.

Mr. Darcy had insisted she could say nothing of Lydia's elopement. She was not even to say Mr. Wickham's name in Georgiana's presence, he warned, the severity of his countenance silencing her questions. For the next several days Elizabeth had been severely distressed but unable to show anything of what she felt. Lonely, frightened and ashamed, she wept alone every night in the inns.

The hours in the carriage had been easier to bear. Lady Matlock — Elizabeth simply could not think of her as "Aunt Eleanor," no matter how the older woman insisted — had been a valuable travelling companion. Seemingly unable to abide silence, the countess filled the long hours with endless questions about Elizabeth's preferences in books and music, her family, and her life at Longbourn.

When Elizabeth mentioned her habit of rambling the countryside unaccompanied, both her companions gasped. "My dear, it is unsafe!" Lady Matlock said. "My nephew would never permit Georgiana to do such a thing. When you walk the grounds at Pemberley you must always take a footman or a maid with you, at the very least."

When Lady Matlock quizzed Elizabeth about her plans for managing Pemberley, she soon discerned how meager was Elizabeth's knowledge. She set about educating both Elizabeth and Georgiana on household management, quizzing them relentlessly as she did so. Inattention was impossible; answering Lady Matlock's questions required considerable concentration and recall of what they had just learned. In this manner the hours passed more quickly than Elizabeth had thought possible.

Only two days after their arrival at Pemberley, however, Lady Matlock received a note summoning her home. "My daughter Margaret — Arthur's wife; he is my eldest, you recall — shall be brought to bed with my first grandchild any day now. I am sorry to leave you both so soon, my dears, but I must return."

For all her commandeering presence, Lady Matlock had been a comfort. Left with only Georgiana and Mrs. Annesley for company, Elizabeth's loneliness threatened to overwhelm her.

I do not deserve to be here. The thought struck often: when she looked out over the pleasing prospect of the lake, which was visible from every window on the south side of the house; when she woke in the deep comfort of the mistress's bedchamber; when she stood in the cavernous front hall or the elegantly appointed rooms with their silk wallpaper and decorated ceilings.

The enormity of her new role as the mistress of Pemberley was equally overwhelming. In those first difficult days, Mrs. Reynolds was single-handedly responsible for helping Elizabeth feel less like an impostor. The housekeeper had been exceedingly welcoming and patient — reviewing the staff, recipes, and household accounts with Elizabeth without once implying concern over the new mistress's ignorance — and never seemed amused when Elizabeth lost her way in the great maze of a house. Elizabeth could not say the same of the housemaids. They had the grace, at least, to lead her where she meant to go and snicker when she was safely out of earshot.

She assumed they must be laughing at her, at any rate. She still became turned around at least daily, though she had been at Pemberley for nearly a week. Mrs. Reynolds never mocked, though, and her cheerful demeanor was partnered with ruthless efficiency and an impressively thorough knowledge of the house. She knew her people well: Elizabeth had never had a lady's maid but she quite liked Sarah Still, who Mrs. Reynolds promoted to the position.

Sarah was a sturdy young woman of nineteen years, raised on the estate. Blond and blue-eyed, with a merry, no-nonsense demeanor and an artistic eye, she chattered happily as she did Elizabeth's hair each morning. Within days, Elizabeth knew more about the staff and local families than she could have learned on her own in weeks.

* * *

"Good morning, Mrs. Darcy. Your breakfast is here." Sarah spoke softly as she opened the bed-curtains a fraction. She needn't have been concerned; Elizabeth had been awake for hours. Sarah met her eyes and smiled. "What will you wear today? The day promises to be very fine indeed."

"The blue muslin, I think." Elizabeth was looking forward to the morning's planned activity. She had initially confined her wandering to the house and nearby grounds, but today

Mr. Harwood was touring her around the estate. The steward was an exceedingly forthright and competent man who appeared to love Pemberley nearly as much as his master did, and his face had lit with delight when she asked him to introduce her to the tenants.

Dressed and breakfasted, she stepped through the side door nearest the stables, where Mr. Harwood waited with a small gig. Georgiana was also there in a smart green riding habit, already mounted and arranging her skirts over Willow's saddle. The sleek bay mare stood perfectly still, looking back once Georgiana took up the reins as though to verify her rider was properly settled.

Georgiana patted the mare's neck and grinned. "Good morning, Elizabeth! I know you and Harwood are going out today in the gig, but perhaps one morning you might join me for a gallop. There is no better way to see the grounds than from horseback!"

"Sadly, I must take you at your word," Elizabeth said. "I never learned to ride properly."

"What! Never! That is very strange indeed," Georgiana said. "Never mind, you must learn. Reynolds here may teach you; he is teaching Mrs. Annesley, you know."

James Reynolds looked over from where he held the bridle of Mrs. Annesley's horse. He took after his mother; he had Mrs. Reynolds's warm hazel eyes and broad, honest face, though he did not share her energetic cheer. Instead, he held himself with a quiet stillness that radiated calm. He seemed more comfortable with horses than people, in truth, which might explain why he had been named Pemberley's stable-master at an astonishingly young age. Elizabeth guessed him to be no older than Mr. Darcy.

"Aye," he said. "I would be very pleased to teach you, Mrs. Darcy. Daisy here is perfect for novices. She's patient and gentle, and she doesn't care to go very fast." He looked past Elizabeth and smiled shyly. "Good morning, Miss Sarah."

"Good morning, Mr. Reynolds." Sarah smothered a silly grin as she handed a large basket to Mr. Harwood. She kept sneaking glances at the stable-master, however; he, in turn, made no attempt at subtlety, openly admiring her rounded, graceful form.

Mr. Harwood shot Mr. Reynolds a hard glance as he stashed the basket beneath the seat. "That's the last of it," he said. "We may leave whenever you wish, Mrs. Darcy."

The estate was vast. The nearest tenants were more than a mile from the main house, the dowager cottage further still. The cottage appeared snug and in good repair but had the look of a building long vacant.

"Aye, nobody has lived at Pemberley Cottage since Mrs. Wickham died about ten years back," Harwood said when Elizabeth asked. "Old Mr. Wickham was Pemberley's steward before me, and a good and honest man he was, too, by all accounts. Took excellent care of the estate. Old Mr. Darcy allowed his widow and her children to live at the cottage as a mark of gratitude for her husband's service."

Elizabeth's knowledge of the history between Mr. Darcy and Mr. Wickham had come entirely from Mr. Wickham's lips; she could not let such an opportunity pass. "Was not the younger Mr. Wickham a favorite of the late Mr. Darcy?"

"Oh, aye. Old Mr. Darcy was young Wickham's godfather. A pity he never knew what a scoundrel that boy became, but young Wickham was always clever enough to keep his sinful activities well away from the estate. He was a charmer, that one. He could tell you the sky was green and the grass blue, and you'd swear it was truth. It's a good thing for us all that the master sees through him."

"Good heavens! I had no notion! I met Mr. Wickham in Hertfordshire; it shall not surprise you, I suppose, to hear he was a favorite of everybody in the neighborhood. He spoke of a living in Kympton. He said old Mr. Darcy meant it for him once he had taken orders, but when the living fell vacant the present Mr. Darcy refused to grant it to him."

"That's true enough, though I'd not fault the master for it. Mr. Darcy would never act dishonorably, Mistress. Never. I know none of the details, but the important part of the story is always whatever young Wickham leaves out. And I don't mind saying old Mr. Darcy had the wrong of it. That boy has no business being a clergyman."

Elizabeth was silent. This was a very different account of Mr. Wickham than her own experience portrayed; he had appeared the picture of sincerity and forbearance in Hertfordshire. *His manners were always so pleasing... but did not Mr. Harwood say his charm kept his godfather from discovering him?*

This unflattering account also accorded with his behavior with Lydia. Perhaps he truly thought nothing of ruining a penniless young woman! *And you already knew he blackened Mr. Darcy's name to all who would listen, as soon as Mr. Darcy could not defend himself. Oh, Lydia! What misery have you brought upon yourself, to be taken in by such a man?*

She shied away from the thought that until very recently she had been taken in herself. Indeed, had she a fortune, she might have been wed to Mr. Wickham by now. Her mother would have been delighted to see a daughter married to any eligible young man, and her father would never have had a reason to suspect him.

Elizabeth was roused from her unpleasant musings when the gig stopped moving before a small but sturdily-built home. Their first visit of the day was with Susan Wright, a recent widow. Harwood pulled the large basket from beneath the seat while Elizabeth knocked at the door. A girl answered, no older than seven or eight, her hair in messy braids and her pinafore smudged with green.

"Good morning, Miss Wright. Is your mother at home?" Elizabeth asked.

The little girl folded her arms. "She's with Mr. Burrell. Who are you?"

"This is Mrs. Darcy," Harwood said, coming up behind her. "We've come with supplies for your family." He lifted the basket.

"Oh! Come in, then. I'm Martha," she said, heading for the table by the window.

"I am pleased to meet you, Martha," said Elizabeth.

In the main room were four more children, the youngest perhaps a year old. The green smudges on Martha's pinafore were peas, Elizabeth realized, watching the girl attempt to feed several spoonfuls to the baby. A tired-looking woman in a simple yellow dress sat before the fire with an older man whose compassionate gaze warmed Elizabeth's heart. As the widow stood to greet the newcomers, Elizabeth was startled to realize she was much younger than Elizabeth had at first assumed; Mrs. Wright could not be above twenty-five!

Mr. Harwood made the introductions, and Elizabeth begged to be introduced to the children.

"My Martha you've met, Mrs. Darcy. She's eight years old," Mrs. Wright said. She pointed to each of the others in turn. "Tommy is six, Rose four, Lily three, and little Charlie is one year just yesterday."

"A very happy birthday to little Charlie." Elizabeth smiled as he stuck his tongue out, still covered in mashed peas. She turned back to Mrs. Wright. "We've brought you some salted pork and fresh vegetables and flour, and there are surprises in the basket for the children as well." Impulsively she caught the woman's hands in her own. "It must be difficult with your husband gone so suddenly. Please tell me what else I may do to help you."

"I thank you, Mrs. Darcy. The food will go a fair way, but we must not rely on charity." Mrs. Wright shrugged helplessly. "I should like to earn my keep, but I cannot leave the children alone all day."

"Is there nobody to look after them?" Elizabeth looked at Harwood, but it was Mr. Burrell who answered.

"What of the Smiths? Their farm is a half-mile distant, Mrs. Darcy. The youngest Miss Smith is fourteen and looking to go into service as a nanny when she is old enough."

"That may do very well indeed. We shall visit them next and inquire. I hope to have an answer for you by the end of the day, Mrs. Wright." She smiled when the young mother squeezed her hands tightly. They left the house with Mr. Burrell, ears ringing with joyful exclamations over the small toys and sweets the children had found in the basket.

"We have all been eager to meet you, Mrs. Darcy," said Mr. Burrell. His voice was deep and soothing. He had thick white hair and kind eyes, and the lines beside his mouth bespoke a lifetime of laughter. "I have been the vicar here for nearly thirty years, and it has never been quite the same since Lady Anne's death. If you mean to keep doing this sort of good for the people, you shall find me ready to aid you at every moment."

"I am delighted to hear it, but surely your own family must claim some of your time?"

"Nay, my wife passed five years ago, and my daughters are all grown and gone. I have only my flock to care for now."

"Then I shall be pleased to have such a devoted partner. Will you not join us at the Smiths' farm?"

The remainder of the day was spent bringing cheer to the tenants and small gifts of food or medicine to several of the poorer families. As much as she enjoyed these visits, Elizabeth's greatest pleasure was in delivering good news to Mrs. Wright: Mr. Burrell had assisted Elizabeth in brokering an agreement which would see Mrs. Wright's children cared for, allowing her to work. Meanwhile, young Lettie Smith would earn Mrs. Darcy's reference for a position as a nanny.

Finally, Elizabeth and Harwood returned to the great house. Elizabeth watched it grow larger as they approached, the graceful lines of pale gray stone warmed to a buttery yellow by the late afternoon sun. It was unquestionably the most beautiful home she had ever seen, and when she was inside, surrounded by its elegant grandeur, she still felt like an interloper. But out among the fields and villages she had felt a deep connection to its people. For the first time, she did not feel so entirely alone.

Seven

The Master Returns

OVER THE NEXT few weeks Elizabeth established her routine. She rose early and walked on the grounds, conferred with Mrs. Reynolds, then took a riding lesson with Mr. Reynolds or visited the tenants. In the afternoon she joined Georgiana and Mrs. Annesley in the music-room or tested her recall of the house. For this she enlisted Sarah's help; her maid named a destination and accompanied Elizabeth as she attempted to find it, returning her to the correct route if she failed.

In this manner Elizabeth soon found her way. She spoke to every servant, learning their names and inquiring into their lives. The maids no longer seemed to be laughing at her; instead, they smiled warmly whenever she came upon them and were perhaps a little disappointed when she required no assistance to navigate the halls.

One of Elizabeth's favorite rooms was the library, with its plush armchairs and tall windows. She particularly adored the wrought-iron spiral stair leading to the balcony, which provided access to a second storey of bookshelves along two walls. The servants soon took to throwing open the curtains every morning and placing fresh flowers on the table beside her preferred chair.

She spent an hour there before dinner every evening, amusing herself by browsing the enormous collection to find anything that might be of interest. She instructed these volumes be shelved by her chair, along with the books she had brought from Longbourn; she hoped Mr. Darcy would not be too displeased at her re-ordering of his library.

She also hoped to influence Georgiana to read more. Her new sister had been timid at first, but as Elizabeth learned to ride and practiced the pianoforte, Georgiana became more talkative. In turn Elizabeth was determined to improve her mind. Sheltered as she was, Georgiana seemed all too willing to allow Mrs. Annesley to direct her.

She will never attract a husband if she cannot carry on a simple conversation, Elizabeth thought, and then started. *Oh dear. I sound just like Mamma!*

The primary benefit of keeping herself busy was to prevent her from thinking too much about her family. News was slow in coming; Elizabeth had been at Pemberley a week before she received a letter from Mr. Darcy.

Darcy House, 15th July 1812

Dear Mrs. Darcy,

At last I am able to give you news of your sister and Mr. Wickham. I have seen them both. As I anticipated, he had no intention of marrying her. She was entirely unaware of this; rather, she was confident they should marry eventually, and was content to remain living with him yet unwed. They have both been persuaded to be reasonable, however.

She now resides with Mr. and Mrs. Gardiner, and we have put it about that she has been at their house since departing Brighton. They will be married in three weeks' time. I shall remain here to ensure the wedding proceeds. I would not put it past Mr. Wickham to disappear in search of greener pastures while we wait for the banns to be published.

Yours ever,

F. Darcy

P.S. You must not speak of Mr. Wickham, or your sister's marriage, to Georgiana. I shall tell her after I return to Pemberley.

Elizabeth had stared at the postscript, deep in thought. *Why all the secrecy? Georgiana cannot know Mr. Wickham very well — she would have been very young when he went away to school, would she not? Of course, she is entirely innocent of the world. Perhaps he wishes only to avoid shocking her.*

It was a relief to know Lydia would be married — for her sisters' sake, if nothing else — but to such a man! For Mr. Darcy to be forced into accepting him as a brother! It left her wretched.

I do not belong here. The thought continued to plague her, followed now by another: *How can such as I deserve to be Mrs. Darcy?*

She consoled herself that she was doing some good for the tenants, with Mr. Burrell proving as eager to aid her as he had promised. He now dined with them twice every week, at her insistence, and his stories were always gratefully received, for he recounted memories of Georgiana's parents as often as he spoke about his parishioners.

He was particularly pleased by his visits with the Wright family, but Elizabeth had seen it for herself: within a week the house was tidy, the children laughing and their mother less haggard in her appearance. Mrs. Wright held her head high and smiled whenever Elizabeth visited.

"I hope you will accompany your sister on her visits to the tenants, Miss Darcy," Mr. Burrell said when Elizabeth had been at Pemberley three weeks. "One day you too are like to be mistress of a great house, and you could have no better model than Mrs. Darcy's care for those under Pemberley's protection."

Elizabeth blushed. "You give me too much credit, sir. I do no more than my sisters and I did at Longbourn."

"Not at all, madam. It has been sixteen years since Pemberley had a mistress, and in all that time none from the great house have taken such trouble to know the women and children. Mr. Darcy is a good man and a good master, but when he visits his attention is for the fields and homes. I hope he may see how much good you have done."

She merely smiled. Mr. Burrell was all affability and wise advice, but he knew nothing of the truth of her marriage.

I shall count myself fortunate if Mr. Darcy does not chastise me for wanting to spend my pin-money on the tenants. She had purchased nothing for herself; she had no need of fine clothes or new hats, and the house was already so elegantly furnished the thought of redecorating was absurd. She had considered buying warm woolen cloth, however, so that the poorest children might have winter garments.

"When do you expect Mr. Darcy?" Mr. Burrell asked.

"We hope to see him here next week," Elizabeth said. "He fell ill in London. An ailment of the digestive system. His physician, Dr. Lindley, believes he shall recover swiftly, but he was forced to delay his return."

Shortly before Mr. Darcy's anticipated arrival, Elizabeth received a letter that gladdened her heart more than anything had yet done.

Longbourn, 6th August 1812

Dearest Lizzy,

I shall take the time to write a proper response to your letter soon, but I cannot wait to share the delightful news with you: I am to be Mrs. Bingley after all! Papa would not give his permission until we knew Lydia was truly married, but Charles insists he would not have let her scandal put him off for anything and would have argued until Papa gave way, even if we had not received word from Uncle Gardiner that she was married yesterday to Mr. Wickham.

You would have laughed at the scene this morning, Lizzy: we were all assembled in the sitting-room. Papa came in and read our uncle's letter aloud, and before he had finished Charles jumped to his feet, saying, "Mr. Bennet, I insist—" and Papa just said, "Yes, yes, you may marry my daughter. Now get along with you. Take your bride-to-be and have your celebration outside, if you must be noisy about it."

We are to be married at the end of September. Charles is impatient and would prefer to marry immediately, but Mamma insisted. Oh, Lizzy, I am so happy! He has repaid all his debt of neglect with such a surplus of attentiveness and care that I can have no reservations. My wedding-day shall be

entirely perfect, I am sure, if you and Mr. Darcy are there.
Please say you shall come! I miss you so!

Your affectionate sister,

Jane

* * *

Mr. Darcy arrived home very late. Elizabeth was reading before the fire in her bedchamber when she heard the crunch of gravel beneath the carriage-wheels. Padding silently to the door, she cracked it open far enough to hear Mr. Darcy's tired baritone float up from the entry hall.

"Good evening, Mrs. Reynolds. I am well, but it has been a very long day. I had no wish to spend another night in an inn. Tell me, is Mrs. Darcy awake?"

"She retired an hour ago, sir, but she may yet be awake. She often reads in her chamber at night. Shall I tell her you wish to see her?"

"Nay, let her rest. I shall see her on the morrow."

Despite his words, the following day Elizabeth saw her husband hardly at all. He rose with the dawn and was already touring the grounds when she awoke. While she breakfasted, he was closeted with Mr. Harwood, reviewing the accounts. By the time she was astride Daisy for a slow turn around the lake he was riding out to the fields to observe the harvest, which kept him away for much of the afternoon.

She had just settled into her favorite chair in the library when she heard Mr. Darcy in the hall. "Mrs. Reynolds, why have all the curtains been opened in the library?"

"Mrs. Darcy likes a bright room, sir. She reads by that window every afternoon before dinner."

Elizabeth froze. The back of her tall chair faced the open door, and her feet were tucked up beneath her; she doubted they knew she was there. *Will he come to find me?*

"I see. Thank you, Mrs. Reynolds. I shall be in my study until dinner," he said. Almost immediately came the sound of a door closing.

Elizabeth stared at the door separating the library from the study. She could not decide if she was more disappointed or relieved. *Is he avoiding me? I suppose I cannot blame him.*

She had received only three letters during the month he was in London, and these contained only essential information. Nothing personal, and no hint of the renewed affection she thought she had glimpsed on their wedding-day. *With such evidence that my family is every bit as inferior as he believed them to be, how could it be otherwise?*

Supper that evening was a stilted affair. Georgiana was cheerful and unusually talkative, for which Elizabeth was grateful. Mr. Darcy asked Elizabeth only a few questions about her time at Pemberley and was satisfied with brief answers, but he listened attentively to Georgiana. He merely lifted a brow when she beamed about Elizabeth's riding lessons, but seemed truly surprised by Georgiana's determination to accompany Elizabeth on visits to the tenants.

"I must say, this is unexpected," he said. "You have not taken such an interest in the tenants before. What prompted it?"

"Mr. Burrell advised me when last he dined at Pemberley. He said Mother visited them often, and I must learn if I am to be mistress of a great estate."

"I see." Mr. Darcy turned a penetrating gaze on Elizabeth. "Do you visit my tenants often, Mrs. Darcy?"

Elizabeth shrugged. "Once or twice a week, perhaps. I find I cannot be satisfied without knowing the widows and their children are well."

"And you have invited Mr. Burrell to dine here?"

"I have asked him to join us twice a week. I greatly enjoy his company. He is wise and grandfatherly."

"Of course. Mr. Burrell is a good man, and he was devoted to his wife and children. Now they are gone, it must please him to have dinner companions again."

After supper the ladies played the pianoforte, preventing any further conversation until Georgiana retired. Elizabeth hesitated, uncertain whether to remain or retire; when Mr. Darcy fixed her with a look, she stayed.

"Does Georgiana know anything about the nature of my business in London?" His tone was cool.

"I gave her no hint, sir," Elizabeth said, her voice sharper than she intended. "You were very clear on that point."

"She seems quite eager to befriend you."

Does he mean that to be a compliment or a complaint? Elizabeth shrugged. "I believe she is lonely. Georgiana is a delightful young woman, but her shyness causes her great difficulty in forming new acquaintances. As you suggested, I am endeavoring to help her overcome it."

His lips pressed together. "What caused you to take up riding?"

"Georgiana insisted. She is correct that the grounds are too vast to enjoy properly on foot, and I am informed you are unlikely to support my preference for long walks in any event."

"I shall certainly not permit you to wander about on your own. This is not Hertfordshire."

"Of course not." She tried to keep her tone even.

Mr. Darcy stood then, pacing restlessly to the window and back. "Do you not find it a remarkable coincidence that your sister and Mr. Wickham departed Brighton together, just on the eve of our wedding?"

Elizabeth started at the sudden shift in topic. *What is this about?* "I had not considered it before. My sister is nothing if not impulsive."

"Perhaps, but Wickham is not. An opportunist, certainly, but he does nothing without motive." He came to stand directly in front of her. "He seemed surprised not to see you."

Elizabeth stiffened. "I cannot imagine why. I have hardly spoken to him since March, unless propriety demanded it."

"Your sister gave me to understand he was a great favorite of yours. She was quite delighted to have stolen him from you." His gaze was unwavering, his voice flat.

Elizabeth rolled her eyes. "My sister is a child. For years she has been eager to best either me or Jane in something — anything, really — though she was most determined to be married first." She fixed him with an equally firm gaze. "I do not deny I found Mr. Wickham charming when I first knew him, but I was never attached to him. Later I began to think of him very differently. Certainly by the time we returned from Kent. Not that Lydia noticed. She sees nothing that does not suit her fancy, and she has a talent for exaggeration."

"Then he had no reason to expect you to be in London?"

"I had assuredly not given him any reason to expect so, if that is what you mean." She could not keep the irritation from her voice. A thought came to her. "You say he does nothing without motive. He has no grudge against *me*, beyond the fact that I accepted *you*. Is it not more likely he wished to harm you in some manner? Had news of Lydia's ruin come even two hours earlier, it would have rendered me unmarriageable. How was he to know Colonel Forster would not send an express as soon as they were missed? But you arrived in London already married."

Elizabeth averted her eyes, pain creeping into her tone. "Perhaps he thought it would harm you to believe I cared for him." *It might have done so if you still cared for me,* she thought. *Mr. Wickham could not have known his actions would destroy whatever remained of your affection.* She was unnerved by the realization that she desired her husband's affection, but its obvious absence was difficult to bear.

Mr. Darcy turned away and stared into the flames. "Perhaps," he said at length. "I shall not keep you any longer. You may retire if you wish."

"Thank you." She did not wish him good-night. After all, would she not see him in her chambers soon? There had been no wedding night. *He must expect to claim his rights as a husband, for all that he hates the sight of me.*

She shuddered; she had been in his company for no more than ten hours complete in three months. She had no desire to welcome a resentful stranger to her bed, but she knew her duty.

Sarah brushed out Elizabeth's hair, leaving it to hang in loose chestnut waves nearly to her waist, and set out the scandalously sheer white silk night-rail Mamma had insisted Elizabeth wear for this. Once she donned it, gooseflesh covered her skin and she could not stop shivering, though the room was pleasantly warm.

It required all Elizabeth's courage to sit by the fire with her hands quietly folded in her lap. She wished desperately to throw a shawl about her shoulders and wrap her arms about herself. She flinched at every sound that might be the knob of the door across the room, which opened onto the sitting-room separating Mr. Darcy's bedchamber from hers. Tonight, for the first time, she had unlocked the door with trembling fingers.

But the knob never turned. Once she thought she heard it rattle, as though her husband had placed a hand before thinking better of it. Eventually the fire burned low and the candles guttered. She wrapped her shawl about herself and wept, knees drawn to her forehead.

Does he despise me so completely? Perhaps he is waiting until we are no longer so awkward with each other. Nay, there is little hope of that. And he requires an heir. So why did he not come to me?

She could not make sense of it. Nor could she ignore the flicker of relief that he had not imposed his body upon her. Finally, she was too drained to sort out her disordered thoughts and feelings. She stumbled to her bed and fell into exhausted slumber.

Eight

The Fall

$\mathcal{M}$R. DARCY'S RETURN to Pemberley caused little change in Elizabeth's routine, as it happened. She took breakfast in her room most mornings, as Georgiana often went riding with her brother and Elizabeth was not yet skilled enough to join them. They were usually returned by the time Daisy was saddled and waiting for Elizabeth's riding lesson. Elizabeth and Georgiana would trade pleasantries while Mr. Darcy looked on, saying little before he excused himself to attend to his correspondence.

Several times Elizabeth noticed her husband standing at the open window of his study, observing her as she rode around the paddock. She was learning to trot, though she struggled to accustom herself to the bouncing gait and nearly bounced out of the saddle on more than one occasion.

"I may soon be forced to admit defeat, Mr. Reynolds," she said on one such morning, pulling Daisy to a halt. "Quite aside of the ridiculous image I present, I am not certain my spine can tolerate such jarring. To say nothing of the very real possibility I shall topple face-first into the dirt."

Mr. Reynolds shook his head. "Nay, Mrs. Darcy. Your seat improves already."

"I would not say you look entirely ridiculous," said a new voice.

Elizabeth's head swiveled. She had not noticed Mr. Darcy approaching. The corners of his mouth lifted slightly as he leaned against the paddock fence.

"Your countenance belies your words, sir," Elizabeth said wryly. "You would not smirk so otherwise."

"Somewhat ridiculous, then." He smiled. "You shall find it more comfortable if you hold yourself just above the saddle and sit down fully only every other step. You might also try loosening your grip on the reins."

"I thank you for your kind advice. I shall apply it at my next lesson. Now, however, I should prefer to dismount and walk for a bit."

Mr. Darcy straightened but before he could take more than a step Mr. Reynolds was there, lifting Elizabeth to the ground. He was a strong man and lowered her easily, setting her down a respectable distance away. Mr. Darcy's smile vanished.

Elizabeth looked at her husband curiously. "Will you walk with me to the hedge-maze, Mr. Darcy?"

He nodded stiffly and they set off in silence. He looked straight ahead, countenance shuttered, and he seemed to be taking care not to walk too close to her. The hedge-maze was some distance away, to the west of the lake; they had nearly reached the entrance before Elizabeth gathered the courage to speak.

"May I know what troubles you?" she asked.

He frowned, and for a moment it appeared he would not answer. Then, without looking at her, he said, "I would prefer to assist my wife from the saddle."

Elizabeth stared at him. *Can he be... jealous? How is that possible?* She had seen no sign he still held any sort of tender regard for her. Indeed, since his return he had never sought her out before this. He spent his days attending to business and overseeing the harvest. She saw him in the evenings, but they both spoke far more to Georgiana and Mrs. Annesley than to each other. And he had never yet visited her bed.

He must have read the surprise and confusion on her face, for his frown deepened. "Perhaps you do not expect me to play the part of a husband."

She flushed. "I do not know what to expect." She turned her head, unable to look at him, and her voice was soon thick with suppressed emotion. "Particularly after Lydia's disgrace. You said once... that we would live apart. After the wedding. You have made no mention of it since, but it is nearly three weeks since you returned, and you have not dismissed Mrs. Annesley. If Georgiana still requires a companion, I cannot believe you wish me to remain here as her sister."

It was his turn to stare incredulously. "You have been waiting all this time to be packed off somewhere?"

Elizabeth shrugged helplessly, tears pricking at her eyes. *It is fortunate,* she thought, *the hedge-maze is so far from the house.* It was not tall enough to conceal them, but there appeared to be nobody near enough to see her discomfiture.

"Elizabeth, I—" He shook his head, gaze directed upward, before facing her squarely. "I am sorry to have caused you such uncertainty. I spoke in anger that day; I have long since thought better of it. As I said on our wedding-day, you are Mrs. Darcy. Your place is here." He gave a small shrug. "I kept Mrs. Annesley on so that Georgiana might have more than one companion. As you say, she has difficulty forming new acquaintances. Perhaps it was a mistake to do so."

"I cannot say if it was a mistake or not. Only that it has caused some confusion for Mrs. Annesley and Georgiana as well. They would not naturally be friends — their ages are too far apart, and they have few interests in common."

He nodded slowly. "I shall speak to them both today. And let me be clear: I wish you to be a sister to Georgiana. As for Lydia, her behavior does not reflect upon you. Lydia's foolishness belongs to her alone."

"I thank you," said Elizabeth quietly. As they made their way through the maze, she added, "Speaking of sisters, I have not yet answered Jane's inquiries about her wedding. May I say we shall attend?"

"Yes," Mr. Darcy said. "I should like that very much."

* * *

The next two days passed far more pleasantly than any before. Mrs. Annesley departed Pemberley with affectionate good wishes. Georgiana and Elizabeth began to spend the afternoons together, and Mr. Darcy offered to join them once the harvest was in. Elizabeth and her husband were still somewhat awkward with each other, but she began to see glimpses of the ease and humor he had shown in Hertfordshire before that terrible day in May.

On the third morning after their walk in the hedge-maze Elizabeth had tucked herself into the window-seat in her bedchamber, nibbling a pastry. It was the first of September and the day promised to be mild and sunny. Outside, Mr. Darcy galloped toward the lake. He rode alone this morning: Georgiana and her lady's maid would soon depart to visit the shops at Lambton, the charming town only five miles distant. Elizabeth had elected to stay behind; her courses were due, and she was achy and irritable.

She continued to sleep alone, for which she was grateful. *Perhaps he truly was waiting until things were less fraught between us,* she thought. Neither of them had said a word about it. Elizabeth could not imagine broaching the topic — what could she possibly say that would not be mortifying? — so she put the thought aside. He would come to her when he was ready; she only hoped he waited at least another week.

An hour later she was dressed and lingering over her coffee when a tremendous thud sounded from the hallway, followed by a crash and a masculine cry. Elizabeth flew to the stairs. Mr. Darcy was sprawled at the bottom, leg twisted at an unnatural angle, blood beginning to pool where his head rested by the shattered pieces of a great porcelain vase.

"Mr. Darcy!"

Hers was not the only cry; the commotion had attracted servants from all over the house. Mrs. Reynolds called for clean cloths and fresh water and dispatched a footman to fetch a surgeon. Mr. Simmons, her husband's valet, bent over him and urgently called his name.

"What is it, Simmons?" Mr. Darcy's voice sounded groggy.

"You took a fall, sir. You struck your head, and your right leg appears to be injured." Simmons looked up at Elizabeth.

"He cannot be moved before the surgeon approves, but we must stop the bleeding. Can you do that, Mrs. Darcy? I will attempt to keep him conscious."

"Yes." Elizabeth took a wet cloth and held it to Mr. Darcy's head. It turned from white to red with alarming speed.

He swatted at her hand. "Why are you speaking of me as though I was not here?"

For the next half-hour they remained there in the hall, entreating Mr. Darcy to lay still when he would attempt to rise. Elizabeth had gone through three cloths before the bleeding truly began to slow. Her skirts were ruined, the floor was a mess of blood and porcelain shards, and Mr. Darcy complained bitterly about the pressure of her cold hand against his temple, but she held on.

Eventually he succeeded in lifting his head. "What the ▨▨▨ is wrong with my leg, Simmons?"

"The bone appears broken, sir. It will need to be set. Please allow Mrs. Darcy to hold the cloth to your head. You are still bleeding."

Finally, the surgeon arrived and took in the scene. "Has he been moved? No? Excellent." His examination was swift and efficient. "Please continue to hold the cloth to his head very firmly, Mrs. Darcy, while I attend to the leg." He looked at Simmons. "I shall need assistance holding him while I set the bone."

Mr. Darcy frowned. "I am well able to tolerate pain, doctor."

"I have no doubt of it, sir, but I should prefer if your man and one or two others help you to remain still all the same. I cannot have you move if I am to bring the bones into proper alignment."

Mr. Simmons, Mr. Reynolds and two footmen positioned themselves, firmly grasping Mr. Darcy's shoulders and legs. There was a sickening grinding sound; Mr. Darcy paled, and his body relaxed as he lost consciousness.

"Good. Better he is not aware of this," the surgeon muttered. "But do not leave your stations, gentlemen. He may yet wake."

Mr. Darcy remained unconscious, however, through the setting of both lower leg-bones, the splinting and wrapping, and the examination and stitching of the head wound. Four men bore him to his bedchamber and cut him out of his bloodied clothes while Elizabeth waited in the sitting room next door. When he was once again clean and garbed, she stationed herself at his bedside.

It was some time before he finally woke. He immediately attempted to rise, then fell back into the pillows with a grunt. "By Jove, Simmons, I feel as though my head has been split with an axe. And what the ▬▬ is that on my leg?"

Mr. Simmons patiently explained his injuries once again.

Mr. Darcy frowned. "Why are you are speaking to me as though I were an imbecile?"

"Of course you are not an imbecile, sir. It is only that — you do not recall it — but we spoke of this several times before the surgeon arrived."

"How severe is your pain?" Elizabeth asked. "The surgeon instructed me to give you some laudanum when you woke. Only a little, on account of the injury to your head."

"Which surgeon was that?"

"Dr. Pierce, sir," said Mr. Simmons.

"I want Lindley."

"Dr. Lindley is in London, sir."

"Then fetch him here. He is a superior physician to any man in Derbyshire and I require his medical opinion."

"I shall immediately send an express, sir, but he cannot possibly arrive for several days."

"Fine. Pierce may attend me until then." He looked at Elizabeth. "Do you know how to administer laudanum?"

"Of course, Mr. Darcy."

"Very well, then. My entire body seems to be throbbing."

Over the next five days Elizabeth rarely left Mr. Darcy's side. Georgiana, who had returned home when her brother was still unconscious, also kept silent, tearful vigil. Mr. Darcy was irritable and cross whenever he woke, and for the first day or two they were obliged to tell him several times what had happened. The head wound healed cleanly, thank the heavens, but the pain in his leg seemed to become worse rather than better.

By the time Dr. Lindley arrived, Mr. Darcy had been complaining for days of burning, shooting pain in both legs and hands. Dr. Pierce blamed the concussion, but Dr. Lindley frowned. He instructed Mr. Darcy to press his uninjured foot against Dr. Lindley's hand and grip the physician's first two fingers. Mr. Darcy had no difficulty identifying where the physician touched him, even with his eyes closed, but both legs and hands were weakened far beyond what would be expected after only five days abed.

"There is more to this than merely a broken leg and a concussion," Dr. Lindley told them. "Though Mr. Darcy has no memory of the fall, it may be that it was due to weakness in his legs."

Mr. Darcy looked annoyed. "I have never suffered from weakness in my legs, Lindley."

"This is indeed new. What can be causing it, doctor?" Elizabeth asked.

"An excellent question. Were it only weakness in the legs, I would look to the muscles. Given that his hands are also involved, and he complains of pain there as well, I suspect a disorder of the nerves. I shall remain in Derbyshire to closely observe him."

He proceeded to prescribe a larger dose of laudanum than Elizabeth had ever seen used. "It is safe enough, Mrs. Darcy," he told her. "With regular dosing through the day, the body becomes accustomed, and the medicine loses its potency. So long as he is not too sedated and he breathes normally, the dose is not too high."

With his pain improved, Mr. Darcy's frustration turned to his enforced immobility. They all adjusted to accommodate him. Harwood met with him daily to discuss the estate and Georgiana had her old piano moved into the next room so he could hear as she played. Elizabeth sat with him in the afternoons to relieve Simmons, sewing or reading as Mr. Darcy frowned at her around his newspaper.

"What do you do in the mornings?" he finally asked her. "It has been a week since I was injured, and I hardly see you before mid-afternoon."

"I improve my riding or visit the tenants. If you wish me to sit with you in the mornings, however, I shall do so."

He stared at her a long moment. "I recall you said you might give up riding when trotting proved too difficult. You have continued?"

"Yes. I applied your advice and had far greater success. In fact, I find I quite enjoy riding."

"You sound surprised."

"I was thrown as a child. I have not been comfortable on horseback since, but Daisy is so gentle. Mr. Reynolds was wise to recommend her, though he says I must have another mount if I am to learn to canter or gallop."

"You enjoy Reynolds's company?" She could not miss the suspicion in his tone.

She shrugged. "Mr. Reynolds is very capable, and he does not shame me for my ignorance or error, which makes him a valuable instructor."

"Hmm." Mr. Darcy continued to stare at her but made no other reply.

* * *

As difficult as those first days were, Elizabeth learned to look on them as easy in comparison to what came later. By the time another week had passed, Mr. Darcy could not hold the newspaper; the week after that, he could not lift his arms or legs at all. Then it became difficult for him to sit upright, even with assistance. The pain climbed his body along with the weakness, and the doses of laudanum grew ever larger and more frequent.

Elizabeth took to sleeping on a sofa in Mr. Darcy's room. Simmons, bless him, spent all of every day with his master — feeding, bathing and dressing him, exercising his limbs, never complaining despite Mr. Darcy's irritability — but even the seemingly super-human valet needed sleep. At night Mr. Darcy's pain seemed to be worse; he slept poorly, waking Elizabeth often with groans of discomfort. He would refuse the laudanum — "I cannot think with that blasted stuff clouding my mind" — but would beg for a dose an hour later, screaming in pain if he delayed any longer.

He was also increasingly surly, particularly with her. When she sat with him in the morning to read the newspaper to him, he said, "Come, Mrs. Darcy, you have such a clear voice — do tell me how my investments are doing. Surely you must have an interest in my income." Another night when she offered the laudanum he said, "Of course my *beloved wife* wishes me to down the wretched potion! I shall be silent and biddable henceforth!"

When she assisted Simmons to exercise his limbs one afternoon he sneered, "Why, Miss Bennet! You take my hand at last. I see it required only my utter helplessness for you to do it."

Grimly determined, she ignored his remarks and pressed on. Simmons gave her a conscious look but said nothing. Mrs. Reynolds entered with a new bottle of laudanum and greeted Mr. Darcy pleasantly.

"Excellent, I see you have brought the poison," he said with exaggerated cheer. "Is it time yet for another dose? My blushing bride would like nothing so well as my insensibility, I think."

Mrs. Reynolds tsked. "Now, Mr. Darcy, you mustn't say such things. You know very well Mrs. Darcy is only doing as Dr. Lindley instructs."

"I know no such thing."

That, at least, is the truth, Elizabeth thought. Mr. Darcy's memory had improved for a time, but in the past week he had begun to demand repeated explanations, as he had done immediately after his head injury. "It is more than an hour until the next dose is due," she said. "Mrs. Reynolds, perhaps you will join me for tea while Mr. Simmons assists Mr. Darcy to complete his exercises."

They departed the room to find Georgiana standing in the hall, wide-eyed with dismay. "I am sorry, Elizabeth, I came to play for my brother, and I could not help but overhear. Does he — ?" She blushed. "Is he always this way?"

"Does he say such terrible things often, do you mean? It has become more common of late. Dr. Lindley believes it is the illness at fault and advises me to think nothing of it." *Let us hope he is correct.* She had not told the physician of her husband's veiled accusation the first evening after his return, when he seemed to think she had been in league with Mr. Wickham, or his pointed questions about her riding lessons with Mr. Reynolds. *He cannot truly believe I wish to poison him.*

That evening she sat before the window in the library to write the letter she had been dreading.

Pemberley, 24th September 1812

My Dearest Jane,

Can it be possible your wedding is only a week distant? How the weeks have flown by! As delighted as I am for you both I am quite wretched today, for I cannot travel to Hertfordshire to stand up with you. Mr. Darcy's condition has not improved, and he requires constant attendance. Dr. Lindley remains in Derbyshire and will not leave until he is satisfied Mr. Darcy is on the mend. (I cannot imagine what his London patients do without him, for he is an excellent physician.)

You must not worry about us, however. Despite these difficulties, we want for nothing. Mr. Darcy receives diligent care and Mrs. Reynolds bullies me into eating and taking leave of the sick-room from time to time. Daisy lures me out of doors nearly every morning, though we do not travel far from the house.

I have visited the tenants only twice in the past three weeks, but Mr. Harwood assures me they are well. Mr. Burrell's visits are a source of comfort and calm amidst the turmoil, and dear Georgiana finally begins to see me as a proper sister, I think. Today she insisted I must ride Willow — her own mare! — that I might learn to canter.

Give my love to all at Longbourn. Next week you must write and tell me if Mamma succeeds in sneaking another dozen guests into the pews at your wedding, as she did with mine!

Your affectionate sister,

Elizabeth

She sealed the letter with trembling hands. She had written nothing untrue but she was lying to her sister nevertheless, as she had lied to Georgiana. *As Mr. Wickham lies — by omitting truths that would alter the story.*

The truth was that Mr. Darcy's comments were becoming increasingly vicious, and they were beginning to wear on her. She had not slept well in weeks and she avoided the mirror; she had no desire to see her own dull eyes and sallow skin.

She did not wish her family to become concerned and journey to Pemberley. She told herself it was because she did not have Mr. Darcy's permission to invite them and because Dr. Lindley could not be certain if Mr. Darcy's condition was infectious. But as she stared at the letter in her hands, she forced herself to acknowledge the real reason.

I cannot bear for them to see me thus — belittled by my husband, unable to respect my partner in life. This sickness does not cause him to think ill of me. It permits him to say what he already believes. She recalled his seemingly easier manner in the few days before his fall and feared it had merely been wishful thinking on her part.

She sighed. *I do not belong here.*

Nine

October

MRS. DARCY, I must speak with you."

Elizabeth looked up from Jane's latest letter. Harwood stood in the doorway, worrying the brim of his hat in his hands. "Of course, Mr. Harwood. Do be seated. What is the matter?"

"I've just heard there is influenza in Lambton, ma'am. Many of our staff have family there. It's been years since we had the influenza at Pemberley, but it was bad. It spreads quickly. Many people died."

"Oh, no! Are any at Pemberley ill?"

"I cannot say, ma'am. I came to you as soon as I heard."

Elizabeth paused. "Does not Mr. Darcy know of this?"

"No, ma'am." Harwood's hands clenched, mangling his hat brim. He forced his eyes to meet hers. "I don't believe Mr. Darcy is in any fit state to decide on matters such as these."

Elizabeth nodded slowly. "I understand."

Mr. Darcy had continued to worsen. In the week since Jane's wedding, his speech had become garbled and his eyes unfocused. "It is as though he were intoxicated," Simmons had said to Dr. Lindley. "Can it be the laudanum?"

"Unlikely," Dr. Lindley had replied thoughtfully. "The dose has not recently been increased. This disease appears to be attacking the nerves and muscles in a progressive fashion. The tongue is now affected, impairing his ability to speak."

Despite difficulty making himself understood, Mr. Darcy persisted with his cutting remarks, though they were no longer directed solely at Elizabeth. He had begun to openly question Elizabeth's fidelity, associating her with both Mr. Wickham and Mr. Reynolds, and had even begun to glower at Simmons and mutter imprecations under his breath.

Most worrisome, however, was his breathing. Just last night she had noticed his breaths came faster and he could not jeer at her without pausing. Simmons was with him now; Mr. Darcy had banished her from the room as they awaited Dr. Lindley.

How am I to keep influenza from spreading? Elizabeth wondered. She had no experience with such a thing, but Mr. Harwood needed her to be decisive — they all did. "We must discover if any of Pemberley's staff or tenants are ill, and who has visited Lambton recently," she said, speaking with more confidence than she felt. "I shall instruct Mrs. Reynolds to inquire of the house staff. You shall speak to the grounds-keepers, stable hands and tenants."

"Very good, ma'am. And if any are ill?"

"I shall ask Dr. Lindley for his advice, but we must try to keep them away from those who are healthy."

For all their efforts, it was already too late. Several of the groundskeepers fell ill; Elizabeth instructed them to remain away from the house. Fortunately, there was little grounds work needed, as it had been raining ceaselessly for several days. Some of the footmen and maids took ill soon afterward, and Elizabeth banished them from the house as well. She instructed Pemberley Cottage be opened for them, and Mrs. Reynolds assigned others to provide their care.

Elizabeth, Harwood and Mr. Burrell saw to the tenants. Elizabeth begged them to remain in their homes and visited frequently, bearing food and medicines. Every day it became more challenging to make her rounds; the rain refused to stop and roads were increasingly treacherous, mud sucking at carriage wheels and causing horses to lose their footing.

Influenza made its deadly, inexorable way through the farms and villages. One of the gardeners died first — an older man with a weak heart — and Mr. Burrell was soon giving last rites in many households. Elizabeth comforted grieving families as best she could before returning to Mr. Darcy's bedchamber, where she felt equally helpless. She lay awake at night, listening to her husband's labored breathing as he slept. His barely-intelligible accusations whenever he awoke in pain, glaring as she held the glass of laudanum to his lips, were no more pleasant.

She knew she must look a fright when the staff began to admonish her. "You cannot see to every sick person on the estate yourself," Mrs. Reynolds told her. Sarah commented pointedly that her stays and dresses were too loose. "You must eat, ma'am," she said.

To appease them, she tried. For three rain-soaked, dreary days Elizabeth remained at the house and ate whatever was set in front of her. She felt utterly useless as she wandered through the empty rooms, unable to settle on anything to do. It had been raining continuously for more than two weeks and she could no longer travel safely to the tenants' cottages, but this knowledge did nothing to ease her mind.

She could not even divert herself by spending time with Georgiana. They played the pianoforte and read aloud to one another, but their conversations were subdued. Even the servants spoke in hushed whispers. The specter of illness and death hung over them all.

On Elizabeth's fourth day of confinement Harwood came to her again, his expression grave. "It's the rains, ma'am. They've drowned the vegetables and wheat just planted, and there's flooding. Some of the stores are spoiling. We at the house shall find it difficult to get through the winter at this rate, never mind the tenants."

Elizabeth's chin lifted. "Then we must discover a way to obtain more food."

She spent the day in Mr. Darcy's study, reviewing the estate's account ledgers. They were more complex than Mrs. Reynolds's household accounts, but with Harwood's detailed explanation she soon felt able to make some sense of it.

"We must grow what we can," she decided. "Any of the gardeners who are healthy must convert the hothouse for the growing of vegetables. Inquire into purchasing grain from the south. Cook can preserve whatever stores we still have. We shall likely be required to store food in our cellars for the tenants as well as ourselves."

The worry on Harwood's countenance did not ease. "How are we to pay for food from the south? It shall cost a pretty penny to transport it in the winter."

"Start with my pin money. We may also leave off enlarging the stables for another year. What we save on salaries and supplies we can divert to the purchase of food. And I shall speak to Cook about limiting the menu."

"Do you not require your pin money for your own needs?"

"I need my people to have food to eat far more than I need new clothes, Mr. Harwood. We shall all be required to sacrifice, I wager, to see this winter through."

"Aye, ma'am. There's another thing, too. The tenants shall struggle to make their rents this winter. It's the sale of last year's wheat that usually sees them through at this time of year, but with the influenza... medicines are expensive, and many have been too ill to work."

Elizabeth sighed. "It may be necessary to forgive the rents this winter. I shall examine the accounts and try to discover if there are any other alternatives."

"Of course, Mrs. Darcy."

Elizabeth spent some time puzzling through the ledger, comparing its entries to those of several previous years to be certain she correctly interpreted the figures. Harwood was right; once the rents were paid, many families would be reliant upon charity if they were to have food and sufficient fuel to heat their homes. She had already heard tales of the occasional snows and freezing rain to come.

I cannot expect them to choose between starving and freezing, not after an autumn such as this. She would tell Harwood to forgive the rents and ask Mr. Burrell to remind the more prosperous tenants that charity toward their neighbors was their Christian duty in times like these.

Suddenly her eyes were arrested by a familiar name in the ledger she held. *George Wickham!* She examined the entry; on

14th August 1808, the sum of three thousand pounds was paid to George Wickham. The annotation read, "In lieu of Kympton preferment."

Can it be? Mr. Wickham had been so eager to paint Mr. Darcy as the worst sort of blackguard for refusing him the position as Kympton's parson when it fell vacant, but if he had already been compensated....

Elizabeth searched through Mr. Darcy's desk, finding no other record of such a transaction. She sighed, disheartened, until her fingers closed upon a key tucked into the very back of the bottom-left drawer. Studying it carefully, Elizabeth guessed it might open the great wooden chest which sat against the far wall. She closed the study door and tried the key. It turned smoothly.

The chest contained what seemed to be decades' worth of important documents, including the late Mr. Darcy's will. Reading it carefully, Elizabeth discovered Mr. Wickham had been bequeathed a legacy of one thousand pounds upon the elder Mr. Darcy's death in 1807. There was also a letter from Mr. Wickham dated August 1808, offering to give up the Kympton preferment in exchange for a lump sum. He was not inclined toward the church, he wrote. He now intended to study the law.

When we met him last autumn, he had no money and no prospects, Elizabeth thought. *He was certainly not a solicitor. How could he have spent four thousand pounds with nothing to show for it?* She hardly needed another reason to dislike Mr. Wickham, but she was now entirely in agreement with Mr. Darcy's opinion of him. *How blind I was! How gullible! Oh, poor Lydia!*

She resisted the urge to snoop further into the documents in the chest. *I must serve as both master and mistress of Pemberley while my husband's mind is incapable of grasping hold of reality,* she told herself. *But if he recovers, he will not thank me for such an intrusion into his privacy. I will open this chest again only if I must.* Sighing, she replaced the documents, locked the chest and returned the key to its hiding place.

* * *

After supper Elizabeth would have gone directly up to Mr. Darcy, but Georgiana forestalled her.

"Elizabeth, I — I feel useless," Georgiana said miserably. "I wish to help but I know not what I can do! You visit the tenants and see to the servants, and then you spend all night and half the day caring for my brother while he shouts at you, and I do nothing but play and read to him!"

"Oh, Georgiana. My dear sister, you are not useless!" Elizabeth regarded the girl with all the seriousness she could muster. "Your brother would never forgive either of us if I permitted you to expose yourself to illness, and it is a great help for you to play and read to him. You may ask Simmons if you do not believe me! It soothes him, and very little can soothe him at present."

"I wrote to my aunt at Matlock," Georgiana said. "I hoped my uncle might be of assistance, but they are not at home. They have been in Scotland these two months, and she says there is influenza at Matlock as well. They have urged my cousin Arthur and his family to join them at Heath Hall. They mean to stay all winter."

It had not occurred to Elizabeth to seek assistance from Mr. Darcy's family, any more than she wished for assistance from her own. "Thank you for thinking of it, Georgiana. I can only hope they all remain healthy."

Georgiana nodded, her chin set at a stubborn angle. "If we are to be entirely on our own, there must be something more I can do. You cannot take everything on yourself, Elizabeth. You are making yourself ill!"

Elizabeth thought. "There is something. Harwood told me the rains have drowned the crops. I asked him to see the hot-house given over to vegetables. Will you talk with Cook and the gardeners about what should be planted, and what must be preserved if we are to feed ourselves this winter?"

"Certainly!" Georgiana's eyes lit up. "I shall see to it first thing in the morning. Shall I discuss the menus with Cook as well?"

"Yes, thank you." Elizabeth smiled. "I do hope Cook is not too scandalized when you tell her we wish to eat as simply as the servants do. You must prepare yourself — we shall all be heartily sick of stew by Christmas, you know."

Georgiana's eyes widened. "I suspect you are making fun so as not to frighten me, but you must tell me the truth. Is the situation truly so serious?"

"It is. Harwood says the tenants shall be hard-pressed to make it through the winter, with the crops entirely gone and the stores spoiling."

"And so many ill or dying…" Georgiana frowned. "My brother cannot help us, can he?"

"Nay, he cannot. I only pray he does not continue to worsen. His breathing frightens me."

A new light of determination shone in Georgiana's face. "Then we must do all we can. Together. I shall be happy to eat stewed turnips every day for a month if need be."

Elizabeth laughed. "You hate stewed turnips."

Georgiana's determination crumbled a bit. "Yes, well, let us hope it does not come to that." She flashed a mischievous grin. "I suppose it is a good thing I shall be the one talking to Cook about the menu. And if you are going up to my brother now, I shall come with you and read aloud to him."

The next few days saw more of the same: the hard, steady rain continued to render the roads impassable, so Elizabeth turned her mind to planning for the future. When the rain finally eased, the damage would be done: there would be no wheat this year, unless they purchased seed to plant spring wheat instead.

But how are we to pay for it? Even if he were able to hold a pen, Mr. Darcy would sign nothing she placed before him. He was suspicious even of Simmons and Harwood.

Instead, Elizabeth and Harwood studied every line of the account ledgers, strategizing how they might afford such a purchase without drawing anything more than the ordinary allowances from Mr. Darcy's accounts.

"Is there no other who might help you, Mrs. Darcy?" Harwood asked. "Lord Matlock, perhaps?"

"Not you, too, Harwood," Elizabeth said testily. "Lord Matlock is in Scotland for the winter. Besides, his estate here is equally damaged by flooding and influenza. I cannot ask him to come and help me sort through this mess when he already has one of his own. Now, is there anything we can sell that it would not injure us to lose?"

Ten

Fever

A FTER SEVERAL DAYS without rain the ground was finally firm enough to ride upon. Elizabeth had Willow saddled, at Georgiana's insistence. Outside she took a deep breath of the cool, crisp air, turning her face to the sun. For a brief period she could pretend there was no flooding, no illness, no accusing husband. Hearing a giggle, she turned to see Sarah and Mr. Reynolds near the stables, standing far too close together.

"Good morning, Mr. Reynolds," she said. Sarah jumped back, cheeks crimson. "Shall we ride? I rely on you to judge if the ground is adequate for cantering."

"Aye, ma'am. Fine morning to you, Miss Sarah." He nodded at the girl with the sort of smile that made Sarah blush again.

I must speak to Sarah, Elizabeth thought. *Mrs. Reynolds as well, I think.* She felt a pang; Mr. Darcy had smiled at her like that once — in May, when he had kissed her hand so tenderly, the night before everything fell to ruin — but she no longer believed it possible he might do so again. She kicked Willow into a trot, eager to escape her own thoughts.

The other thoughts which occupied her were unfortunately no more cheerful. The dry weather had done nothing to slow the spread of influenza. On the contrary, the disease spread more rapidly as people finally left their homes after three weeks of heavy rain. Those most vulnerable were the elderly, the infirm and the very young. Elizabeth knew she must prepare herself to learn of many more deaths when she visited the tenants on the morrow. It was imperative she stop at every home, but she had never dreaded her duty more.

As it happened, the following day Elizabeth did not stop at every tenant's home. She knocked at Mrs. Wright's door in the morning to be greeted by a sobbing Martha, who flung her arms around Elizabeth's waist.

"He's gone, Mrs. Darcy! He's gone and there's something wrong with Mamma!"

Elizabeth rushed inside, Harwood close behind her. Mrs. Wright sat before the dying fire, rocking back and forth, little Charlie cradled tightly against her chest. His small body was motionless and ghostly white. His mother's eyes were tightly closed; as Elizabeth came close she heard the fierce whispers of fervent prayer.

"Find Mr. Burrell," she told Harwood. "Tell him he must come directly." As he hastened to obey, she placed a hand on Mrs. Wright's shoulder. "Mrs. Wright? Please, Mrs. Wright, look at me."

There was no response. Elizabeth sat beside the woman and wrapped an arm about her. "Susan." The rocking slowed and the whispering stopped. "Susan, I am so sorry." They rocked gently together. "I am so sorry."

Mrs. Wright raised her face; tears streamed unheeded down her cheeks. "He was burning up with fever. I put him in a cold bath, but that only made him shake so hard he couldn't breathe. As soon as I took him out, he was hot again. But he still couldn't breathe. He just gasped — for hours, it seemed — slower and slower. Until finally he didn't breathe at all." She began to sob. "Why would God take my baby from me? He already took my William! Why did He have to take my Charlie too?"

Elizabeth had no answer. She held Susan Wright tightly in one arm and wrapped the other about Martha and the other children; they huddled close, tearful and frightened. Three-year-old Lily climbed onto Elizabeth's lap, burying her small face against Elizabeth's neck. Harwood and Mr. Burrell found them that way a quarter of an hour later: two women and five children — only four of them still living — holding on to each other as though for dear life.

Mr. Burrell said the last rites. Mrs. Wright washed and dressed Charlie's body for burial as Elizabeth spoke softly to the other children, trying to ease their fears before tucking them into bed. It was nearly dark before she finally returned to Pemberley, exhausted and heartsick, to find Mrs. Reynolds waiting with tea and a determined expression.

"Mr. Harwood told me about the Wright boy. You need food and a proper night's rest, ma'am. I will sit up with Mr. Darcy tonight. You must sleep in your own bed."

"Mrs. Reynolds —"

"I insist, Mrs. Darcy. You look entirely wrung out."

Elizabeth sighed. "Very well." She sat with Mr. Darcy for an hour after supper but allowed herself to be ushered to her own chamber when Mrs. Reynolds arrived to shoo her away. Sarah had not yet finished banking the fire when Elizabeth crawled under the counterpane, too tired even to close the bed-curtains. Within moments she was asleep.

The sun was well up when she awoke. Her first thoughts were of Susan Wright holding the body of her sweet baby boy; tears gathered instantly in her eyes. Still yawning, she padded over to the fireplace, hoping the contents of the breakfast-tray would distract her.

Clearly, I need more rest than even Mrs. Reynolds realized. She smiled wryly to herself. *She is like to tie me to this chair if I attempt to visit the tenants again this morning.*

Mrs. Reynolds, indeed, looked prepared for battle as they sat down for their daily conference. "Nay, ma'am, you shall have no cause to bark at me today," Elizabeth said. "I have determined to remain quietly at home and conserve my strength. How does Mr. Darcy?"

Mrs. Reynolds gave a satisfied nod. "A little better, I think, ma'am. His breathing seemed easier last night, though the pain is still very bad."

Harwood seemed equally pleased when she did not ask for the gig to be prepared. She had taken to meeting with him daily, as Mr. Darcy had done before his illness struck, and for once he brought her no fresh catastrophe. "The hothouse is coming along well, ma'am," he said, "and we expect a large shipment of grain and vegetables to arrive next week. Cook already has a small army preserving everything in sight."

When she entered Mr. Darcy's chamber her reception was not so favorable.

"Why, Mrs. Darcy. I missed you last night. Tell me, whose bed were you warming while Mrs. Reynolds took your place?"

"My own, sir. Mrs. Reynolds insisted."

"Alone?"

"Of course. How are you? Your speech is clearer, and Mrs. Reynolds tells me your breathing seems improved."

"Never better, Mrs. Darcy. Perhaps you would prefer to administer my morning dose of poison? The burning pain shooting up my back tells me it is nearly time."

Elizabeth kept her face expressionless as she measured out the laudanum and helped him sip from the tiny glass.

"Ah, the sweet savor of thick-wittedness." Mr. Darcy fixed her with a glare. "Tell me, wife — quickly, before this toxic brew saps my intellect — how empty shall I find my coffers when I can once again read the account ledgers? I notice you do not favor *me* with a close view of your newest fashions. I wonder, do you model them for Reynolds?"

"I have purchased no gowns to show you, Mr. Darcy."

"A likely story! Did you not marry me for my wealth?"

Elizabeth was suddenly exhausted; tears pricked at her eyes again. She caught Simmons's compassionate glance as she turned away. "I shall leave you to rest," she said. "I shall return when Dr. Lindley arrives."

Dr. Lindley was encouraged by the improvements in Mr. Darcy's speech and breathing. "It suggests you may regain the use of your other muscles," he said. "If there is any silver lining here, it is that you have had no ability to do further injury to your leg. The bones have knitted well." Mr. Darcy's leg was indeed perfectly straight, if too thin; Simmons was instructed to exercise it regularly with the other limbs. "Take heart, Mrs. Darcy," said Dr. Lindley as he prepared to leave. "This is a promising sign."

Elizabeth sat with Mr. Darcy for a time, listening to Georgiana play. After luncheon she made her way to the library, where she dozed off in her favorite chair. The nap seemed to do her good; she felt almost rested when she sent Simmons to his bed that night, taking her station on the sofa. When Mr. Darcy's groans woke her in the early morning, however, her limbs complained as she levered herself up.

One night in my own bed and I am as creaky as an old woman, she thought. She could feel a headache coming on. *Let us hope Mr. Darcy sleeps for the remainder of the night.*

In the morning the headache was much stronger, and her entire body ached as well. Dimly, she heard Simmons calling out for Mrs. Reynolds.

What is the matter? She attempted to sit up — *is something wrong with Mr. Darcy?* — but the effort exhausted her.

Mrs. Reynolds placed her hand on Elizabeth's forehead. "Mrs. Darcy! You're burning with fever! Quickly, we must get her to her own room. Oh, I hope the master does not fall ill!"

What does that mean? Mr. Darcy is already ill. Elizabeth realized she was being carried and lifted her eyes to find Simmons's face. He appeared distressed. *Mr. Darcy will not like you carrying me,* she thought. But her head pounded and she was sleepy; she rested her head against his shoulder.

"Better it's me than another man, ma'am," Simmons said grimly. "Here now, you must rest."

What? Oh. Perhaps I spoke. She felt the soft warmth of her mattress beneath her and closed her eyes. Then Sarah was there, lifting her head.

"Here, Mrs. Darcy, you must drink this." Sarah held a cup to her lips, refusing to remove it when Elizabeth turned her head.

Elizabeth sipped, just to make the girl go away. She grimaced; the liquid was bitter.

"It's willow-bark tea, ma'am," Sarah said. "It will help with the fever. Please, you must drink it."

Elizabeth was too tired to argue. Slowly she choked the tea down. *Perhaps she will leave me alone now.* But she did not; Sarah placed a cool, wet cloth on her forehead — *that feels nice, at least* — and stationed herself at Elizabeth's bedside.

After that, Elizabeth lost track of time. She woke with her mouth parched, skin hot and dry, and Sarah helped her sip cool water before peeling the sheet away and placing wet cloths on her arms, legs, neck and forehead. She begged for more blankets to stop the hard, shaking chills, furious when Sarah refused. She vaguely recalled Dr. Lindley questioning her closely about whether she was with child. She might have shouted at him but could not recall precisely.

Eventually she woke in a dark room, sweat pouring down her body. She threw off the covers and felt at her night-rail. *Good heavens! Why am I wearing the gown for my wedding-night?* It was damp, as was the sheet and pillow beneath her. *I need a bath. Or, at the very least, a clean night-rail.* She sat slowly, feeling suddenly light-headed.

"Mrs. Darcy?" Sarah's voice was groggy.

"Sarah? I am sorry to wake you. I meant only to get this sodden thing off."

"Mrs. Darcy!" Sarah's strong hands were supporting her. "You're soaking wet, that's certain. But your fever has broken at last — thank the Lord! We were afraid for you, ma'am."

At last? "How long have I been ill, Sarah?"

"Five days. Sit here while I get you another night-rail, then I shall change the bedding." Sarah guided her into the chair beside the bed, bringing her a proper night-rail and a glass of water. "Sip that, now. You've taken hardly anything for days."

By the time the bed was made up with dry linens, Elizabeth was nearly asleep again. Fortunately, her fever did not return; the next day she sat up for longer periods and took as much water and broth as she could hold. When she awoke the following morning, she felt almost like her usual self.

Dr. Lindley entered the room looking gray and haggard. "I am pleased to see you looking so well, Mrs. Darcy. You are fortunate. Your fever was very high for several days."

"Have I had influenza?"

"You have. Most likely you were infected at the Wrights' home. Mrs. Wright and her children were also ill."

"Oh no! Did any — are they well?"

"Yes, I understand from Dr. Pierce that all recovered but the youngest child."

Elizabeth sagged with relief. "That is excellent news." She gave him a frank look. "And you — are you well?"

He smiled. "I shall take your concern as a positive sign. I am well enough; it is only that I have slept little over recent days. Between you and your husband, it has been a worrying time."

"My husband?" Elizabeth's stomach knotted with dread. "What is wrong?"

He grimaced. "Influenza. You were exceedingly ill with it, but you were healthy beforehand. He, however, was not. He shall be fortunate to survive."

Oh, dear God, no. "Did I pass it to him?"

"I regret to say that is the most probable scenario. You could not have done so knowingly, of course."

"I must see him."

"Mrs. Darcy, you are not yet fully recovered yourself. You should remain here."

"Absolutely not. If my husband is near death, I belong by his side. Sarah, help me. I must get dressed."

Twenty minutes later, with Sarah trailing close behind on Dr. Lindley's orders, Elizabeth pushed through the door to Mr. Darcy's chamber. She stopped in her tracks. Only Sarah's arm around her shoulders kept her upright.

Mr. Burrell stood beside the bed, head lowered, praying aloud. Mr. Darcy's hand lay, white and still, on the counterpane. Mr. Burrell turned; like Dr. Lindley's, his face was lined and haggard.

"Mrs. Darcy. You have come just in time."

*E*leven

In Sickness and in Health

ELIZABETH FELT her blood pool in her feet. "Is he —?" Her throat closed. She could not say the word.

"He is asking for you, Mrs. Darcy."

Elizabeth sagged against Sarah's strong grasp. "Thanks be to God. I was afraid —"

Realization dawned on Mr. Burrell's face. "Nay, nay. My deepest apologies for frightening you. Your husband is very ill indeed, but he has not yet left us."

"He asked for me?" *Incomprehensible!* Elizabeth steadied herself and moved to the bed, taking Mr. Darcy's hand in both of hers. It was warm — not cold and lifeless! — and his breathing was slow and steady, eyes closed, damp hair sticking to his brow.

"He said, 'Where is my Elizabeth?' They were the first comprehensible words he has spoken in days."

Elizabeth chided herself for the hope that surged through her even as she thought, *He cannot mean me. He has never called me his Elizabeth.*

Dr. Lindley spoke from behind her. "His fever broke this morning. He has been in a great deal of pain, I confess. His breathing was so labored I was forced to reduce the dose of laudanum. He bears close watching; we are not yet out of the woods."

"I thank you for your vigilance and care, Doctor. I shall remain with him. You — and you, Mr. Burrell — should both get some sleep. I shall have someone fetch you if he seems to be worsening."

"Mrs. Darcy, I really must insist you return to your bed. You are not well enough to be up and about."

"Dr. Lindley, while I appreciate your advice and respect your opinion, if my husband wishes my presence then I shall remain."

"Go, Lindley, and snatch a few hours of sleep," Mr. Burrell said tiredly. "I shall remain and watch over them both."

Dr. Lindley's countenance clearly conveyed his disapprobation, but he departed.

Elizabeth smiled at the vicar. "Thank you, Mr. Burrell."

He snorted. "No thanks are required. I have come to know you well enough to understand that when your mind is fixed on a thing, there is no swaying you."

She dropped her gaze to Mr. Darcy's hand, still enveloped in hers. *He speaks no more than the truth. It is only my own obstinacy that has put me in this wretched situation.*

She had taken a decided dislike to Mr. Darcy after their first encounter. He had been abominably rude, true, but she had collected every one of his faults and failings, imaginary or otherwise, and had no scruple at sharing them with every-body. She had clung to her poor opinion even after he began to behave respectfully toward her in Hertfordshire and again in Kent. It was not until his proposal that she had permitted herself to see him in a more beneficial light, and then only a little.

It had been no different with Mr. Wickham, at least in the beginning. So charmed was she by his flattery and pleasing manners that she overlooked every instance of duplicity and explained away his pursuit of Miss King, for whom he felt no affection, just for her suddenly acquired dowry. Only when his behavior was so egregious it could no longer be ignored did Elizabeth see him for what he was.

Mr. Darcy looked younger in sleep; gentler, too. *I should never have accepted his proposal,* Elizabeth thought. *What was I thinking, to be so selfish? I cared only for my own needs. In return for his sincere affection, I saddled him with a wife who despised him, even when I knew how miserable it would make him. I deserve every bit of his anger and disdain.*

"I am ashamed to say you are correct, Mr. Burrell," she said at length. "Obstinacy is a failing, indeed."

"Now, child, you must not be too severe upon yourself." He placed his warm hand over hers. "That same obstinacy has led you to do a great deal of good for a great many people who rely on your protection. We call it perseverance when you do good with it." He winked. "And I daresay your husband is even more obstinate. That is why I expect him to pull through. If he is unwilling to die, then live he must."

An hour later, Elizabeth was nibbling on a thick slice of soft bread with butter — her first solid food in a week — when Mr. Darcy stirred.

"Elizabeth?" His voice was gravelly with sleep. "Where is my Elizabeth?"

Elizabeth stood, her heart thudding. She could not seem to find her voice. She said nothing as Mr. Darcy's searching gaze traveled past her.

"She is here, Mr. Darcy," said Mr. Burrell from beside her.

This time Mr. Darcy's eyes found her before sliding away again. "No. She was here. Before. Where —?" Suddenly his gaze fixed, and he smiled. "There you are, my Elizabeth."

Elizabeth followed his gaze to the window. Nobody stood there; outside there were only the bare branches of a great oak tree, with the lake beyond. Simmons caught her eye from across the room and shook his head with a gravely resigned expression. *So this is not the first time,* she thought.

Mr. Darcy's gaze did not waver. "Will you not come to me, love?" he said. "I have waited so long. Why do you keep yourself apart? Do you not see how I long to touch you? To taste your sweet lips, and feel the soft curves of your body beneath me?"

A flush suffused Elizabeth's entire body. *It is not me. It was never me he wanted.* The growing bulge where his legs joined beneath the coverlet was unmistakable.

"My angel, tell me you are as eager as I to feel the press of your naked flesh against mine! You must come to me, my Elizabeth, I beg you!"

Tears sprang to Elizabeth's eyes. She fled the room before anyone could see them fall.

* * *

The following week was misery piled upon misery. Elizabeth learned the hothouse vegetables did very well, but the grain delivery had been a disaster: half the grain arrived covered in black mold, rendering the entire shipment worthless. Harwood had traveled to London to have it out with the seller. He remained there now to personally oversee the quality and transport of a new shipment.

There had been several more deaths among the tenants in the ten days since Elizabeth had last visited the Wright home. Young Lettie Smith, who had cared for the Wright children, was among them. Susan Wright now appeared a shadow of herself — dazed and unkempt, she scarcely acknowledged Elizabeth's presence. When she moved or spoke it was very slowly, as though it required tremendous effort, and she had visibly lost weight. Little Martha had done her best to feed herself and her siblings, but she clung to Elizabeth with a ferocity that revealed her desperation.

Once again, Mr. Burrell came through with the solution: the vicar at Lambton and his wife were childless after more than a decade of marriage. They welcomed the Wright family into their home without hesitation. Elizabeth missed seeing Susan and the children — Lambton was nearly five miles from Pemberley, too far to visit as often as she had before — but they would all be well cared-for and the children would be educated.

Meanwhile Mr. Darcy grew increasingly agitated, even as his physical condition rapidly improved. His breathing eased and his appetite returned. Then, as Dr. Lindley had hoped, he began to regain strength in his muscles, beginning with his neck and torso. The pain continued, particularly in his legs and back, but Dr. Lindley refused to increase the dose of laudanum.

"We must wean you off the laudanum very slowly if we are to do it safely, Mr. Darcy," he said. "So long as you continue to improve, your dose must be reduced."

"Lindley, you fornicating toad!" Mr. Darcy shouted. "I am paying you an exorbitant fee, no doubt, and I am in pain, damn you! As my physician, you must give me what I need!"

Elizabeth's mouth dropped open. She had never heard such offensive language from Mr. Darcy! Even Simmons's eyes widened.

Dr. Lindley was unfazed. "You may abuse me all you like, sir. As your physician, I must do my utmost to provide you with the best and safest care, even when it does not conform to your wishes. I have instructed your valet and your wife that you are not to have a drop more than I prescribe, nor are you to be given your dose even five minutes before its time. I shall see you again tomorrow."

Within days, the sound of Mr. Darcy shouting became common in the family wing of the house. He shouted at Simmons if he dripped soup down his chin, or when his exercises were painful. He shouted at the maids when his room was too warm or too cold. He shouted at Elizabeth whenever she happened to be near him, it seemed. He even shouted at Georgiana once, for reading too quietly for him to hear; she ran out of the room and did not return.

The nights were the worst, however. After all the others had gone to bed, when only the two of them remained in his bedchamber, her husband spoke to "my Elizabeth." His eyes always fixed near the window, appearing to see a woman who was not there. Sometimes he quoted sonnets to entice her; once he sang an Italian love song, his rich baritone filling the room. He complimented her fine eyes, her silken hair, her luscious breasts. He longed to stroke her creamy skin. Sometimes his invitations were so explicit Elizabeth fled into the sitting-room that separated their chambers, covering her ears even as she wept into a pillow.

And always, when he perceived Elizabeth next to his bed in the wee hours of the morning — the tiny glass of laudanum in her hands — he berated her.

After a full week of such nights, Mrs. Reynolds and Sarah had begun to second Dr. Lindley's exhortations that Elizabeth give the nighttime duty to another. Thus far Elizabeth had refused, though she was exhausted; she could not bear the thought of anyone else knowing how greatly her husband desired another woman. *Simmons has already been witness,* she reasoned, *but he spends all of every day with Mr. Darcy. It would be cruel to subject him to the nights as well.*

* * *

It was Simmons's afternoon off, and Elizabeth was sitting with Mr. Darcy. Mrs. Reynolds had proved too fond of the master — he had successfully cajoled her into giving him an extra dose of laudanum just three days ago, to Dr. Lindley's manifest displeasure — so now only Elizabeth and Simmons were permitted to administer it.

Mr. Darcy was peering at the mantel-clock as Mr. Burrell entered; he had demanded it be moved into his line of sight. "It is six minutes to two, is it not, Mrs. Darcy?"

"Yes, it is." Elizabeth was usually grateful for the distraction of a visitor, but today there was no reprieve.

"How are you feeling, Mr. Darcy?" Mr. Burrell said.

"Exceedingly poorly, Mr. Burrell. I am in enormous pain, which my lady wife knows well. But she seems to take delight in tormenting me, for she will not relieve my suffering."

"I cannot imagine Mrs. Darcy intends you to suffer!"

"How can it be otherwise, when she refuses to give me my laudanum?"

Elizabeth kept her tone calm and reasonable. "I shall give you the next dose precisely at two o'clock, Mr. Darcy. As you know, Dr. Lindley has been very strict in his orders."

"You see, Burrell, what a wretched woman I have been deceived into marrying?" He glared at her. "You swore an oath to obey, madam! Not to Dr. Lindley, nor to any other man. To me! I demand you bring my laudanum at once!"

"Only five minutes more."

"Your impudence is extraordinary, *Mrs. Darcy*. You abandon your vows with the vicar looking on! Very well, since you have no scruple in flouting your sacred duty before him, shall we catalog the other violations?"

"That is entirely unnecessary," Mr. Burrell said, but Mr. Darcy paid him no heed.

"You vowed to love me — but we both know that for a lie. You did not trouble yourself even to pretend affection. No, once you had secured me, you acknowledged your hatred openly."

"Mr. Darcy, please —"

"You vowed to honor me. What have you stolen while I lay in this bed, unable to prevent you? What purchases have you made? How many of my books have you sent to your indolent father? How many gifts to your wretched mother? How much more of my money have Wickham and that harlot I paid him to marry wheedled out of you? — Yes, I name her a harlot. Your sister was eager to open her legs for the most worthless man in England!"

Elizabeth was on her feet. "Mr. Darcy! Stop this!" This was worse than that awful day in May.

He scarcely paused for breath. "You vowed to cherish me! Ha! Tell me, *wife*, why are your gowns so large of late? Do you think to hide the bastard in your belly? That cannot possibly be my get, so do not think to pass it off as a Darcy. Give it to its father, wherever he is by then."

"How dare you! I would *never*—"

"You may fancy yourself Miss Elizabeth Bennet when you lay with him, but you swore a vow before God! You are *Mrs. Darcy*, damn you, and I will not have you parade your lover around under my nose! James Reynolds can go hang, for all I care, but he shall not do it here, and he may take his bastard with him!"

Blood thundered in Elizabeth's ears. Before she could say anything, the mantel-clock chimed delicately, twice.

Mr. Darcy's head swiveled to read the hands. "You said precisely at two o'clock, madam. And yet you stand across the room. Can you not obey even Dr. Lindley?"

"That is enough, sir!" Mr. Burrell growled. "I shall do it, Mrs. Darcy. What is the dose?"

Elizabeth barely choked out the words. "Four full spoons and one half-full." She stalked out of the room, slamming the door behind her, and raced down the stairs to the library.

Mr. Burrell found her ten minutes later, crumpled and sobbing into her favorite chair.

"Thank you for permitting me to handle the laudanum, Mrs. Darcy. No woman deserves to hear such things from her husband, much less be forced to remain in the room." When she only nodded, he said, "Does he often speak so?"

It was some time before she could reply. "He implies such things. He makes sneering remarks. Never outright accusations before now." She shrugged. "Dr. Lindley says I must ignore it. That it is the illness, or the laudanum, that makes him behave so."

"But you believe it to be more than that." He waited for a response; when she said nothing he added, "Mrs. Darcy, if there were no truth to his words you would be fuming, not sobbing. I wish to help you, but first I must understand."

Elizabeth shook her head, though she could not have said if she were more unable or unwilling to speak.

"Are you with child?"

"No!" Her response was immediate.

"I cannot believe you a thief. I could easily comprehend, though, if you do not love your husband."

She sighed. "He spoke the truth. I do not love him."

Mr. Burrell handed her a clean handkerchief. "Tell me, Mrs. Darcy. What is truth, and what is imagination?"

She told him. From her first encounter with Mr. Darcy at the Meryton assembly to his astonishing proposal and everything that had happened since, she held nothing back. She made no excuses for her prejudice, her family's failings, or the selfishness that had justly led her husband to despise her as she had once despised him.

"It was a mistake to go through with the marriage. I do not deserve to be the mistress of Pemberley," she said tiredly. "I have known it since I arrived."

Mr. Burrell's reply was sharp. "What you do not deserve is to be treated like a criminal, for doing nothing more evil than consenting to marry a man you do not love. Such marriages are exceedingly common. There is nothing extraordinary in a woman choosing to marry for security. Your husband's disappointment does not justify him."

Elizabeth blinked. "Are you not going to counsel patience and wifely submission?"

He seemed surprised. "Not at all. You have thoroughly chastised yourself for what you have done. You need not submit to his chastisement for what he *imagines* you have done. In fact, I suggest you limit your presence in the sick-room, so long as he continues thus."

No, I must not return. How can I be alone in a room with him after that? She smiled wryly. "Dr. Lindley will be pleased. He has insisted I sleep in my own bed and leave another to see to the laudanum overnight."

Mr. Burrell gave a satisfied nod. "Then we are agreed. But I must also ask... forgive the presumption, but have you considered that the mistake of going through with the marriage can be reversed?"

Elizabeth looked at him quizzically. "I do not understand you."

"If you like, I can look into the possibility of obtaining an annulment. It would require the bishop's approval, and Mr. Darcy's, though after witnessing his behavior today I expect he would agree."

An annulment! How could that be possible? "I — I am not certain. I would need to carefully consider such a step."

"Allow me to investigate, if nothing else. You need not go through with anything you do not choose to."

"Very well. Thank you, Mr. Burrell."

Twelve

Reclaiming Joy

SEATED COMFORTABLY atop Daisy's back as the horse ambled alongside the lake, Elizabeth frowned at the sky. The clouds had been high and uniform when she awoke but now a low, dark mass threatened.

"Are you well, Elizabeth?" Georgiana asked gently, her expression concerned. Even Willow, usually so spirited when Georgiana rode, seemed subdued.

In the two days since Elizabeth had last been inside Mr. Darcy's room, she had often sought Georgiana's company. Now she sighed and nodded at the clouds. "I fear our excursion shall be cut short. But I do not suppose that was what you wished to know, is it?"

Georgiana blushed, speaking to her lap. "I could not help but hear some of what my brother shouted the other day. Elizabeth, I am so, so sorry. I have never known him to speak like that to anyone! And for him to say those hateful things to you…"

"You need not apologize for him, my dear. I cannot say why he believes such things, but he is entirely convinced." She paused, debating whether to burden Georgiana with her feelings. *She deserves an honest answer,* she decided. "As to your question: I am not particularly well, for all I have slept soundly and endured no baseless accusations for two days. I expected to feel at least a *little* more at peace by now, but how can I, when so many of those for whom I am responsible are exhausted and grief-stricken?"

It was mid-November; the rains had eased considerably in the three weeks past and the influenza was finally begin-ning to loosen its grip on the estate. Pemberley Cottage no longer housed convalescing servants, and only two of the tenant families still suffered with the illness. But, as Harwood had predicted, many had died. Fewer than before, he said, but it still seemed far too many to Elizabeth.

"Perhaps we may bring them cheer." Georgiana grinned. "I know! We shall send Mr. Reynolds and Sarah around to everybody. They are both so deliriously happy you cannot help smiling when they are near!"

It was true. Mr. Reynolds had proposed once Elizabeth and Mr. Darcy recovered from the influenza. Sarah — always a lively, talkative girl — now seemed to overflow with joy, and even Mr. Reynolds wore a bashful, almost giddy grin. Eliza-beth's mornings now began listening to Sarah eagerly recite her plans for her wedding-day as she twisted and pinned up Elizabeth's hair.

"I have a better idea," Elizabeth said. "I cannot understand why I did not think of it before. We shall bring everybody to them. Sarah's father is a widower; he has not the first notion of hosting a wedding-breakfast, I am sure. We must host one at Pemberley."

"Oh, Elizabeth! What a delightful idea! Mrs. Reynolds will be beside herself. We must speak with her directly!"

"Indeed we must," Elizabeth said as she felt the first drops of rain.

They had little time to prepare, but the enthusiasm of the entire household more than made up the deficit. Elizabeth declared they must open the ballroom; no other room in the house would hold such a crowd as they expected, for Elizabeth had invited every tenant and servant on the estate. For a full week Pemberley was bustling: footmen uncovered and arranged furniture; maids burnished the silver and polished the floors to a mirror shine; the kitchens were a constant hive of activity. Georgiana took charge of the decoration and Mrs. Reynolds oversaw the menu.

Elizabeth also insisted that Sarah wear one of her gowns, ignoring the girl's protests of being undeserving of such finery. The seamstresses added a gracefully flowing over-skirt to Elizabeth's ivory silk so it would better fit the taller girl. *This dress deserves a happier fate than it shall have with me,* Elizabeth thought, recalling her own nervousness when she had first worn it. It seemed a lifetime ago that she and her aunt and uncle Gardiner dined at Darcy House, and she had hardly donned it since.

On the twenty-fifth of November, Mr. Burrell beamed like a proud father as he performed the ceremony in Pemberley's chapel. The pair had eyes only for each other as they spoke their vows, and Mr. Reynolds scandalized the onlookers, so energetically did he kiss his delighted bride. Afterward Mrs.

Reynolds and Mr. Still tearfully embraced the couple. Then the whole party scurried through the rain to the great house, the other maids hefting Sarah's trailing skirts as they ran.

An hour later Elizabeth stood near the fireplace, surveying the ballroom with satisfaction, when Georgiana joined her.

"This is the most delightful wedding-breakfast I have ever attended, Elizabeth!" said Georgiana. Suddenly she clapped her hand over her mouth. "Oh! I should not have said that. I would never wish to disparage your mother's hospitality."

Elizabeth laughed. "Nay, I quite agree with you. This is far more enjoyable than my own." She doubted the enormous room, with its elegant silk wallpaper and crystal chandeliers, had ever hosted such plain-spoken, simply dressed folk, but laughter rang from the walls and there seemed to be a smile on every face. Her heart had not felt so light in months.

Her pleasant mood lasted until evening. As she readied for dinner, the indistinct sounds of Mr. Darcy's shouting could be heard from the master's room. With a sinking heart, Elizabeth dismissed the maid and opened the door to the sitting-room that separated their chambers; she could clearly make out his tirade. Her fists clenched as Mr. Darcy railed against "that harlot's wretched party."

"She spends every cent I have on that filthy lover of hers! And were that not enough, she subjects me to the ignominy of hosting *peasants* in my family's ancestral home!"

That is enough! Elizabeth went in search of Mrs. Reynolds.

"I would like my belongings moved to the furthest room from Mr. Darcy's on the family side of the house," she said once she had located the older woman.

"Why, Mrs. Darcy! Are you quite certain? Surely there is nothing wrong with the mistress's chambers?"

"They are too near the master's chambers, Mrs. Reynolds. I have no wish to hear his every shouted epithet. I beg you — place me as far away as you can."

"If you insist, ma'am, but that room is quite small — and decorated for a man. Most often Mr. Darcy's cousin, Colonel Fitzwilliam, uses it when he visits."

"I do not object to a masculine room, nor a small one. I merely desire a quiet one. Please see to it immediately."

* * *

"I thank you for your kind welcome, Mrs. Darcy. Mr. Burrell has told me somewhat of your troubles. Before I may make a determination about whether an annulment may be granted, I must ask you some questions which shall seem intrusive and difficult but are necessary. I assure you I shall keep your answers in confidence."

Mr. Burrell had called with his bishop. The men were of an age, but where Mr. Burrell was all grandfatherly warmth, Bishop Searle was coolly patrician — assured, businesslike, and superior.

Not unlike Mr. Darcy, Elizabeth thought. *As he was, at any rate.* She was privately glad it had taken so long for him to come; after two weeks of proper sleep and blessed silence in her bedchamber, her equanimity was much restored. She had not ventured into Mr. Darcy's room since that awful day when he had "cataloged her violations."

"I understand you greatly disliked Mr. Darcy at the time he proposed marriage to you," said Bishop Searle.

She blushed. "I did, I confess."

"Tell me, what caused you to form such an opinion? And why, if you detested him, did you agree to marry him?"

Elizabeth repeated for the bishop what she had already told Mr. Burrell, though her story now held more logic and less self-loathing. He questioned her closely as to her state of mind: did she feel pressured to accept? What did she imagine Mr. Darcy would have done if she refused? Did she have reason to think him a man prone to violence?

"Nay. At that time, I did not believe him likely to retaliate with anything more damaging than words. I would have felt safe to refuse him — I would have done so, in truth, were it not for my father's ill health."

"Tell me of your father's health when Mr. Darcy applied to him."

"He had very recently been feverish with pneumonia; he was beginning to recover when we arrived at Longbourn. Mr. Darcy spoke with him the following day." *And his mind was as sharp as ever,* she thought.

"So he was not yet recovered?"

"Nay. He was short of breath even when sitting, and tired easily with any activity."

Bishop Searle frowned. "Was he inclined to consent to the engagement?"

"He encouraged me to give it up." When the bishop lifted a skeptical brow she added, "I have long been his favorite. He could not bear to see me wed to a man I did not respect and admire."

"And yet he gave his consent, despite this?"

"Papa told me Mr. Darcy was the kind of man to whom he should never dare refuse anything." The truth of it rankled. "Mr. Darcy is greatly my father's superior, you understand."

"Why did you not give up the engagement?"

She shrugged. "Nothing in my family's circumstance had altered. My father's lungs have not fully recovered. Even now my sister Jane worries for him, and she is the most likely of any of us to hope the best."

"Then why do you seek an annulment? Shall your mother and sisters not be equally destitute if he dies?"

"I have not yet determined whether I wish an annulment, Your Excellency." Her fingers laced and unlaced in her lap. "I do not like to think of abandoning a man who remains in the grip of a severe illness."

"I see. Let us say Mr. Darcy recovers and his behavior to you continues as it is now. Would you then wish to proceed?"

"Perhaps. I would now be risking only my own reputation and prospects. My sister Jane has since married an amiable man of good fortune, who I trust will ensure my mother and sisters are adequately cared for if my father dies."

"I understand. So had your sister already been married, you would have refused Mr. Darcy's proposal?"

"Yes."

He nodded. "What do you understand of the conditions under which an annulment may be granted, Mrs. Darcy?"

"Only a little, Your Excellency."

"There are several: lunacy, if present before the marriage; use of force; marriage without legal consent; and fraud."

"Mr. Darcy was entirely sane when we wed, and I did not feel myself to be forced."

"Yet you tell me you would have refused were it not for your concern for your family's welfare, which at the time had no other prospect of security. And, more to the point, that your father was not yet recovered from a serious illness and did not believe he could refuse, despite his objections to the match."

"That is true." Put that way, Elizabeth could see she had been trapped — perhaps more by society's expectations than Mr. Darcy's willful behavior, but trapped nevertheless.

Bishop Searle stood. "I appreciate your candor, madam. I shall speak with Mr. Darcy now, and Mr. Burrell shall give you my decision once I have reviewed all the pertinent information and prayed over the matter."

The men were gone for nearly an hour. Elizabeth resisted the impulse to slip upstairs to the sitting-room, where she might have eavesdropped. She could hear Mr. Darcy's shouting voice at one point, though she could make nothing out. Eventually, the two clergymen descended the stairs, deep in quiet conversation; they bade her a respectful farewell before departing the house. She made her way to the second floor; Mr. Darcy was still shouting.

Her teeth worried at her lower lip. *What shall I do if the bishop approves? What is my promise worth, if I ask him to unmake it?* She listened a moment more before retreating to her own chamber. *What shall become of me if I do not?*

* * *

For the next week she fretted. *Would it be better to have the decision taken out of my hands? Simpler, perhaps; but how shall I live with his fury when he finally regains full control of his limbs? Perhaps he shall banish me.* The thought of living alone in the country, far from Mr. Darcy, made her smile.

In the end, however, the bishop did not make the decision for her.

"I have received a letter from Bishop Searle," Mr. Burrell said. "He shall approve an annulment on the basis of fraud."

"Fraud?" Elizabeth could not disguise her astonishment. "How is that possible?"

Mr. Burrell appeared distinctly discomfited. "Mr. Darcy... did not sign his legal name in the register."

"What?"

"He signed only his initials: 'F.D.' The vicar at Longbourn did not take note of it at the time."

Why would he deliberately sign the register improperly? Could this have been his desire all along? Divorces were rarely granted except in cases of adultery. Had her husband wished to preserve other options for ending the marriage?

"Ordinarily, such an oversight would merely be corrected," Mr. Burrell went on. "In a case such as this, well... I shall say only that Mr. Darcy was eloquent in his dissatisfaction and that after his interview, Bishop Searle's sympathies lay entirely with you."

Elizabeth found she could not meet his eye. "Mr. Darcy must admit his register entry was fraudulent, I suppose, and agree to the annulment?"

"Yes, he must. Do you wish to proceed?"

"I cannot yet say." She could not keep still; a few steps took her to the window, where the lake sparkled in the sunlight. "Dr. Lindley..." She turned, sighing. "Dr. Lindley says Mr. Darcy's strength is returning, nearly as quickly as it fled. He can sit unaided and hold a cup, and Simmons is able to get him to a chair far more often. His pain is also improved, and he is... well, exceedingly unhappy, truth be told, about the laudanum being reduced, but he tolerates it. Dr. Lindley is hopeful that his mind will also be restored, given time."

"Are you also hopeful?" Mr. Burrell's voice was gentle.

"I cannot say," she admitted miserably. "Might he ever be able to think well of me again? What came before this illness was hardly pleasant, but for the briefest of times I thought we might overcome it."

The way he had looked at her on their wedding day — the way he had spoken — all had given her reason to hope. Until the messenger arrived. *And then, just before he fell, he seemed to want to be a proper husband…. Unless I was mistaken?*

"You need not decide today, or even this month. We may wait to see how he recovers, if you prefer."

Elizabeth nodded. "If his mind does recover, he may even learn to look on me with kindness."

"I shall pray for such an outcome."

Thirteen

Parting Shots

NE WEEK REMAINED until Christmas, but Elizabeth did not feel much like celebrating. How could she know if Mr. Darcy would make a full recovery? *Even if he does, how shall our marriage ever be anything more than a sham?* Dr. Lindley was exceedingly pleased with his patient's progress, but Simmons had warned Elizabeth to avoid the sick-room while Mr. Darcy was awake: "He flies into a rage if he hears your voice, ma'am."

Fortunately, Georgiana had enough Christmas cheer for them both. She directed evergreen boughs be draped on every conceivable surface, gaily tied with holly sprigs and white ribbon; planned a Christmas menu; wrapped gifts for the servants; and played Christmas songs every evening after dinner. Elizabeth found herself singing along on Christmas Eve, fingers wrapped around a steaming cup of spiced cider.

"*Venite adoremus, venite adoremus, venite adoremus, dominum.*" Georgiana sighed as she lifted her fingers from the keys. "I do like *Adeste Fideles*, but I should like it better in English. Such a pity it has never been translated!"

"I agree," Elizabeth said. "Then again, perhaps one day it shall not be considered improper for young women to learn to speak Latin. Or even Greek! We ladies might then have no such conundrums."

Georgiana giggled. "Why should it be improper, I wonder? Did not Roman women speak Latin?"

"I had not thought of that!" Elizabeth laughed. "Some of them must have done so, I suppose. Though if we are to be properly revolutionary" — she leaned forward, lowering her voice to a dramatic whisper — "do Greek women not speak Greek even now?"

"Why, Elizabeth!" Georgiana pressed her hands to her heart in mock horror. "How could you permit such unfeminine words to cross your lips?"

Impulsively Elizabeth hugged the younger girl. "I am so proud! Your education in the fine art of teasing has been shockingly neglected before now, but you are making great strides."

Georgiana ducked behind the pianoforte and brought out a wrapped gift. "Your musical education has been similarly inadequate, dear sister, but I admire how diligently you have practiced."

Elizabeth unwrapped new music for the pianoforte. "Oh, Georgiana!" Leafing through it, she said, "I am most grateful, though you must help me with it. I fear this is too much for my meager skill."

"Not at all! You have also made great strides. I believe you shall play it very well."

"I shall endeavor to justify your faith in me. And if I am to stretch my boundaries, then you must stretch yours as well." She produced a small, wrapped rectangle from her pocket.

Georgiana gasped as the bright paper fell open. "A novel! Elizabeth, thank you again and again! Our library contains so few, and I have never had the courage to ask Fitzwilliam if I might purchase any."

"Pemberley's masters have cared little for either poetry or prose, I find," Elizabeth said dryly. "The library is all dull academic tomes. *Cecelia* is a classic. I hope you enjoy it as much as I did."

When Elizabeth retired to her bedchamber, two volumes awaited her, stacked neatly alongside the writing-desk. She had purchased them months ago for Mr. Darcy to read as he recovered from his fractured leg: *Römische Geschichte* by Berthold Niebuhr. Elizabeth could not fathom why Mr. Darcy would wish to read such enormous books about the history of Rome — in German, no less — but his enthusiasm for them in May was unmistakable, and Simmons verified he had not yet purchased them himself.

Dare I give him a gift? She had not wrapped them; had, in fact, been debating with herself all day about them. Finally, she picked up a pen and opened the first volume. *Perhaps he may accept an olive-branch if it comes in written form.*

She knew little enough about Roman history, but Papa had told her as a child of the Empress Livia, devoted wife of Octavian and ambitious mother to a long line of Emperors. Before she could think better of it, on the book's end-paper she wrote:

To Mr. Darcy — Octavian of the Pemberley Empire —

Know that I have ever sought to preserve and protect you and all you hold dear.

— your Livia, Elizabeth Bennet Darcy, Christmas 1812.

She wrapped the books, tying a neat bow, and tiptoed down the hall. She knocked very softly on Mr. Darcy's door; it was a relief to see Simmons's face on the other side.

"I do not wish to disturb," she whispered, "only to leave something for him."

She padded to the bed; Mr. Darcy's features were peaceful in repose. His cheeks had filled out again — he had become far too thin, once his tongue became so affected he could manage only fluids without choking — and his color was improved. She placed the wrapped volumes on the bedside table, careful to make no sound.

Happy Christmas, Mr. Darcy, she thought. Nodding her thanks to Simmons, she slipped back down the hall to her bedchamber.

* * *

Another week passed, but Elizabeth was no closer to making a decision. *Tomorrow shall bring us a new year. Dare I believe it shall bring new hope as well?*

Mr. Darcy continued to make excellent progress physically: he could stand now with assistance, though he lacked the strength to walk, and his pain was greatly improved. He was not yet free of the laudanum, but the end was in sight, Dr. Lindley had said this morning.

"And how fares his mind?" Elizabeth asked.

"His mind has not recovered as swiftly as his body," Dr. Lindley admitted, frowning. "But he no longer rants at me if I speak of you, and he is generally less excitable."

"Does he still see a spirit-woman every night?"

"Simmons does not believe so. His master has not spoken to any imaginary persons in perhaps two or three weeks, he says."

Perhaps Harwood may begin to take estate matters to Mr. Darcy again, Elizabeth thought, settling into her favorite chair.

The tenants and staff fared tolerably well: the meals were repetitive and simple, perhaps, but there was sufficient fuel to warm homes and the influenza had finally departed. Susan Wright had even begun to come around; Elizabeth had visited the Lambton vicar's family just yesterday. Susan's demeanor was spiritless, and she needed encouragement to join their conversation, but she had lost both the vacant expression and the profound sluggishness. The children were well-fed, well-scrubbed and seemed happy enough, though Martha's eyes still took on a haunted look whenever Charlie was mentioned. Elizabeth had hugged the girl tightly before leaving.

Elizabeth eagerly opened Jane's latest letter. For three months she had devoted her mornings to estate matters and Mr. Darcy's business correspondence, saving letters from her family for the brief period in the afternoon when she could curl up, undisturbed, in the library. Jane's letters were a particular source of pleasure. Her sister was truly happy at Netherfield and wrote fondly of the rest of the family and the neighborhood goings-on.

Netherfield, 26th December 1812

Dearest Lizzy,

Happy Christmas, my dear sister! I hope you, Mr. Darcy and Georgiana had a joyful day. Charles and I were delighted by your news that Mr. Darcy's health improves at last. Such tidings can only add to our pleasure in the season. After services we spent the morning quietly at Netherfield and then enjoyed a merry dinner at Longbourn. Charles's sisters and Mr. Hurst did not, perhaps, enjoy the dinner quite so much as the rest of the party, but they were not ungracious.

I wish I could fill the rest of this letter with such happy news, but alas I cannot. I must now confess I have kept the truth of Papa's failing health from you. I know you do not take our mother's reports with complete seriousness — for which I cannot blame you — and I did not wish to add to your distress. Perhaps I hoped Papa might also make a miraculous recovery, but in vain, it seems. Dr. Burke says he has a cancer of the lung. He may live another month, perhaps two, but not likely more.

It seems cruel to ask you to leave your husband just when he begins to recover — I cannot imagine he is well enough to travel himself — but I must own I long for your company and comfort, and of course Papa misses you terribly. Our mother is surprisingly calm. She has said hardly a word about being turned out by the Collinses to starve in the hedgerows! But I cannot guess how long it will last. I pray you may travel to Hertfordshire as soon as possible!

Ever your loving sister,

Jane

Elizabeth stared, uncomprehending, at the paper she held in trembling hands. She read the letter again, and then a third time. *Papa is dying? And Jane kept it from me!*

She had not seen any of them since her wedding-day. Her father was not yet entirely recovered, she had told Mr. Darcy that morning. His lungs were weak, and he tired easily. *But it was more than that, was it not? He looked so distinguished in his waistcoat and jacket! But he required new clothes because his usual ones hung so loosely on him.* She had seen it at the time — had observed the hollowed cheeks and pallid skin — but had not permitted herself to think about what it might mean.

I must go home directly. Pemberley did well enough that Harwood could manage without her, even if Mr. Darcy was not yet able to provide direction. And Mr. Darcy had neither wanted nor required her care in weeks.

She folded the letter with shaking hands and half-ran up the stairs to Mr. Darcy's chamber. Taking only a moment to compose herself before rushing inside, she barely registered Simmons's startled expression. "Mr. Darcy, I apologize for disturbing you, but I must speak to you urgently."

He regarded her coldly from his chair by the window. "Mrs. Darcy, how kind of you to make an appearance. It has been more than a month, has it not? Why, pray tell, have you abandoned your duty to your husband?"

"Mr. Burrell advised me to stay away from your sick-room, as my presence seemed to make your difficulties worse. Dr. Lindley agreed. He has not yet given me leave to visit you. I do so now only because of the urgency of my request."

"I cannot think why you would believe yourself entitled to ask anything of me."

"My father is very ill — far more so than he was last spring. I have just had a letter from Jane, and she fears he shall not live long. I must return to Hertfordshire immediately."

His answering smile made Elizabeth shiver. It was exceedingly unpleasant, mirroring the sudden, vicious satisfaction in his eyes.

"Please do. You may take everything you brought with you last July."

Elizabeth hesitated. "I thank you."

"And do not plan on returning." At her quizzical look he lifted one of the heavy volumes of Roman history at his side. "Are you truly stupid enough to think I would believe these lies? That you have sought only to protect Pemberley? For months you have usurped my authority. You stole from me and shamelessly carried on your adulterous affair before you infected me with influenza. My death would have been very convenient for you, I am sure, but you shall not get another opportunity. Take your lover and be gone."

She stared, as though seeing him clearly for the first time. *His mind is lost.*

Suddenly the decision over which she had agonized was easy to make; she felt unnaturally calm. "I see," she said. "You have no evidence of my guilt, but I cannot convince you of my innocence. I shall be gone within the hour. You have my best wishes for your full recovery."

* * *

Within minutes Georgiana, Mrs. Reynolds, and Sarah were all assembled in Elizabeth's room.

"I am leaving Pemberley immediately and for good," she said to stifled gasps. "My father is dying, and Mr. Darcy is not able to see my actions as others do. He has made it clear I am not to return, and I am in full agreement."

"Mrs. Darcy, you must not give up on the master," said Mrs. Reynolds.

Georgiana put a gentle hand on the housekeeper's arm. "Nay, Elizabeth is right. Fitzwilliam is beyond sense. We have all seen it; is that not why the bishop was here?"

"Yes. He came to determine if he had sufficient evidence to grant an annulment."

"I do hope he shall grant it. Oh, no, that sounded awful! I meant it only for your sake, Elizabeth. You do not deserve to be treated as Fitzwilliam treats you."

"Thank you, Georgiana. Yes, Bishop Searle agreed to grant an annulment if both myself and Mr. Darcy desire it. I shall notify Mr. Burrell I wish to proceed."

"Very well. I shall arrange for the carriage to be readied," Mrs. Reynolds said sadly. "Are you certain you wish to leave today? You shall have no more than an hour of light."

"Mr. Darcy will not tolerate my presence another night, I think," Elizabeth said. "I am grateful to you, Mrs. Reynolds, but I must go. Take heart; I shall be well."

"Mrs. Darcy," asked Sarah when Mrs. Reynolds had gone, "may Mr. Reynolds and me go with you as well? You know how the master feels about my James. It's a wonder he hasn't already thrown us out."

"Of course, Sarah. You shall come with me to Netherfield. If Mr. Bingley cannot offer you a place, then I shall help you both find a position elsewhere."

"And you must take Willow," said Georgiana. "Sarah, go tell your husband to ready her as well as the carriage-horses and your own things."

Sarah hastened to obey; she disappeared before Elizabeth could object. "Georgiana, you cannot do this. Your brother will be furious! He will believe I stole her."

"I shall tell him as often as necessary that she is my gift to you. You are becoming a horsewoman and you must have a proper mount. You cannot refuse, you know. I shall not listen to a word of it."

Elizabeth embraced her, tears spilling down her cheeks. "I care not what the law says. You shall always be my sister!"

"And you shall be mine." Georgiana sniffled. "You must write to me very often. I shall contrive with Mrs. Reynolds to ensure Fitzwilliam never sees your letters."

"Naturally I shall write to you! And you must tell me how the tenants and servants do." She caught Georgiana's hands. "I beg you will visit Mrs. Wright and the children in Lambton from time to time. I worry for Susan."

"I shall. I promise to do all I can to care for the tenants as you would."

Elizabeth's things were collected and her trunks speedily packed and loaded. James and Sarah Reynolds waited with Willow by the carriage as she made her farewells. She looked across the lake and gardens, taking in the view for a final time. *I do not belong here, but I shall miss it all the same,* she thought.

She turned back to the house; the fading sunlight threw deep shadows across the stone. Mr. Darcy watched her from his window, expression flat and unyielding, making no response to her nod of farewell. As the carriage rolled away, she said good-bye to Pemberley with a heart that beat more lightly with each passing moment.

I am going home!

Part Two

Darcy

Fourteen

The Harlot is Gone

ARCY'S EYES followed the carriage until it was out of sight. "The harlot is gone," he said, making no effort to disguise his satisfaction. "Simmons, please call for Mrs. Reynolds. I wish to see her immediately."

"Right away, sir."

Simmons has become very formal of late, Darcy thought. Charles Simmons had been his valet for a dozen years; he had earned the right to speak his mind and had regularly done so before Darcy became ill. Now he was as tight-lipped and rigid as any gawky, newly-trained servant. *What has happened to him?*

"How may I serve you, Mr. Darcy?" Mrs. Reynolds curt-seyed. Curtseyed! *What the ▮▮▮ is going on here?* She kept her eyes trained on the floor, but she had clearly been crying. *She cannot have developed a fondness for the harlot.*

"Now *that woman* has departed, I wish you to restore Pemberley to its former state."

Confusion was written on his housekeeper's features. "I am sorry, sir, but I do not understand you."

"Sell every stick of furniture she purchased. Put everything back into its proper place. I want no evidence she was ever here." He frowned. "This is not a difficult charge."

"I believe Mrs. Darcy already returned the books to their former places in the library, sir."

"Do not call her that."

"I'm sorry, sir."

He nodded. "Your error is understandable. Please see to my instructions."

"There is nothing of that nature to be done, sir. Mrs. — she — made no changes to Pemberley."

"I know what I saw, Mrs. Reynolds." *Why would she lie to me?*

"As you say, sir." She curtseyed again and turned to leave.

He spoke before he could think better of it. "Why are you curtseying?"

"You are the master, sir. Good evening, sir."

As though she has not known me since I was four. Mrs. Reynolds had never curtseyed to him. She was more like a doting aunt than a servant, in fact. *Why does she now refuse to meet my eye? Could she be involved in the harlot's schemes?*

"Why was she crying, Simmons?"

"Her son just departed, sir. She does not expect to see him again."

"And why is that?"

"Your opinion of Mr. Reynolds is well known, sir. He is not welcome here at Pemberley, and servants are not permitted holidays of sufficient duration for Mrs. Reynolds to visit him in Hertfordshire."

Plausible, I suppose. "Thank you, Simmons. That will be all for now."

Mr. Burrell called the following morning. With none of the usual pleasantries he said, "Mrs. Darcy sent a note before she departed yesterday."

"She is not Mrs. Darcy."

"I see. You also wish to petition for an annulment, then?"

'Also?' She wishes an annulment? "I do."

"Very well. I shall notify Bishop Searle. He must convene a formal ecclesiastical trial, but he indicated he shall support a petition alleging fraud."

"Fraud? Not adultery?"

"Adultery is justification only for divorce. There is insufficient evidence in this case to support any other justification for annulment."

"Divorce? Nay, I have no desire to see it splashed about in the newspaper that I have been cuckolded in my own home." *Ah! Naturally she wishes an annulment. She must preserve her reputation if she is to ensnare another wealthy man.* "I am willing to do whatever I must to end this sham of a marriage quietly."

Burrell nodded. "Excellent. I shall notify you when the trial is scheduled."

Even Burrell is all business now, Darcy thought after the man had gone. *What has the harlot done to my people?* His eyes fell on Niebuhr's volumes of Roman history. *'I have ever sought to protect you and all you hold dear,' she claims. Lies.*

He had never quite been able to throw the volumes into the fire, though after reading the inscription he had been sorely tempted. Her talent for maintaining the fiction of the devoted wife was unparalleled — she had purchased these volumes knowing how eagerly he desired them. He had not read even a page, however; it felt too much like conceding victory.

* * *

Darcy stewed until tea-time, when Mrs. Reynolds brought in the tray.

Why does my housekeeper now act like a simple servant girl? "Stay for a moment, Mrs. Reynolds. I neglected to ask yesterday — what did *that woman* take with her?"

"Only her own things, sir, as you instructed."

"I did not observe many trunks on the carriage. Is another to be sent today, or was it sent yesterday?"

"I know not what you mean, sir. All she owned fit into those trunks you saw."

That cannot possibly be true. "I see. And what did she own, precisely?"

She shrugged. "Only her clothes and books and the music Miss Georgiana gave her at Christmas, I believe."

"Can we not ask her lady's maid? Summon her here."

"Sarah went with her, sir."

"Is she so loyal to *that woman,* that she would leave my service?"

Mrs. Reynolds's chin lifted. "Sarah is loyal to her husband, as she should be. She would never have stayed, with him leaving."

"Explain."

"She is Sarah Reynolds now, sir." She gave him a dubious look. "Do you not recall? They married — oh, six weeks past now."

He vaguely remembered a large party in the house; the knowledge that peasants were dancing in his mother's ballroom had incensed him. "Who was invited to the wedding-breakfast, Mrs. Reynolds?"

"Oh! Why, every man, woman and child on the estate, sir. Mrs. — *she* — insisted the people needed some joy. The meal was simple, but it was a lively time for us all." She smiled fondly. "I cannot recall that I ever saw my James so happy as he was that day."

Sarah Still married James Reynolds? Surely the harlot's maid would know her mistress was bedding him. Incomprehensible! "How much of my money did *that woman* spend on the wedding-breakfast, pray?"

"Only her own pin money, sir. She was always spending it on food and medicine for the tenants and servants. I do not know that I ever saw her spend a penny on the usual things fine ladies buy. She never bought a stitch of clothing, you know, aside from the fabric and trim we added to the gown she gave Sarah. She did buy several books, but mostly those were gifts."

How is that possible? Did she hide her thievery so well? "And jewels? What became of her wedding-ring?"

"I cannot say, sir. She never wore any jewelry but that one ring and a garnet cross."

He knew the cross; it had been around her neck every time he saw her, except their wedding-day. "What of the horse your son was riding? Was that not Georgiana's?"

"I believe so, sir, but I must ask Miss Georgiana."

"Never mind. I shall ask her myself."

"No need, brother," Georgiana said, entering the room. "It was indeed Willow. I gave her to Elizabeth as a gift." She turned a gentle smile to the housekeeper. "Mrs. Reynolds, I wish to speak to my brother alone. Will you ensure we are undisturbed?"

"Yes, Miss Georgiana. Mr. Darcy." She bobbed a curtsey to him and closed the door gently behind her.

Georgiana faced him squarely, tightly gripping the back of the chair opposite. "Elizabeth was exceedingly kind to me and took great care of the tenants and servants. She deserved something in return, and Willow was the only thing of value I could give her." She paused, appearing to gauge his reaction. When he made none, she went on. "Besides, she has made great progress in her riding, and her family has no proper riding-horses. And Willow liked her very much."

With some effort Darcy unclenched his jaw. "I am grateful to hear she was kind to you, sister. Please, join me for tea." He indicated the chair.

She did not move. "She was kind to everybody. Including you, brother." Her eyes flashed with anger. "Far kinder than you have been to anybody these last several months."

"What are you talking about?"

"You have shouted at all of us, Fitzwilliam. We are too loud, or too slow, or conspiring against you, or any number of failings. Have you not noticed that only Simmons or Mrs. Reynolds bring the tea-tray? That only the head housemaid cleans your chambers, and only Harwood assists Simmons to lift you? Have you actually *looked* at Simmons? Do you not see his exhaustion?" She furiously scrubbed tears from her cheeks. "Elizabeth did everything she could to keep you from abusing all the staff, and I shall do the same."

He blinked at her stupidly. Georgiana was never angry. She never chastised anybody, least of all him. *Abusing all the staff?* He had certainly noticed the servants all spoke to him with excessive formality. Though now he thought on it, he realized she was right; he saw only a few of Pemberley's many servants. "Georgiana, I —" He could not finish the sentence. He had no idea what to say.

She was not done, however. She took a deep, steadying breath and pulled a slim rectangular box from her pocket. "Before she left, Elizabeth entrusted me with these. She knew you would believe she stole them, and Willow. She did not want you to shout at any of the servants, not even Simmons or Mrs. Reynolds, over them."

He opened the box; nestled inside it were his mother's sapphire necklace and the matching ring.

"I told her they were hers — that though you might now regret it, they were your gift to her. She said she could not accept a wedding-gift that was given unwillingly, especially now the wedding is to be undone."

He frowned. *That harlot is not entitled to my mother's jewels.* They agreed on that much, at least.

"Fitzwilliam — I do not understand any of this. Did you truly marry her against your will? And why? If you did not wish to marry her, why not simply end the engagement?" Her eyes were accusing. "She seemed so lost and sad, even at the first. Were you cruel to her even then?"

"I was no more cruel than she deserved," he snapped. "I knew she did not love me, but when her harlot of a sister ran off with Wickham on the very day of our wedding, I knew she had played me for a fool."

"What?" All the color drained from his sister's face and she wobbled, nearly falling into the chair. "What has Wickham to do with any of this?"

"Did you not know? Lydia Bennet eloped from Brighton with George Wickham. She has no fortune — none of the Bennets do. Were it not for my intervention, Wickham would never have married Lydia. But *that woman* appeared to like him very much indeed, when I first knew her in Hertfordshire. I can only assume they were colluding together."

"Elizabeth never mentioned his name." A thought struck her. "Is that why you went so suddenly to London?"

"Yes. I instructed her not to tell you. I am surprised she did that much."

She was silent for a time. "You were right about him all along, then. He wants whatever he can get. I suppose that is why he convinced me to elope with him at Ramsgate — for my thirty thousand pounds."

"Correct. It was fortunate I made an unexpected visit before you could run off with him. So with that scheme thwarted, he joined with *that woman* to force my hand. They both came into money that day."

Georgiana shook her head firmly. "Nay, brother. You have convinced me only that *he* is wicked. You have no proof Elizabeth has done anything terrible, and I cannot share your suspicion. I have seen her do too much good."

"You cannot know the things she has done to me, Georgiana, but —"

"Oh, I know very well what you *think* she has done. We all do. You have been shouting it for months. But I saw no evidence of any of it. Ask Simmons, if you think me too naïve and trusting. Or Harwood." She stood and turned to leave. "But do not ask unless you are willing to hear them, brother. If you are only going to shout at them, I beg you to keep silent."

The tea grew cold in his cup as he sat, staring out the window at the winter trees and the lake beyond. *Have I truly been shouting at everybody?* He could not credit her assertions about the harlot — she was only sixteen, after all, far too naïve to take the proper measure of an actress as skilled as *that woman* — but she would not have lied to him about the servants. He squirmed; there were some who regularly mistreated their staff, but his father had drilled into him from a young age that he must always treat them respectfully.

I must speak to Simmons. And Harwood. And I must show Georgiana the evidence of the harlot's theft and adultery. She cannot be allowed to remain in that woman's thrall.

Fifteen

Revelations

ARCY CURIOUSLY REGARDED his valet. Georgiana's chastisement yesterday — *'have you even looked at Simmons?'* — had shamed him more than he desired to admit. Particularly now, when the bright sunlight streaming through the window highlighted the man's pallor and the sagging purple skin under his eyes. Grim lines were carved deep around his mouth — lines that had not been there six months ago, Darcy was certain.

"Are you well, Simmons?"

Simmons glanced up from where he held Darcy's foot in his hands. This was their morning routine: Darcy pushed or pulled his leg against Simmons's resistance until he became fatigued. *Simmons appears to be much stronger than he was,* Darcy thought. *Or perhaps I am only much weaker. Perhaps both.* Simmons had regularly lifted him for months, after all.

"As well as can be expected, sir."

A political response. "You appear exhausted. How do you sleep?"

"Better now, sir. Now you sleep the night through without waking, that is."

"But not before?"

"Not since I took over the night duty."

Darcy frowned. "Why not give the night duty to someone else? You would already have been here all day."

Simmons avoided his eyes. "The nights were... particularly difficult, sir. I did not wish to trouble anyone else."

"Difficult? What do you mean?"

Simmons set down his foot. "Nothing, sir. I should not have mentioned it. Will you try to walk?"

Darcy studied him. *There is a great deal he is trying not to say,* he thought. *Perhaps he expects me to shout.*

"I would have you speak the truth to me, Simmons," he said.

Simmons's expression was wary.

"Georgiana tells me my behavior these past months has been abominable. I do not recall it. I recall very little of these months, in truth." He waited until Simmons met his eyes. "I have relied on your frankness for years. I ask you to be frank with me now. You have my word there shall be no retribution for what you say."

Simmons seemed to debate with himself. "Very well, sir. Will you stand?"

Darcy levered himself up from the chair somewhat unsteadily, putting his arm across Simmons's shoulders. "What did you mean, the nights were difficult?"

"You were exceedingly agitated at night, sir. Your pain was more intense — you screamed with it, though the mistress bore the brunt of that. By the time I took over the pain was not so bad, but you slept poorly, and you threatened me and called me all sorts of terrible names when I did not give you the laudanum early."

"What names did I call you?"

"I shall not degrade us both by repeating them, sir. Will you try a step or two?"

Darcy glanced sidelong at him. *That bad?* He tried a step; his foot dragged and he started to go sideways when he put his weight on it. Simmons held him upright, his arm like an iron bar across Darcy's back. *He is definitely stronger.*

"Was that the worst of it, or is there more?"

"You… saw things, sir. Things that weren't there. People. You spoke to someone every night for more than a month." Simmons's cheeks suddenly flamed scarlet.

What could I have said, to make him blush like a maiden to recall it? He tried to remember, but nothing came. He took another step. This time his body did not threaten to topple.

"And, of course, you accused us all of trying to kill you. At first you talked of the laudanum as though it were poison. Then you were convinced you would die if we did not give you more. I don't think there's one of us you didn't threaten over it." Simmons smirked. "You even called Dr. Lindley a fornicating toad."

Darcy was not yet done with the laudanum; another two weeks yet, Lindley had said. Something about the last bit being the most difficult. The pain was largely gone, but he often found himself wishing for another dose. Grimacing, he took a third step. "I have not been kind to Lindley, have I?"

"It seems not to bother him. He says that people who take laudanum regularly are often exceedingly ill-mannered when they are not sedated."

Darcy turned carefully, leaning on Simmons for balance. "I have put you through a great deal, I fear."

"No more than most, sir, and less than some." Simmons's eyes were on the ground.

Three steps back to the chair. He took the first gingerly. "Do you refer to the harlot?"

Simmons winced. "I never saw that the mistress was unfaithful, sir. And Reynolds was smitten with Miss Sarah. Even a blind man could see that."

"What about the money she spent?" Another step.

"I know nothing of any money, sir."

A third step and he braced his hands on the arms of the chair, easing himself into it. His legs were shaking. "Thank you for your honesty, Simmons. I shall try for five steps this afternoon. In the meantime, send Harwood to me. Tell him to bring the ledgers."

"Very good, sir."

* * *

Harwood arrived promptly, carrying three ledgers and a thick sheaf of papers.

"What are the papers?" Darcy asked.

"Receipts, Mr. Darcy. I imagine you shall want to verify the ledger entries."

Darcy lifted an eyebrow. *He expects me to question them?* He opened the estate ledger, finding the last of his own entries in August. Carefully he read the subsequent ones in

167

Harwood's confident hand. There were fewer than he had anticipated.

Why are there no payments after September toward the expansion of the stables? Where are the entries for the winter rent collections? And where are the harlot's purchases? He had expected entries for furniture, art and carriages.

Perhaps they are in the household ledger. He reviewed Mrs. Reynolds's ledger with equal care, but nothing was unusual except that expenditures for meat and vegetables had been reduced. The only new expense was laudanum from the Lambton pharmacist.

The third ledger was slim, the leather unblemished. "The mistress kept a record of her pin money," Harwood said.

Darcy opened it. The entries were in the harlot's rounded, feminine hand, lacking the elegance he expected of a well-bred young lady. The first entry was in early September, just after his fall. "Did she spend nothing before this?" he asked.

"Nay, sir. She did not touch her pin money until after your injury."

A bookseller. His preferred London bookseller, in fact. The note read, "2 vol Roman hist & 2 novels."

He read further, brows drawing together in confusion. *October... medicines for fever and pain... Vegetable seeds? Why vegetable seeds? Wheat, barley, and rye? What the* ████

That note read, "Returned for blight — new shipment + potatoes, onions, turnips" in tiny script.

November... fabric, ribbon and lace — yes, Mrs. Reynolds mentioned those. For the gown. Pastries and chocolates, yes... Why would she purchase hothouse flowers? Why not simply cut them from the hothouse?

In December there were various small purchases that looked to be gifts for her family. Nothing he could see might have been intended for Wickham.

Darcy methodically matched the receipts to the various entries, growing ever more baffled and angry. "Where is the rest?" he demanded finally.

"What do you mean, sir? That's all there is."

"Harwood, *that woman* nearly bankrupted the estate while I was confined to my bed. I may not recall everything that happened during my illness, but I recall that much quite clearly. Where are the rest of the expenditures?"

Harwood shook his head firmly. "No, sir. The ledgers are accurate — I'd stake my life on it. We were worried there for a time after the flooding, I own — the mistress had no access to the accounts, of course — but she made her pin money stretch like nothing I've ever seen, especially from a fine lady. And we all agreed to tighten our belts a bit. What harm is there in boring stews day after day, if it means we can all eat this winter? We hadn't sorted out how to pay for new wheat seed this spring, mind you."

"Why should we require new wheat seed? And why did she buy vegetable seed and grain?" He lifted her ledger. "This is nonsensical."

Darcy listened in growing amazement as Harwood detailed the events of last October — influenza, flooding, crop destruction, food spoilage — the deaths of tenants and servants alike, with more to come if something was not done. He learned of the vegetable garden now flourishing in the hothouse and the forgiveness of winter rents.

"I have no authority to make what changes the mistress did," Harwood finished. "And if you'll forgive me, sir, you were in no fit state to decide on any of this. She saved us all from a lean, freezing winter, no question."

Can it be? He scrubbed his face and looked again at her ledger. *Food and medicine. Flowers...* He checked the date. *For the wedding, most likely.* "What of her relationship with Reynolds?"

"There was never anything between them, sir. None of us can fathom how you came to that idea."

"I watched him sneak her into the stables for months, Harwood."

Harwood shook his head again, his expression resolute. "Begging your pardon, sir, but you could never have seen any such thing from your bed." He shrugged. "I'll own you might have seen Reynolds and his missus sneaking in there recently. I did advise Mrs. Reynolds to see them married quickly on that account. Just after you had the influenza, that was."

I know what I saw. Simmons also said he had seen things that were not there. *Is every person in my employ lying to me?*

* * *

Darcy carefully walked across the room and back to his chair.

"Excellent!" Lindley said. "I noted a bit of unsteadiness when you turned, but you have made such tremendous progress, I have no doubt that will soon disappear. Your reflexes are normal, and your arms seem to have regained their full strength, which bodes well for the legs."

"How much longer?"

"Who can say? Your condition is highly unusual. But with the pace of improvement in the last month, I should wager you may be walking without difficulty — perhaps even able to sit a horse again — within another month. And after tonight's dose you must stop taking the laudanum."

Darcy nodded. He still craved it, but even that was slowly receding.

"Now I must examine your mental state," Lindley said. "Tell me the date and day of the week."

"Tuesday the nineteenth of January 1813."

"Excellent. Do you feel safe, or does it seem like others might be conspiring against you?"

"I am perfectly safe."

"Do you sometimes see things others do not appear to see?"

"No. Why do you ask?"

"You had difficulty with these questions when I examined you not three weeks ago, Darcy. And that examination was markedly improved over previous months. Recall that you have suffered an acute disorder of the nervous system which affected nearly every muscle in your body and caused excessive pain, requiring very high doses of laudanum. You had barely begun to recover when you contracted influenza. You were severely delirious for more than a month."

"Simmons tells me I saw things that were not truly there. Everyone tells me I believed things that are not true."

"You did indeed. Delirium can make a man temporarily insane. Agitation is common. Hallucinations and intense suspiciousness may occur when the delirium is severe. When you were recovering from influenza, you insisted I tried to kill you by denying you laudanum. I was attempting to keep you breathing, but you could not believe me."

There was a knock on the door; Simmons admitted Mr. Burrell.

"I have come with information about the trial, Mr. Darcy, but I am happy to wait outside."

"No need. We are speaking of nothing you have not heard. Lindley was telling me about delirium." He turned back to the physician. "I have several memories of — well, of Mrs. Darcy — that I have been advised may not be accurate."

"You have no true memories of her, Darcy, only insanity," Burrell interjected. He ignored the surprised faces surround-ding him. "For months — even before you fell ill! — you accused her of lies, infidelity, and theft, with no more evidence than your own suspicion and the behavior of her sister and that worthless young Wickham. You publicly degraded her from the very moment you first saw her! And when you finally discovered she disliked you for it, you humiliated and threatened her!"

Darcy felt the blood leave his face in a rush. *He cannot know about the assembly in Meryton. Unless…. Dear God, did she hear what I said of her? How many others?* He recalled her mother's frosty demeanor. *Everyone must have known of it.*

Burrell gave Darcy no opportunity to respond. "I stood in this very room last November while you ranted on about her 'broken vows.' She had no scruple flouting the oaths she had sworn before God, you said, when she was only following Lindley's orders to give you the laudanum precisely on time."

Burrell's glare intensified. "I have no doubt that, had you been capable of it, you would have struck her then. And the worst of it was, she blamed herself! I insisted she stay away from you because she could not believe she deserved better than to be treated like a common whore — by the man who swore the very same oaths to God, I might add! — after she damn near killed herself taking care of you and everybody else on this estate!"

A stunned silence filled the room.

He believes I would have struck her? After she nearly — no, that cannot be. Everyone was looking at him, Darcy realized. His voice was a croaking whisper. "Lindley — is that true? Did she nearly kill herself?"

"The influenza nearly killed her," Lindley said somberly, "but she had worn herself into the ground by then. From the day you were injured she was at either your bedside or a tenant's. She slept on that sofa, when she could sleep. You were awake screaming for hours in those days. I'm told that when tenants fell ill, she carried food and medicine to them through pouring rain, on treacherous roads."

He looked to Burrell for confirmation, who nodded, still glaring. Lindley continued. "More to the point, nobody could convince her to eat properly. She lost weight even before she contracted the influenza. Afterward, she was in this room the moment she could stand without falling. She followed my orders without fail if they were for you, but she ignored every order I gave to see to her own health."

Darcy's memories were too hazy to recall her so; when he had last seen her she appeared healthy, but by then she had avoided his rooms for more than a month. Ever since that day in November, when Burrell believed he would have laid hands on her. He shuddered. "And the babe? How fared the babe?"

"Babe? What are you talking about?" Lindley looked at him, perplexed. "Oh, yes! I had forgotten you believed her with child by another man. You were so certain I examined her when she fell ill, to be sure it was only influenza and not a septic pregnancy." He gave Darcy a meaningful look. "She was not with child. She was, in fact, a virgin."

"Then —" his head fell into his hands. *What have I done?*

"You already know she accepted you because of her father's illness," Burrell said, his voice implacable. "After you convinced your friend to abandon her older sister, she knew no other way to protect her mother and sisters if he died. She had little reason to think well of you, apart from what your cousin and friends said in your favor. But she dared to hope if you loved her, you might one day forgive her mercenary motives. And if you were as good a man as they said, she might one day come to love you."

Darcy could not meet the man's gaze; he bent double, his hands covering his face.

He heard Burrell stand. "If I were a younger man, I would seek a new position. You believe yourself her superior, Darcy, but she is farther above you than you can imagine. The trial is at ten o'clock on the ninth of February. I shall expect to see you there."

The door opened and closed. Lindley's voice was gentle, as was his hand on Darcy's shoulder.

"Darcy, I do not believe it is your nature to be deliberately cruel. If you have behaved cruelly to your wife these past several months, the delirium — combined with the influence of the laudanum — is primarily at fault. But delirium alters your memories — even those from before your illness. You must therefore question *everything* you think you know from at least the six months past. Your strength will return in full if you continue to exercise. Your mind is much improved, but for now you must not trust it fully. I shall return in a month to assess your progress."

The door opened and closed again; when Darcy finally lifted his head, he was alone. *I never deserved her.* The truths he had been told by Georgiana and the servants in the days following her departure had been difficult to hear, but he had not truly accepted them. For two weeks his mind had clung to the belief that what the others had seen was an elaborate act on her part. *I know what I saw,* it had insisted. *I know what she did.*

'Question everything you think you know.' If those other truths had been difficult, the ones he heard today were shattering. Between them, Burrell and Lindley had demolished everything he had ever known to be true of — well — what was he to call her? She was not truly Mrs. Darcy, and she was not Miss Bennet. His gut twisted when he thought of her as Elizabeth.

I had no right to call her by that name. I never even asked permission. I thought I loved her, so I thought myself entitled. But did I? Burrell was right. The moment I learned she did not like me I berated and abandoned her. I never forgave her, but my pride would not permit me to release her.

His eyes fell on Niebuhr's *Roman History.* He opened the first volume, staring again at the inscription.

To Mr. Darcy — Octavian of the Pemberley Empire —
Know that I have ever sought to preserve and protect you and all you hold dear.
  — your Livia, Elizabeth Bennet Darcy, Christmas 1812.

Livia. She had styled herself after the Empress Livia Drusilla, dutiful and beloved wife of Octavian. *And I wanted to throw this into the fire.* His heart felt like a thousand jagged shards.

He had a sudden urge to race to Hertfordshire and throw himself at her feet in penance, but what good could that possibly do?

He would appear at the trial and admit his guilt; he had, indeed, been lying when he vowed to love, honor and cherish her. *She nearly killed herself to protect me and all I hold dear, and I reviled her for it. She deserves to be free of me. The least I can do is let her go.*

Sixteen

Anniversary

DARCY SAT at the breakfast-table, a plate of eggs congealing before him as he stared at the newspaper in his hands. He had read none of the articles; had not, in fact, made it past the date: *9th July 1813*.

His mind presented him with a series of images: a lovely chestnut-haired woman wearing flushed cheeks and a pale yellow gown, walking toward him on her father's arm; his mother's oval sapphire nestled just above the swell of her breasts, tiny diamonds sparkling with every breath; the same hope and fear that beat in his heart reflected in her warm brown eyes as she lifted her face to be kissed.

"Are you well, Fitzwilliam?" Georgiana's voice was gentle, as though she were speaking to a skittish horse.

He lowered his paper and glanced around. *No servants, at least.* "I keep imagining she permitted me to kiss her once. Did that —?"

"Yes, that memory is true. It was one year ago exactly, at your wedding." She smiled. "You both looked a bit terrified."

"I was, certainly." *She was crying,* he remembered. He had never asked why. He rubbed absently at his chest; the shards that were all that remained of his heart sliced at him whenever he spoke of the Empress.

"Richard arrives today," his sister said. "He shall want to hear the full story. I suggest you tell him. It will do you good." She rose and kissed him on the cheek. "I am for Lambton this morning, to call on the vicar and the Wright family."

"Please give Mrs. Wright my regards." Darcy had barely been aware of the Wright family before the Empress came to Pemberley. The Empress had taken the young widow under her wing and, with Burrell, had rescued the woman and her children from destitution — twice, to hear Georgiana tell it. The family now thrived in the vicar's home, but Georgiana still called once each month, as a promise to the Empress.

She had not been gone thirty minutes before Darcy heard a commotion in the front hall. "Darcy!" came his cousin's jovial, booming voice. "Come down here and greet me, you slug-a-bed!" It was an old joke between them; they were both in the habit of rising with the dawn.

He embraced his cousin with a grin. "At last, the good Colonel Richard Fitzwilliam graces us with his presence! Did you walk beside the horse all the way from Matlock?"

"Naturally! What is a holiday without a half-day's hard march?" Fitzwilliam gripped his shoulder. "I had your man hold Brutus for me. Shall we ride?"

"An excellent idea." On horseback he could speak freely. *Likely why Fitzwilliam suggested it.*

His cousin was studying him carefully, though he tried to be subtle about it. *What did my aunt tell him?* His aunt and uncle had visited in April, after the snows finally cleared and the roads from Scotland were passable. Aunt Eleanor had seemed particularly anxious to assure herself he had returned to full health, while Uncle Henry had quizzed him minutely about the estate. *No doubt to verify I am fit to manage it.*

His new stable-master brought Caesar around. The great blood-bay stallion pranced and tossed his head, nipping the hand holding his leading rein. Darcy waved the man away, taking hold of Caesar's bridle until he settled and then giving him a good knee to the belly as Darcy cinched the girth strap. Never did Darcy regret his suspicion of James Reynolds more than when he rode. His new man was a solid, knowledgeable fellow, but he had not Reynolds's way with the horses, and Caesar was a temperamental bully to everyone but Reynolds and himself.

Once they were well away from the house they slowed to a walk; both horses were blowing after their gallop. "You seem as fit as you were last year, Darcy," Fitzwilliam said. "If I did not trust Georgiana's account, I would not believe you were ever unable to move of your own accord."

"I have entirely recovered, but I spent fully four months confined to bed. It came on quite suddenly, not long after I returned to Pemberley last August. Then it steadily worsened over two months and receded over another four. It was not until February that I could navigate the stairs; March, before I could ride."

His mind showed him another image: staring down the long staircase on the eighth of February, gripping the railing as a vague, jumbled memory flooded him — tumbling down to the sound of crashing; searing pain in his right leg; the Empress's face hovering upside-down above him; Simmons's insistent voice.

It had taken years, it seemed, to make it down the stair that first time. He was expected at the trial, however, so he had gritted his teeth and accepted Simmons's assistance.

Darcy shook himself; Fitzwilliam regarded him oddly. "My apologies. Did you say something?"

"I asked if you have difficulty with your memories."

He stared at his cousin. "What have you been told?"

Fitzwilliam snorted. "Not enough to satisfy me. Darcy, I am a *soldier*. I have seen men with gaping head wounds; men screaming in pain years after losing a limb to the surgeon's blade; men so far gone with fever that they talked to the walls and accused their best friends of conspiring against them. I have seen things you cannot even conceive. Nothing you can say will surprise me."

"I have done all those things, I am told." He sighed. "I remember little of it. Lindley instructed me not to trust my own memories. I rely on Georgiana and Simmons to confirm that events happened as I recall. My memories appear to be correct from the beginning of the year — since the day the Empress departed Pemberley, in fact."

"The Empress?"

Darcy flushed. "Miss Bennet, now. I could not think what to call her, once I discovered 'the harlot' was entirely wrong. Then I read her inscription, and she has been 'the Empress' in my mind ever since."

Fitzwilliam's brows lifted nearly to his hairline. "I think you had better tell me the whole story from the beginning."

Darcy hesitated. *Georgiana thinks it will do me good.* More, he found he wanted to tell it, specifically to someone who was neither under his protection nor paid to provide a service. Fitzwilliam might be his only remaining friend, now Bingley had cried off.

Darcy could hardly blame the man; his sister-in-law had returned to Hertfordshire with what must surely have been a tale filled with horrors. Darcy had received Bingley's last letter, declaring him unforgivably deplorable in his treatment of both sisters, the day after Burrell and Lindley had torn his carefully constructed world to pieces.

"I went about everything all wrong from the beginning," he said, rubbing his chest.

Fitzwilliam nearly swallowed his own tongue when Darcy described his first encounter with Elizabeth Bennet, and the cutting remark he had made to Bingley about her appearance. "You spoke those words aloud? In a public place?"

"I can hardly believe it myself. It was not long after the business with Georgiana and Wickham at Ramsgate, but that is no excuse. It was insupportable. Even worse, she heard me, though I did not know it until much later."

He detailed his internal struggle with the inexplicably growing attraction he had felt over the following months to an entirely unsuitable woman, and his flight from Hertfordshire in an attempt to escape it.

"Then we visited Aunt Catherine in Kent, and there she was." He shook his head and plunged grimly on.

"I cannot countenance my own hypocrisy," he said after recounting his disastrous proposal. "In the very same breath

I confessed my affection and disparaged her family, never once doubting she would accept me. And only a few months before, I took such satisfaction in separating Bingley from her sister Jane!"

Fitzwilliam paled. "The young lady you told me about was Miss Bennet's *sister*? Good God, Darcy!" There was a long pause; Fitzwilliam appeared deeply discomfited. "I suppose I should tell you Miss Bennet heard that story from me. It must have been the same day you proposed. She seemed unwell afterward."

This was news. *But it explains a great deal.* Darcy groaned. "She remained at the parsonage that evening, do you remember? With a headache. Because she had just learned of my interference. She must have been furious, so naturally I took the opportunity to make her an offer of marriage."

He laughed humorlessly. "When I first discovered she had always hated me, my pride could not withstand the blow. Now I marvel that she could bring herself to accept me at all. I cannot fathom how desperate she must have been to protect her family."

"How did you learn she hated you?"

Darcy told the tale. "I behaved like a spurned schoolboy. I called her an actress and a fortune-hunter, and stormed off when she failed to grovel. She sent me a letter the following week, attempting to explain her reasons for accepting me." He grimaced. "I have replied with far greater sympathy to inquiries from my solicitor than I did to that letter."

"Why not simply end the engagement? Your reputation could certainly withstand a minor scandal."

"My pride would not permit it." He sighed. "In her letter she asked to begin again, and once my anger had cooled, I felt I must at least make the attempt. In truth, however, I cannot say I behaved very well. When she dined at Darcy House with her aunt and uncle, I treated her as a common acquaintance. The wedding gave me some fleeting hope, but no more than an hour after we spoke our vows, we learned her youngest sister had run off with Wickham."

Fitzwilliam laughed. "Are you in jest? *George Wickham* became your brother-in-law?"

"He did. Naturally I was forced to bribe him to marry the girl. Meanwhile he spent the weeks we waited for the banns to be read making all sorts of insinuations about his intimacy with the Empress. I was not inclined to be charitable toward her by the time I returned to Pemberley."

"What did you do?"

"I avoided her. I told myself I was needed on the estate, but the truth was I could not tolerate the wretched mixture of anger, suspicion, and yearning I felt whenever I was near her. Only a few days before I fell, she told me she expected to be sent away."

Fitzwilliam lifted a brow. "Why would she have expected such a thing?"

Darcy snorted. "I told her I would ensure we saw as little as possible of each other after the wedding. That was in May, before I ran away like an angry child. I never retracted that statement. Not until she spoke of it, at any rate. By then more than three months had passed."

"Then you fell."

"Then I fell, and my behavior degraded from petty avoidance to outright cruelty." Fitzwilliam listened in silence as Darcy bitterly described the hateful accusations he had flung at his then-wife, and the truth he had been incapable of believing until after she had gone.

Darcy hauled in a deep, cleansing breath. He had never told this story before — had never revealed this much of himself to anybody — and it seemed a great weight had lifted from his shoulders.

"In March I began to attend services in the chapel again. Burrell's sermons have been about the sanctity of family and the responsibility each man has for his fellows," he said. "I can feel the eyes of every parishioner drilling into my back. We all know what he is truly saying."

"Do your tenants and servants know the truth, then?"

"They know our marriage was annulled and I was at fault. They still call her 'the mistress,' though they will not speak of her unless I ask. I can hardly deny I did not treat her as she deserved, and to them she is an angel of mercy."

"I cannot suppose you ask them to speak of her often."

"Not at first, but after the trial I began to do so. Georgiana encouraged me. To help me test my memories, she said, but I think she did not wish to be the only person willing to speak well of the Empress to my face. I had many amends to make to the servants — I was hateful to all of them for a time — but it was asking them to tell me of the Empress that began to restore their trust in me, I think."

"Have you seen her since she departed?"

"Only once, very briefly. At the trial. She did not speak to me or even look in my direction. I can hardly blame her. The last time I spoke to her was the afternoon I told her to leave and never return, when I still thought of her as 'the harlot.' The trial focused only on my fraud in signing the register, so she did not know I finally understood how wrong I had been about everything."

Fitzwilliam looked at Darcy in surprise. "Does she remain ignorant of your recovery?"

Darcy nodded. "I have not been able to bring myself to write to her. What could I say? I never treated her properly." He shrugged. "Bingley ended our friendship months ago, which is entirely natural, as she is now his sister-in-law. He did marry Jane Bennet in the end. I have no other reason to visit Hertfordshire."

"And you love her still." It was not a question.

Darcy considered this. "I am not certain I ever truly loved her. I admired her, certainly. Her utter lack of deference was bewitching. But what I saw as flirting was, in truth, defense against what she perceived as my disdain." He caught himself rubbing his chest again and shook his head. "If I had loved her, I could not have walked away from her last May, no matter how angry I was."

"You do not speak of her as an indifferent man would."

"Shame and regret are not love."

"Freeing her when you wish to keep her with you, because you harmed her too badly to be borne, surely is." Fitzwilliam cocked his head. "Can you imagine loving another? Taking another wife?"

"Nay. Pemberley shall pass to Georgiana's firstborn son. I have made my peace with that."

"You would rather see your ancestral estate pass out of Darcy hands than marry another woman who can give you sons of your own? Say no more to me of not loving Elizabeth Bennet. I shall not hear you."

"Very well, if it satisfies you to hear it: I shall love Elizabeth Bennet until I die. But I do not deserve her."

"Debatable. Your behavior thus far has unquestionably been abominable, but your abject misery and self-loathing suggest you may be capable of reform." Fitzwilliam smirked. "Do you still wish to throw yourself at her feet?"

Darcy snorted. "Every day."

"I believe I can aid you. She deserves to hear your apology, at the very least. You have avoided that duty for six months, and you are entirely correct — a letter would be insufficient. But it is unlikely she will want to speak to you, and if Bingley has also cut you then you must have an excuse to be in the neighborhood and meet with him."

"What are you plotting now, Fitzwilliam?" Darcy's heart was pounding at merely the thought of seeing the Empress again.

"My father has a few mares to sell, and Bingley has begun a proper breeding program at Netherfield with the assistance of your former stable-master. I shall sell the mares, perform some reconnaissance, and drop a word or two in your favor. With luck he will agree to see you, even if she does not."

"I would be grateful for news of her, if nothing else."

"Excellent. Let us give these beasts another run, and we shall plan our campaign."

* * *

Were it not for Georgiana and Caesar, Darcy would have spent the next two weeks prowling the house like a caged animal. As it was, to keep from crawling out of his own skin he took long rides every morning, saddling Caesar himself in the early light. He returned hours later, in time to accompany Georgiana on her visits to the tenants.

His sister had eagerly taken up the Empress's mission to provide assistance to those most in need. She visited every tenant, but her most diligent care went to the widows with young children, the elderly without family, the infirm and injured.

With Burrell's aid, and eventually Darcy's, she had brokered mutually beneficial arrangements between neighbors. She had gifted chickens or goats to the poorest families, recruiting other tenants to teach them how to care for the animals.

She had even pestered Darcy until he agreed to provide small loans to widows and young women looking to make do for themselves. He had been astonished at first when these loans were invariably repaid on time and in full, but the results were inarguable: the women and their children were now well-fed and healthy, able to provide charity rather than depend upon it.

Darcy had recently assigned Georgiana the responsibility of making these small loans. She had blossomed in the past year; now seventeen, she carried herself with greater assurance and judgment. She had even begun to read more. She regularly corresponded with the Empress, he knew, though she took pains to disguise it from him. He pretended to be unaware, not wanting to intrude on a valuable friendship.

Long rides and visits could occupy him for only so long, however. Darcy had begun silently cursing Fitzwilliam's continued silence and concocting plausible reasons to travel to Hertfordshire when a letter finally arrived.

Meryton, 26th July 1813

Darcy,

You are surely too hungry for whatever intelligence I may provide to tolerate the usual preliminaries, so I shall skip straight to the meat. I have seen the Empress; she resides with the Bingleys at Netherfield. Apparently, her return to Hertford-shire was exceedingly timely: Mr. Bennet died shortly after the annulment — a cancer of the lung, I understand. She was wise to be concerned for her family's future, it seems, but Bingley has not been called upon too greatly. The fourth sister, Kitty, also lives with him but Mrs. Bennet and the third sister, Mary, now reside in Meryton with Mrs. Bennet's sister, Mrs. Phillips, and her husband.

As for the eldest sister: how you could have failed to mention Mrs. Bingley's extraordinary beauty is beyond me. Bad enough that your Empress heard of your attempts to separate Bingley and his Hertfordshire lady-love from my lips; worse that her sister is a truly angelic creature. When I arrived she was graciousness itself, despite being very near to her confinement. She was delivered of a daughter yesterday who shall be named Elizabeth. Bingley is giddy with delight.

The Empress is much changed from when I met her in Kent. Her manners are as charming as ever, but she lacks the "joie de vivre" she displayed so artlessly then, and her merry wit is entirely absent. That she remains in full mourning must be partly to blame. I have yet to meet a neighbor who does not inform me that she was her father's favorite child.

From the tavern gossip, I learn she is no longer considered too far above some of the local men, all of whom eagerly await the day she begins to wear half-mourning. The women roll their eyes and remark that if any of these ambitious fellows could see past her wealthy brother-in-law, they would notice she shows no interest in marriage whatsoever.

She was understandably reserved with me, though she asked after my mother and Georgiana. She wanted some courage to ask after you, I think, but seemed genuinely pleased to learn you are fully recovered. She has kept the habits she learned at Pemberley, too. Mrs. Bingley mentioned she spends her mornings seeing to Netherfield's tenants or riding out in lieu of the long walks she once favored.

Bingley is very well. He was particularly gratified to hear of your recovery; I believe he misses you, despite his righteous anger on behalf of the ladies all those months ago. His breeding venture is quite a success: Reynolds seems more horse than man, and he has helped Bingley build an impressive stable in record time. After I dashed Bingley's hopes by revealing Brutus's gelded status, he bid me to ask if you would consider allowing him to purchase Caesar's stud services. He did not explicitly say he desires you to bring the horse yourself, but Bingley is too transparent for subtlety.

I shall remain in Hertfordshire until I must return to my regiment. Frankly, my friend, you need allies. Quite aside from the Empress herself, the general prejudice against you is exceedingly strong. I have shared as widely as possible the truth of Wickham's compensation in lieu of the Kympton living — it was the single detail he omitted, naturally — and I mention your noble qualities whenever I can.

I shall send this express in deference to your certain impatience and expect your arrival in Meryton upon its heels. Until then I remain

Your faithful friend and cousin,

R. Fitzwilliam

$\mathcal{S}$ eventeen

Meryton

$\mathcal{Y}$OUR CUFFS are straight, man. Stop fidgeting."

Darcy forced his hands to stillness. He stood with Fitzwilliam at the door to Netherfield, waiting on Bingley, but it was the butler who answered.

"I thought we were to meet Bingley outside," Fitzwilliam muttered as they were ushered into the drawing-room.

"We were," Darcy replied. Then he was through the door and the breath left his body with an audible whoosh.

The Empress turned, a half-formed smile — clearly meant for Fitzwilliam — freezing in place as their eyes locked. She was dressed modestly in a black crepe gown devoid of frills, chestnut curls threaded with black ribbon. Her lovely face lost all color and she wobbled until Mrs. Gardiner stepped in front of her, catching her arms and blocking his view.

"Darcy!" Bingley hurried toward him, grinning sheepishly. "I am very glad to see you. I apologize for not meeting you outside just now. I had not recalled we were expecting Jane's aunt and uncle Gardiner this morning. They arrived only a half-hour ago."

"Lizzy and I are going up to visit Jane and the baby," said Mrs. Gardiner, steering the Empress out of the room.

"No apology is necessary, Bingley," said Darcy, trying to recover himself. "We do not wish to intrude on your family party. We shall be happy to visit at a more convenient time."

"Not at all, Mr. Darcy. I welcome the opportunity to speak with you," said Mr. Gardiner. His amiable expression was belied by the note of steel in his voice. "Kitty, my dear, now would be an excellent time to ensure your things are all in readiness. Then please join your aunt in Jane's room."

When only the four men remained, Mr. Gardiner said, "What brings you to Hertfordshire, Mr. Darcy?"

"That is my fault, I fear," said Bingley. "I hoped he would bring his excellent stallion to breed with my mares."

"Caesar is unwilling to be ridden by any but myself or Mr. Reynolds," Darcy added.

"I see." Mr. Gardiner gave him a long, direct stare. "Are you truly going to require me to ask?"

Dimly, Darcy recalled this man was in trade. Under other circumstances he would never have tolerated such a direct challenge from his social inferior, but Mr. Gardiner was also the Empress's uncle — the man she trusted most, after her father.

"I only wish to apologize, sir," he said quietly, holding Mr. Gardiner's gaze. "I treated her abominably, for reasons I can now see were entirely delusional. I owe her a great deal — all of Pemberley does. I ask nothing else, only that she allow me to say it. She need never lay eyes on me again."

Mr. Gardiner's features softened a fraction. "I understand you were gravely ill."

Darcy nodded. "I lost the ability to move at all — even to breathe or swallow properly. My physician tells me I would not have survived if my breathing had not already begun to improve before the influenza caught me in its grip."

He wanted no blame to fall on the Empress, however. "I was delirious for months, and it made me hateful. No woman should be forced to endure what she suffered, particularly when her husband is the cause. She was right to leave."

"Very well," Mr. Gardiner said at length. "That you are willing to humble yourself to me is no small thing. We are here to collect Kitty for a journey to the Lakes, but I shall speak to Lizzy before we depart. It must be her decision to hear you or not, mind you."

"I understand, sir."

They chatted companionably about the Lakes. Darcy and Fitzwilliam had both visited many times, given the proximity to Derbyshire, and they argued good-naturedly about all the best sights until Mrs. Gardiner reappeared. She took the seat next to her husband, who spoke a quiet word in her ear.

Mrs. Gardiner favored Darcy with a determinedly pleasant smile. "You may recall we hail from the same county, sir," she said. "I grew up in Lambton as a girl. My father was the vicar for many years."

"Delightful village," he said. "The present vicar and his wife have my enduring gratitude for taking in a young widow and her children who were my tenants. Your niece deserves all the credit, however — I was insensible with fever and pain at the time."

At Mrs. Gardiner's exclamation he detailed the Empress's efforts on behalf of Pemberley's people. "I learned of all this in January, after my mind began to be restored. It was thanks to her more people did not perish of illness and starvation. She has been a great influence on my sister Georgiana."

Mrs. Gardiner regarded him thoughtfully. They made small talk about the many beauties of Derbyshire's untamed wilderness while Mr. Gardiner went to collect Miss Kitty and, presumably, to speak to the Empress, who remained above stairs with Mrs. Bingley. Darcy and Fitzwilliam soon took their leave, promising to call again when Bingley was free to discuss the horses.

As they settled in the carriage, Darcy tried unsuccessfully to recall his opinion of the Gardiners the previous year when they had dined at Darcy House. Mr. Gardiner had impressed Darcy a great deal just now. The man was shrewd and fiercely protective, but kind-hearted and gentlemanly. Darcy was sorry not to have the opportunity to know the couple better.

Fitzwilliam's hearty voice interrupted his thoughts. "Well done, Darcy. Are you up for a repeat performance?"

"What are you talking about?"

"You really ought to call upon your other acquaintance in the neighborhood, you know. Make yourself agreeable."

Darcy was still recovering from the unexpected confrontation with Mr. Gardiner. Fitzwilliam was right, however; the other calls were both expected and necessary, so they went. Darcy even made an effort at congenial conversation, aided by his cousin's calculated silence unless directly addressed.

He shared anecdotes of St. James's with Sir William Lucas and expressed his sincere condolences to Mrs. Bennet on her husband's death. Fitzwilliam, he discovered, already had an invitation to dine the following evening with Mrs. Bennet and the Phillipses, which was politely expanded to include Darcy. He gratefully accepted, which evidently surprised his would-be hostess.

Darcy's reception at Longbourn was decidedly cooler. Its new master was Mr. Collins, who, it seemed, continued to share Lady Catherine's disapproval of Darcy's marriage to Elizabeth Bennet. Nor could the former parson countenance the subsequent annulment.

Mrs. Collins, Darcy remembered, was the Empress's close friend. The cheerfully pragmatic and unassuming woman he recalled from Hertfordshire and Kent was gone. In her place was a respectable matron who treated him with guarded civility. Mrs. Collins accepted Darcy's congratulations and best wishes with equanimity, but after the prescribed quarter of an hour had passed, she clearly wished him to depart.

That evening he sat with Fitzwilliam in the local tavern, drinking with men who hoped to woo his Empress when she came out of mourning. *She deserves better than any of us,* he thought later as he fell, exhausted, into bed.

Early the following day Darcy rode to Netherfield, where Bingley was to meet him outside the stables. "Please ask Mr. Reynolds to join me," he told the groom who greeted him.

Reynolds emerged with a wary expression, stopping a good ten paces away. "What can I do for you, Mr. Darcy?"

"Bingley asked me to bring Caesar here today to discuss stud services. You are the only other man he will allow near him. I did not wish your groom to be injured."

"Fair enough. Are we waiting for Mr. Bingley, then?"

"We are. I came early because I wished to apologize to you for my unjust and untrue condemnation of your character. My only excuse is illness. I was not in my right mind, but I slandered you to all within hearing. I now understand you did nothing to deserve it."

Reynolds nodded. "I thank you, sir."

"I also wish to extend my congratulations. I was told you married Sarah Still last year."

Reynolds looked past him; the smile that lit the man's face was filled with affectionate warmth. "Aye, funny you should mention that. Here comes the missus now."

Sarah Reynolds gave Darcy a wide berth, and not because of Caesar; it was not the horse she regarded so warily. She gave him the barest nod of greeting. "I've come to fetch Miss Bennet," she said to her husband, pointedly turning her back to Darcy. "Mrs. Bingley is asking for her."

"She's grooming Willow," Reynolds said, cocking his head in the direction of the stable. "Should be finished soon." He caught his wife's hand, pressing it briefly.

She smiled and walked on. When she reached the stable door, Darcy was struck by a sudden jolt of recognition. *That's her. That is who I saw from my window the day the Empress left. Reynolds was meeting her in the stable, just as Harwood said.* Reynolds's fond gaze followed his wife into the building. *He is smitten, all right.*

Darcy had eventually come to believe Harwood, though it was not until that wretched morning with Burrell and Lindley that he realized his steward was correct: Darcy could never have seen the stable while he remained confined to his bed.

Now he truly understood. *I saw the Empress entering the stable while I was ill, but that was only a hallucination. Then, when I saw young Mrs. Reynolds in truth, my mind perverted reality to fit its own narrative. It was never the Empress.*

"I am heartily glad you and your wife have found an ideal situation here with Bingley," he said aloud.

Reynolds turned surprised eyes to him, and Darcy smiled.

"I have never had interest in creating such a program, but you are the perfect man for it." His smile became wry. "Sadly, I have had no luck convincing Caesar to behave like a gentleman with anyone else, but Lindley tells me grooming a horse is excellent exercise. If I do not do it, he looks feral."

Reynolds grinned and came forward. Caesar lowered his head to be scratched. "Aye, his get will be a handful if they're anything like their sire," Reynolds said fondly, "but I can't wonder Mr. Bingley wanted him. He's magnificent. Aren't you, you great bully?"

Just then Bingley appeared. "Tell me a number, Darcy, and I'll pay it."

"He is not for sale, Bingley."

His friend sighed. "I feared you would say that. Very well then, how many foals do we want, Reynolds?"

"Three, I'd say."

The Empress and young Mrs. Reynolds passed them then, headed for the house. Darcy fought to keep his attention on the conversation. The men spent an hour negotiating stud fees and selecting the mares to be bred; a satisfying morning, so far as it went, but Darcy returned to the hotel frustrated nevertheless. He was not going to see the Empress without an invitation to the house, it seemed.

I must be patient, he told himself. *She will hear me when she is ready.*

* * *

"How badly did you behave on your previous visits, Darcy?" Fitzwilliam asked with a grin. They awaited Bingley outside the stables. Bingley was eager to show off his horses; Darcy was to have his pick of the lot while Caesar remained with Reynolds.

Darcy rolled his eyes. "Very badly, it seems. Can you let nothing rest?"

"And miss such a perfect opportunity? Never!" Fitzwilliam casually backhanded him. "To hear the ladies tell it, you are a man transformed. Were you truly so unsociable before?"

They had dined the previous evening with the Phillipses and Mrs. Bennet. It had nearly killed Darcy to make pleasant conversation in that company for two hours together, all the more so when the matrons began to wax poetic about him: *'How remarkably altered is his disposition!' 'I do not believe I ever saw him smile before today!'* Fitzwilliam, delighted, had egged them on and had not let up since.

"I must own I was," said Darcy. "Though were it not for my inauspicious beginning, I might have been forgiven."

"I would not wager on that. Your present efforts at social discourse are barely adequate in a modest country society." Fitzwilliam grinned. "I suspect you went about glowering at everybody, privately bemoaning the tedious gatherings and inferior company."

This was far too close to the mark for comfort; Darcy lifted a brow, but Fitzwilliam just laughed, undeterred.

"Good morning, Darcy! Colonel!" Bingley's greeting was a welcome interruption.

"Mr. Darcy! How delightful to see you again!"

Lord, give me strength. Miss Caroline Bingley hung on her brother's arm, simpering from twenty feet away.

"You must introduce me to your handsome friend, Mr. Darcy," she said, turning her most ingratiating smile on Fitzwilliam.

"This is my cousin, Colonel Richard Fitzwilliam. The son of the Earl of Matlock," he said, emphasizing his uncle's title. Sadly, it did not have the intended effect; she soon returned her full attention to Darcy.

"I came to visit with dear Jane and the baby, of course, but when I learned Charles was to see you this morning, I knew I *must* join him! It has been positively an age since we met! Where have you been hiding yourself?"

"Pemberley."

"Come, let us go inside," Bingley said. His voice held a note of desperation. "Darcy, I should first like to show you Mercutio. He is there in the farthest stall, as he does not take to crowds. Colonel, would you —?"

"I shall be very happy to introduce Miss Bingley to Ginger here," Fitzwilliam said, stopping before the first stall.

"Caroline arrived last night, entirely without warning," Bingley said in a quiet rush. "Jane is beside herself. First you, then my sister. Jane is rightly refusing to play hostess, but her peace is exceedingly disturbed."

"I am sorry my visit here has made things difficult for you, Bingley." He had been in Hertfordshire three days; it could be no coincidence that Miss Bingley suddenly displayed an interest in her niece, when she had never shown the slightest evidence of maternal impulse. Nor had she ever approved of Bingley marrying a woman as socially insignificant as Jane Bennet. "Shall I take myself off to London?"

Bingley barked a laugh. "No indeed! I have a larger favor to ask. Keep Caroline away from Jane."

"I owe you that much, I suppose." Darcy grimaced. "Very well, but you must invite me to dinner if I am to divert her attention."

Bingley was happy to agree, but Darcy's scheme to see the Empress gained him only three more hours in Miss Bingley's clutches. The Empress remained above stairs with her sister, to Miss Bingley's evident delight.

"She is avoiding me, Fitzwilliam," Darcy sighed heavily as they returned to the inn.

"If you call Miss Bingley's fixation on your every utterance 'avoidance,' I fear to know what you would term 'attention.'"

"The Empress." He directed a baleful glare at his cousin's cheeky grin. "The Empress is avoiding me."

"She rides out every morning. Were I you, I would make an effort to happen upon her on horseback. If she knows she can readily flee, she may be willing to stay and hear you."

That makes a perverse sort of sense. Darcy smiled. "Then Mercutio and I shall get acquainted in the morning."

* * *

Several days went by before Darcy finally crossed paths with the Empress on her morning ride. By then he and Fitzwilliam had been invited guests at Netherfield every day. She had been unable to remain above stairs whenever he was in the house, but he had spoken to her only a handful of times and her responses were the picture of rote politeness.

On Saturday morning Darcy was bent low over Mercutio's hoof, extracting a jagged stone, when the Empress rounded the corner of an abandoned cottage. She pulled Willow to a halt, staring at Darcy as though he might attack at any moment. He stood, Mercutio forgotten, his mind utterly blank as she wheeled the bay mare around.

No! "Empress, wait!"

Her head swiveled, brows knit. "Are you speaking to me?"

"I am. After you left, I —" He scrubbed his hand through his hair. "When I understood how terribly I had misjudged — well — everything, really — I could not think what to call you. I reread your inscription; you signed it 'Livia.'" He shrugged helplessly. "In my thoughts you are the Empress."

There was a small silence. "You might have chosen a far worse name, I suppose."

He winced. "I had, as you surely know. Empress — Miss Bennet — I wish wholeheartedly to apologize. From the first moment of our acquaintance, I was boorish and conceited. It never occurred to me you might dislike me, despite having myriad reasons to do so. I was arrogant in my proposals and heartless in my behavior to you last May. I cannot think on my own conduct without abhorrence."

She turned the horse and looked steadily down on him, her seat confident, her back straight. *Like a queen. Like an Empress.*

"Go on," she said.

"I should have allowed you to explain. I should have tempered my pride with compassion for the untenable position in which I placed you. I should never have abandoned you, neither before our wedding nor after it." He shook his head. "I should have believed you when you said there was nothing between you and Wickham, but I could hardly see straight for jealousy! And I — I know not how to express my horror at my behavior while I was ill. I —"

"Mr. Darcy, you were not in your right mind, for *months*. Dr. Lindley explained it to me many times."

"I cannot so easily dismiss my guilt. I had already spent far too long nurturing suspicion and anger. The accusations I made when I was ill were certainly more terrible than any I entertained before, but... surely you must have seen it."

She nodded, her expression stony.

"You saved me. You saved Pemberley. You kept my people fed and warm and safe when I could not, and you nearly sacrificed yourself in the process. I can never repay you. I do not deserve your forgiveness, but I beg you to give it, if you can."

The silence stretched long as she looked away, deep in thought. "Is that all you wish from me?"

"It is already more than I have a right to ask. Say the word and I shall vanish from your life forever. But if you *can* forgive — even a fraction — I beg you would allow me to start afresh." He flushed at her pointedly lifted brow. "I know I have no right to anything. And I know I beg more generosity from you now than I was willing to bestow when you asked to begin again in your letter to me last year."

He took an involuntary step toward her and was relieved when she did not withdraw. "I have no expectations," he said, though he could not keep the note of desperate hope from his voice. "I merely pray you will allow me the opportunity to be a better man than I have been." With an effort he shut his mouth and stood still, fearing to breathe as he awaited her judgment.

Her gaze shifted back to the horizon. "I have never found comfort in the notion of forgiving and forgetting," she said at length. "We are not made to forget those wrongs done to us, as though they never happened. There can be no truly clean slate, no wholly new beginning. Perhaps it only means we must not carry grudges if we are truly to forgive." Her eyes returned to him, pinning him in place with the intensity of her expression. "I cannot forget what you have done, Mr. Darcy. But that includes the words you said just now. I did not believe you capable of humility. If you are sincere in your desire, I shall not banish you, but I am not yet ready to forgive."

"I thank you, Miss Bennet."

She made a face. "That name sounds wrong on your lips." She tossed her head. "You may call me Empress instead."

He hauled in a deep breath, fighting the grin that threatened to split his face apart. "It shall be my honor."

Eighteen

Starting Afresh

CONVERSATIONS with the Empress were noticeably less stilted after that, Darcy observed with relief. She had not yet forgiven him, true, but she no longer appeared to be avoiding him, which was an improvement in itself.

Two weeks after he threw himself at her feet, Darcy sat in Netherfield's drawing-room after services, trying to appear at least somewhat more at ease than he felt. Mrs. Bingley, who had been in confinement since the birth of the Empress's namesake, was soon to make her first appearance at a family gathering. He had not seen her since the wedding, and then only briefly. He had no notion how to act around her, much less an infant.

Caroline Bingley hovered over his shoulder, pretending interest in the book he held. He had not turned a page in fully five minutes, which deterred her not at all.

"I say, Mr. Darcy," she said, "I cannot make out anything of Mr. Niebuhr! I must have a stern conversation with my old language-master. He declared my German exceedingly fair."

"That was over six years ago, Caroline!" laughed Bingley. "You have uttered not a word of the language since."

"Well, perhaps I must apply to Miss Eliza to aid me. We all know her to be a great reader."

The Empress smiled serenely. "I can be of no assistance, Miss Bingley. I never learned to speak German."

"What? Never! I suppose you think it unnecessary."

"I confess I have no opinion on the necessity of German."

"Why, Miss Eliza! You, without an opinion? Mr. Darcy, *you* must share my astonishment. Not even two years past, we relied on Miss Eliza Bennet to have a pert opinion always at the ready!"

He shrugged. "Two years past she was also advising you to tease me — as punishment for expressing a pert opinion of my own, as I recall." He looked a question at the Empress. "I notice she does not tease anybody now."

"I have lost my enthusiasm for it," she said quietly, avoiding his gaze. "My father loved to laugh at folly and nonsense. He taught me to do the same. I have since learned that when both parties do not share the humor equally, such laughter is merely mockery. I have no wish to behave so cruelly."

Darcy spoke without thinking. "Certainly, it is cruel where there is an intent to wound, but I confess I always rather enjoyed being laughed at by you. My cousin is the only other person who ever does. Fitzwilliam would say I occasionally require a proper set-down."

Her cheeks colored and she looked away. *She did not like you then, you great idiot,* he thought. *Do you not recall? That was battle, not flirtation!* He felt his own cheeks redden.

"I should hope we are all wiser than we were then," said Bingley. His countenance brightened. "Jane, dearest! And our beautiful little Beth! Is she well?"

"Very well," said Jane Bingley. She smiled fondly at her husband, who had raced to her side and was now allowing his daughter to wrap a tiny fist around his finger.

"May I?" asked the Empress. Mrs. Bingley placed the baby in her aunt's waiting arms.

"Jane, dear, are you sure you are quite ready to end your confinement? You must rest!" came Miss Bingley's voice, pulling Darcy's gaze away.

There was the barest hint of annoyance in Mrs. Bingley's tone. "I am exceedingly well rested, Caroline."

Darcy cordially greeted Mrs. Bingley and made pleasant small talk for several minutes. Then, recalling his promise to keep Miss Bingley engaged elsewhere, he offered to explain the German about which she had been so curious. He could not hide his amusement when she dismissively refused, only for Mrs. Bingley to declare herself eager to know what he was reading.

He glanced at the Empress. "This part is about the Roman Emperor Octavian and his wife Livia. I had not known she divorced her first husband to marry him, nor that her son — who would become the Emperor Tiberius — was not Octavian's."

He was interrupted by the sound of a fussing infant.

"Is Roman history so distressing?" he asked, chuckling.

The Empress smiled. "Nay, it is only that our little miss prefers to dance. Shall we dance together near the window, where we shall not disturb your Mamma?" She carried the baby over to the window and gently swayed, bouncing and humming absently.

Darcy had some difficulty finishing the tale. This sight of the Empress — of her tender, playful smile — robbed him of coherent thought.

Bingley caught him staring. "I say, Darcy," he said eagerly, "would you like to hold our little Beth? — No, you must, I saw you smiling at her! Elizabeth, bring her here. Allow Darcy a turn."

The Empress took in his panicky expression and schooled her features, but he could see the grin threatening to break through. She handed him the baby and he stared down — such a tiny thing, her entire body cradled in his two hands! Beth looked at him with dark blue eyes and waved her arms.

How do women hold these creatures without breaking them? He was paralyzed, afraid to move lest he somehow damage her.

"They are not made of glass, you know," said the Empress, laughing. "Here: you must support her head — her neck is not yet strong enough to hold it — but you simply tuck her into your elbow like so. And now if you are very fortunate, you may use your free hand to read while she sleeps."

"Why, Miss Eliza, I never knew you had such remarkable skill at nursing!" Miss Bingley crooned. "Shall you also be the governess, when the children are older?"

Darcy bristled; so did the Bingleys, he noted. The Empress merely smiled, unperturbed. "I suppose I shall. I always did believe I should end an old maid and teach Jane's children to do their sums and play the piano very ill indeed."

"What, shall you never marry? Surely there must be *one* man in England who meets your standards!"

"I have learned the necessity of mutual respect and love between marriage partners, Miss Bingley. I shall not marry unless I am certain of both, and I pray you shall be guided by my experience to do the same."

Miss Bingley took the Empress's hand with exaggerated sympathy. "Naturally — but poor, poor Eliza! How difficult it must have been for you to enter into so unequal a situation! I cannot wonder that it proved too much for you. Longbourn is so modest and the demands on the mistress of Pemberley so great!"

"You are greatly mistaken if you believe Miss Bennet was overmatched by the responsibilities of Pemberley's mistress, Miss Bingley," Darcy said, unable to quell his anger. "Quite the reverse, in fact. While I was ill, she was both master and mistress, and she succeeded brilliantly."

Miss Bingley's eyes widened. "Oh, Mr. Darcy, of course I never —"

"I must also admit I quite agree with Miss Bennet on the necessity of mutual respect and love between marriage partners," he went on in a more reasonable tone. "I shall never marry without them. I find in their absence, I am a terrible husband."

He fixed Miss Bingley with a flat, unblinking stare, willing her to finally understand. A defeated awareness entered her eyes and she awkwardly excused herself. Nobody spoke. Darcy risked a glance at the Empress, to find her regarding him thoughtfully.

"Thank you, Mr. Darcy," she said quietly. "Shall I take Beth from you?"

"Nay, it is her father's turn now," said Bingley. He gave Darcy's shoulder a hearty clap before scooping his daughter into his arms and twirling her around the room.

* * *

When Darcy arrived at Netherfield the following morning, Caroline Bingley was gone.

"She said she had many pressing engagements in London, and departed immediately after breakfast," said Bingley with evident satisfaction. "Now, Darcy, you must come and stay at Netherfield. You have no more excuses; the colonel returned to his regiment two weeks ago!"

Darcy lifted a brow at his friend. "How does Miss Bennet feel about the prospect of my staying in the same house?"

"She is in complete agreement." Bingley was grinning.

Darcy was rendered momentarily speechless. "That is… unexpected," he finally managed. "I thank you for your kind offer. I shall have Simmons make the arrangements."

Just then the Empress poked her head in from the hall. "I thought I heard voices! I suppose you have already had your daily gallop, Mr. Darcy?" She was wearing her riding habit, he realized.

"Mercutio and I were out very early this morning, yes. But if you desire company and Caesar is not wanted, I should be glad to join you."

They rode together in companionable silence for several minutes. "I must thank you, Mr. Darcy, on Jane's behalf," the Empress said suddenly. "It is not politic to say such things, I know, but I believe she might have resumed her confinement if you had not convinced Miss Bingley to depart."

He allowed himself a small smile. "I confess I was thinking primarily of your comfort, madam, and my own. That your sister has also benefited is exceedingly gratifying. And I must thank you in turn — I understand you made no objection to my joining your family party at Netherfield."

"After yesterday, it seemed wrong to insist you remain at the inn at Meryton," she said. "I do not believe I have ever witnessed you defend another person at your own expense. That it was *me* you defended made your apology these two weeks past somehow more... not more believable, precisely. More authentic, I suppose."

He grimaced. "I have little enough experience admitting my faults to myself, and virtually none at admitting them to others."

"None? Nay, sir, I have a clear memory of you boasting to me of your resentful temper, in the drawing-room at Netherfield these two years past."

His own memory of that conversation was remarkably detailed. "Boasting, you say? Miss Bingley declared me to be 'a man without fault.' I could hardly allow such nonsense to stand."

"You said, 'My good opinion, once lost, is lost forever,' with such pride! As though an implacable nature was a sign of virtue. Aye, I name it boasting."

"I was thinking of Wickham at the time."

She paused. "I see. In such a case I imagine it is wisest to maintain a poor opinion — to avoid being taken in."

"That may be the most ungenerous speech I ever heard you make with regard to him."

"I have learned a great deal more about him," she said sourly. "Harwood had nothing kind to say, and I discovered your agreement to compensate him in lieu of the Kympton living in your account ledger. He told me it was his dearest wish to become a clergyman, you know."

Darcy sighed. "Would that I had revealed what I knew of him long ago! Had his character been known, he could not have imposed upon your sister in such a way. But I thought it beneath me to reveal my private actions to the world."

Her look was serious. "I do not think any warning could have dissuaded Lydia. Will you tell me what you did for her? I know it must have cost you no end of mortification to claim him as a brother."

"At first I was merely determined to avoid scandal. When he implied you were somehow involved... I recall jealousy and rage, but I no longer recall how much I felt then and what came later, with my illness." He shrugged. "I certainly resented the necessity of tying our lives together."

When she made no reply, he went on. "As to what I did for your sister: I applied first to Georgiana's former companion, a Mrs. Younge, who I discovered much too late was a close associate of Wickham's. It was several days before she gave him up, but at length I was able to see both Wickam and your sister. As you know, he had no intention of marrying her. I convinced Colonel Forster not to pursue him for desertion and purchased his commission in a northern regiment of the Regulars. I also purchased his debts — again — and settled one thousand pounds on your sister, in such a way he cannot access it."

She nodded. "I guessed as much, from Lydia's letters. She is with child again, and finally beginning to suspect hers is not the only bed he visits. I cannot imagine their life together can possibly be happy." She shook herself. "Enough about Mr. and Mrs. Wickham. Do you fancy a gallop?"

She touched her heel to Willow's flank without waiting on his reply. Grinning, he gave chase.

* * *

Darcy could not recall ever feeling as discomfited by the thought of a dinner party as he did this evening. It had been more than a year since he last entered Longbourn as an invited guest. Then it had been his own engagement party, and he had been warmly received by all in attendance. Now it was to welcome Jane Bingley back into the society of the neighborhood, and he was included as a matter of propriety rather than preference.

"You look as though you are preparing to march into battle," murmured the Empress as he handed her down from the carriage.

"I do? How so?"

"Your posture is tense, and you are wearing that disdainful scowl I recall so well from the first several months of our acquaintance."

Darcy started. *Disdainful? Is that truly how others see me?* "It is only that I am… uncertain of my welcome this evening," he said quietly.

She gave him a frank look. "If you wish for others to like you, then you must attempt to be likable."

"I never had much success on that score." He managed to keep his tone rueful.

"A little congeniality goes a long way. Think of something pleasant so you stop scowling, perhaps." She took his offered arm to go into the house. "And as you may have noticed, most people enjoy talking of themselves. Ask questions and listen to the answers. Seek something to admire about every person you meet and tell them when you find it. It is difficult to dislike someone who gives you a sincere compliment."

Think of something pleasant. Darcy's mind conjured the expression on the Empress's face as she danced with little Beth in her arms in the drawing room at Netherfield, more than a week ago.

"Much better," whispered the Empress, releasing his arm to greet Mrs. Collins.

The lady of the house embraced the Empress and welcomed Darcy graciously. He thanked her for inviting him and was surprised to realize he was truly grateful. *Mrs. Collins is a loyal friend,* he thought. *If she can be kind to me, she must have received a favorable report from the Empress.*

It was more difficult to find something to admire in Mr. Collins. The younger man's inflated sense of self-importance had not benefited by his elevation to the gentry. Closer observation revealed a quality Darcy had never noted before, however. The man was devoted to his wife, who encouraged him to give the newcomers a tour of his garden before they lost the light. Mr. Collins had worked hard to improve the gardens, it was clear, and was justly proud of them. Darcy made a point of telling him so and was rewarded by a thaw in Mr. Collins's chilly demeanor.

Darcy was exhausted by the time the gentlemen joined the ladies in the drawing-room after dinner. He had exerted himself to smile, converse, and generally be more amiable than he could recall in a lifetime of social gatherings. He had not been seated near the Empress, though Bingley had been near enough to come to his aid when Mary Bennet began making pronouncements on the certain evils of pride. That Darcy was the intended target of her speech was obvious by the manner in which she looked to him for his reaction, though she spoke loudly enough for nearly all the guests to hear.

"I once believed where there was a real superiority of mind, pride would always be under good regulation," Darcy said mildly into the tense silence. "I was fortunate to learn better. Had my behavior been less appalling — both before and during my illness — and had those who attended me been less honest with me during my recovery, I might never have known how greatly I erred."

"A man cannot help what he is raised to believe," said Bingley. "I have rarely seen anyone born to great wealth and consequence who is not proud. I cannot agree that it was to your benefit to have been on death's door, Darcy, but you are indeed fortunate to have such friends."

Darcy smiled wryly. "A man in my position rarely hears the difficult truths necessary for him to better himself. I thank you, Miss Mary, for providing me the opportunity to apologize to everyone assembled for my offensive behavior during my previous visits to Hertfordshire. I was, as you say, too proud."

There were polite murmurs from around the table, and Mary Bennet had the grace to blush.

"That is very gracious of you, Mr. Darcy," came the hearty voice of Sir William Lucas. "I believe I speak for many here when I say we are grateful to have the opportunity to make your better acquaintance. I understand you had a difficult autumn at Pemberley last year, what with the influenza and flooding. How does the estate now?"

"Very well, I thank you. Miss Bennet did an excellent job of seeing my people through the crisis. Come spring we were able to replant the fields, and my steward writes of a plentiful harvest."

Conversation resumed around the table, and it was not long before Mrs. Collins signaled the departure of the ladies. Mary Bennet was already seated at the pianoforte when the gentlemen joined them. The concerto she played sounded ponderous to Darcy's ear, but he forced himself to follow the Empress's advice. *Miss Mary practices every bit as diligently as Georgiana,* he thought. *It is not her fault she did not have the benefit of studying with the best music-masters.*

Darcy approached Mrs. Collins where she stood with the Empress. Before he could do more than praise his hostess's excellent dinner, the Empress spoke in a low voice.

"I must apologize for my sister, Mr. Darcy," she said.

"Not at all. Your family and friends are protective of your well-being, which is entirely as it should be." He nodded to Mrs. Collins with a small smile, which she returned.

Sir William Lucas joined them. "Well, daughter," he said to Mrs. Collins, "I believe you have enough young people here for a proper dance. What say you? Could we persuade Miss Mary to play a jig, do you think?"

"I would not object, Papa," said Mrs. Collins, "but I think we should not ask her. Jane may not feel quite up to it, and some of our guests are not fond of dancing."

"You mean Darcy, I suppose," said Sir William. "Come, Darcy, surely you will make an exception? Many of the ladies are married, true, but it makes for a lively evening. Why, at the court of St. James's —"

"I shall certainly dance, sir," Darcy cut in. "Indeed, I shall be pleased to partner any of the ladies here, including your lovely wife." He turned to the Empress, fighting to suppress a smile. "Shall I entreat your sister Mary to play for us?"

The Empress looked puzzled for only a moment. Then the teasing light which had been gone from her eyes for more than a year sparked faintly. "Let us both go," she said. "Pray excuse us, Charlotte." When they were out of earshot, she flashed a small grin. "Desperate times, Mr. Darcy?"

He chuckled. "Desperate indeed, Empress."

Nineteen

Back on the Horse

SEVERAL DAYS after their evening at Longbourn, at which Darcy had kept his vow to dance with every willing lady, he stood next to the Empress at the breakfast-room window.

This had become their routine. Every morning since Darcy had taken up residence at Netherfield two weeks past, they had observed the sky after breakfast. If the weather promised fair, they rode out together. Today, however, the sky was full of lowering clouds, the air damp with the promise of rain.

Darcy frowned. "That does not look auspicious."

"It may hold off until mid-morning," said the Empress. "I say we chance it."

"You are going out regardless, I suppose." At her jaunty nod he sighed, "Very well, let us get the beasts saddled."

They galloped a few miles across the fields before slowing the horses to a walk. "Tell me about your parents," said the Empress. "You have seen mine in all their ridiculous glory, but I know almost nothing of yours, besides what Mr. Burrell and Mrs. Reynolds told me."

This had also become routine. Once they had tired the horses, they talked — about childhoods and families, neighbors and friends, travels and favorite books. Darcy found himself disinclined to be as circumspect as one was expected to be with a mere acquaintance and was delighted when the Empress followed suit. Their conversations bore almost no resemblance to those he recalled from any time in their past, except perhaps during the short weeks between her acceptance of his proposal and his childish abandonment of her. He hoped they were finally becoming friends.

Darcy smiled. "My mother — well, Georgiana is like her in almost every respect: same fair coloring and slender build, same mild, sweet temper, same generous heart. Of course, the daughter of an earl was considered a very eligible match for my father. Their marriage did not begin as a match of affection, but eventually their devotion to each other was so obvious strangers remarked on it. To me it seemed the most natural thing in the world.

"Mother also doted on me — probably to excess, in truth. I was the only child for twelve years, after all." His smile grew wistful. "She was so delighted to be with child again! Mrs. Reynolds said Mother would sing all day to the baby growing inside her. I was away at school most of that time. I had been home a month when she died."

"How did it happen?"

"Puerperal fever. She died only two days after Georgiana's birth. It broke my father. Before, he had been a serious man but a good one: he loved his wife, cared for the estate, treated others with respect and generosity. But after she died, he was hollow — as though the spark that animated him had gone with her. He loved Georgiana, but I think it pained him to see my mother in her face."

A detached part of his mind wondered at himself — he had never spoken of this before, not even to Fitzwilliam. *Why am I telling her?* The answer came instantly: *because I can trust her with my life.*

The Empress nodded. "I believe Georgiana felt the weight of your father's grief. It led her to live in terror of imposing on anyone. Or it did, at any rate. She seems to have grown more confident in recent months." She lifted a brow. "I expect by now you know we continue to correspond."

"I do." He smiled indulgently. "She does not seem to have discovered I am aware of it."

"I am grateful to you for permitting her to carry on, then. She tells me she was eleven when your father died. As awful as it was for her, I can only imagine for you it must have been worse. Such an enormous responsibility — Pemberley and the guardianship of a young girl."

Darcy nodded. "It happened so suddenly — Father rode out alone one morning to observe the harvest. His horse stepped in a hole and went down with its leg broken, and he was thrown headfirst into a boulder. He was barely conscious when we found him. His skull was cracked, and his neck was injured so badly he could not move his arms or legs at all. Within twelve hours he was dead. I was twenty-three, and terrified every day for — well — years, really. I thank God for

Harwood and Uncle Henry. I would have floundered without their guidance."

She was silent for a moment. "It must have been equally terrifying to fall and then lose the ability to move your limbs." Her look was sympathetic rather than pitying.

"It was. It was worse than the pain, I think, and the pain was excruciating."

They both fell silent. Then a large, heavy raindrop struck Darcy's hand; the next landed nearly in his eye. "It appears we shall not escape the rain after all," he said. "We must get back."

They went as swiftly as they could, but the sky was unforgiving. Within minutes they were being pelted with rain like bullets — hard and stinging, leaving them soaked.

"If I catch my death, you have my permission to remind me you warned against this," she shouted.

"I shall certainly do so," he shouted back. "I shall hover around your sick-room and make such a nuisance of myself you shall be desperate to be rid of me!"

Netherfield came into view, hazy through the downpour. They slowed as they reached the house, where thick turf gave way to dirt turning rapidly to mud. The Empress was ahead of him, head down, gown clinging to her body in heavy folds. She clearly intended to ride directly into the open door of the stable. A man stood there, peering out through the rain — Reynolds, most likely, on the lookout for their return.

Suddenly Willow stumbled, her front legs sliding before buckling underneath her. Darcy's heart stuttered as her rider tumbled forward, landing in a heap against the fencepost.

"Empress!" *Dear God, no!* His boots were ankle-deep in mud before he was aware of dismounting. In a few steps he knelt at her side, heart hammering in his throat. His Empress was not moving.

Please let her be well. Darcy's hands shook uncontrollably as he ripped off his gloves to feel for the pulse under her jaw. The breath left him in a sudden rush when he felt the strong and steady thrum beneath his fingertips.

"Miss Bennet!" Reynolds knelt at her head, feeling gently along the back of her skull. "She is not bleeding."

"Thank God for that. I shall get her inside while you see to the horses," Darcy said, inclining his head toward Willow.

Reynolds gave him a hard look.

"I shall never harm her again. I swear it."

With a nod that clearly said he would hold Darcy to that vow, Reynolds moved to run his hands over Willow's legs.

Darcy bent over the Empress, rubbing her hand in both of his. "Empress?" He gently brushed the wet hair from her face. "Elizabeth? Elizabeth, please wake."

Her brows knit and she stirred slightly. "What happened?" Her eyes opened only a moment before she squeezed them closed. "Mr. Darcy? My head is pounding."

"Willow slipped in the mud and you were thrown. Are you well enough to walk? Here, let me help you sit."

She clutched his shoulder. "Nay, I am too dizzy to stand, I think. And my left ankle aches. I hope it is not broken."

"We shall see to the ankle once we are inside. You must forgive me, Empress — I have no choice but to carry you." He lifted her into his arms, taking excessive care to be sure of his footing before taking a step in the thick mud.

The Empress turned her head toward the stables. "Wait! Willow. Mr. Reynolds, how is Willow?"

"She's fine, ma'am," said Reynolds. "You must get inside."

Darcy began barking orders the moment he crossed the threshold; Bingley would forgive him the presumption. "Is there a physician in Meryton? Call for the apothecary, then, immediately. And find Sarah Reynolds. Tell her to meet me in Miss Bennet's room. She must be made dry and warm as soon as possible."

He flew up the stairs. Young Mrs. Reynolds appeared from the servants' stair only a moment later. Ignoring the settee in the sitting room, Darcy made straight for the bedchamber and laid the Empress in her own bed. A moment later he was pushing up the hem of her heavy skirts.

"Mr. Darcy!" Mrs. Reynolds tried to pull him away.

"Her ankle is injured. I mean only to determine the extent of the injury," he said, unlacing her boot. "She also struck her head, I believe. Please help her off with her bonnet and get her some dry clothes."

The Empress hissed as Darcy carefully removed the boot. He prodded gently at her ankle before slowly moving her foot in each direction. The ankle appeared swollen but otherwise intact.

"Ah! That is quite painful," she said.

"I do not believe it is broken." He released her, knowing he should leave but unwilling to do so. Mrs. Reynolds's glare as she placed a clean shift and a simple day-dress on the bed finally reminded him that he was also soaked to the skin. "The apothecary shall arrive shortly," he said. "I shall be just down the hall if I am required."

In short order the apothecary confirmed a sprained ankle and a concussion, ordering his patient to remain in bed. Darcy prowled the corridor for the next several days, asking after the Empress so often Mrs. Reynolds stopped answering to his knock. He was forced to be satisfied by the faint "She's fine, Mr. Darcy!" that drifted through the door.

On the fourth day Sarah Reynolds swung open the door and planted herself in the doorway. "You must stop this, Mr. Darcy!" she hissed. "You have no right to enter her chamber! You are *not her husband*, and I will be hanged before I allow you to badger her!" She slammed the door in his face.

He retreated to his room, cheeks burning. *She is entirely correct. I have no right to anything.* He slumped into the chair before the fireplace. *What am I doing? I must leave her be.*

On the fifth day, as Simmons helped Darcy into a clean jacket after his morning ride, the man smirked. "Miss Bennet has asked to see you."

Darcy met his valet's amused eyes in the mirror. "I beg your pardon?"

"Mrs. Reynolds asked me to tell you Miss Bennet would like you to visit her sitting-room this morning."

Darcy was at the Empress's door in seconds. "Come in," she said at his gentle knock. She was perched on the settee, left foot propped on a stool, a book in her lap. "I understand you have been keeping your promise to make a nuisance of yourself, sir."

He grinned sheepishly. "Guilty as charged, I fear. I found it quite... difficult... not to see for myself you were well."

"I am well enough. I cannot put much weight on my foot, and it gives me a headache to read for very long, but if I am to expire it shall be of boredom."

"May I sit with you?"

"Please. I should like you to read aloud, if you would be so kind. Georgiana and I have agreed to read the same book and discuss it, but she is halfway done and I have yet to begin!"

She handed him the volume on her lap: *Belinda,* by Maria Edgeworth.

He looked at her skeptically. "I do not read novels as a general rule," he said.

"I noticed," she said dryly. "I hoped you might make an exception."

I shall enjoy her company, at least, he thought. Very soon, however, he found he wished to know what would become of young Belinda Portman, and they spent many pleasant hours over the next few days in reading and discussion.

* * *

Ten days after the Empress's accident, the apothecary was satisfied with the ankle and permitted her to walk and even ride, if she kept it tightly wrapped. Darcy was up at his usual early hour, dispatching a message to see the horses saddled before entering the breakfast-room. He stopped in the doorway: Jane Bingley sat at the table, clearly waiting for him. She nodded; the footman closed the door, leaving them alone.

"Please sit down, Mr. Darcy. I believe it is past time we discussed Elizabeth."

He sat warily, taking in the unusual severity of her countenance. *She looks very much like her father,* he realized. Mr. Bennet had been unrelenting with his questions when Darcy had applied for the Empress's hand, and Mrs. Bingley now wore an identical expression.

"I am not fool enough to believe you came here merely because of a horse," she said. "I would like to know your true intent in returning to Hertfordshire."

"I wished to personally apologize to your sister." It was not the whole truth, but it was true enough.

"You might have done that months ago."

Darcy grimaced. "I had not the courage then. Everything was still too raw — for her too, I imagine. And it was several months before I could rely on my memories to be truthful."

"Are your memories of last summer truthful?"

This cannot be good. "They are."

"Why did you marry Elizabeth? I have no difficulty understanding why you might have asked her in the first place, but afterward? When you discovered why she accepted you?"

"That is... complicated." He could not meet her eyes. "I told myself it was primarily to preserve my reputation, and Georgiana's. I also had no desire to subject your sister to the sort of malicious gossip that attaches to a young lady when her engagement is broken."

Mrs. Bingley gave him a look of frank disbelief.

He flushed. "More recently I have come to understand I could not give her up. Part of me still hoped to make her love me, I think."

"Is that why you gave her your mother's necklace?"

He swallowed hard. "Yes." His heart had done a little flip when the Empress entered the church wearing it, and only half a year later he had been so certain she never deserved it! *I was a fool.*

"She was terrified, you know. When she opened it."

Darcy's eyes snapped to Mrs. Bingley's. *Terrified? How could that be?*

"You were very severe upon her. I believe you called her a 'fortune-hunting Jezebel,' or your aunt did. She feared the necklace was a test — one she would fail by wearing it."

He had berated himself for months after his mind began to recover, trying to imagine what it must have been like for her — his anger, his silence, his accusations — but this had never occurred to him. *If she feared to wear it that day...* "You convinced her otherwise," he said.

"I thought you were more likely a wounded animal than a vengeful brute."

"You were entirely correct." He nodded slowly. "More so than I could see at the time."

"Are you here now for the same reason you married her?" Mrs. Bingley waited until Darcy met her eyes, steady and stern. "Do you hope to make her love you?"

His throat closed. "Yes," he rasped.

"You must stop. Immediately," she said, her tone flat.

Just like that? He stared at her.

"You cannot *make* any woman love you, Mr. Darcy. You must *invite* her to do so. Last year you showed Elizabeth your affection, but not your trust — not when it mattered. She will never accept your invitation without it."

"I do trust her."

"To care for others, certainly. But do you truly trust her judgment? Or that of anyone around you, without first giving your advice?"

That is Lady Catherine's failing, he thought. "I do. I trust my cousin Richard, for example. And yes, I trust your sister's judgment."

"How many horses are being saddled at this moment, Mr. Darcy? One or two?"

"Two."

"Did my sister ask you to have Willow saddled for her this morning? Or did *you* decide she ought to ride again as soon as possible?"

Why would she not wish to ride today? He did not trouble to mask his confusion.

Mrs. Bingley's voice was firm, accentuating every word. "When you make the decision for another, it means you do not trust their judgment. You declare your understanding superior, and their right to choose unworthy of respect."

She is not speaking only of the Empress, he realized. Darcy sat beneath her hard, unwavering gaze like a scolded child. "I never thought of it that way. I was taught to rely only on my own judgment, and that I must judge for all those under my protection."

"Surely last year's events have demonstrated the folly of believing your judgment to be inevitably superior. And I beg you to reconsider the breadth of who you believe falls under your protection."

He swallowed. "An excellent point. You are too generous to name Bingley, but I greatly overstepped in my interference between you. It was wrong of me; I hope you may forgive it."

She nodded. "I have already done so, but I shall not find it so easy to forgive if you overstep with Elizabeth. If you love her, you must trust her to judge what is best for herself. She is not too proud to seek advice; she will ask your opinion if she desires it. However, you *must* respect her right to choose — even if she does not choose you, in the end."

* * *

Darcy sat for some time after Mrs. Bingley left him. *How many horses are being saddled? Two. How did I not see the presumption?* He had been fully prepared to insist she ride; all his arguments were marshaled and ready. *Just like Lady Catherine.* He shuddered.

'You must trust her to choose,' her sister had said. *'Invite her to love you.'*

How does a man invite a woman to love him? He wished he had asked.

His thoughts were interrupted by the Empress's arrival. "Good morning," he said. "How does your ankle?"

"Very well. It does not ache at all this morning."

"That is excellent news." *Invite her.* "What think you about riding? I have not yet gone out, if you would like to join me."

"I thank you, but I must own I am exceedingly nervous at the prospect. My ankle is improved, but I still suffer headaches from striking my head against the fencepost."

He stifled his initial response. *Save your advice, man.* "I believe I know what you are feeling. When I first descended the staircase at Pemberley last February, after so many long months... I required some assistance, I confess. Neither my legs nor my courage were quite equal to it on my own."

Her eyes widened. "Truly?"

"I recalled falling that day. Not all of it — mostly pain, and your face above me — but my heart was pounding as though it had just happened."

"You were so confused. It took ages for the wound in your head to stop bleeding," she said, eyes distant. "Even when it did, I had to hold your head in my lap to keep you from sitting up." She shook herself. "What think you — should I ride today?"

She is not proud, he thought. "The sky is clear today and the ground is dry, and you cannot go above a walk until your ankle is fully healed. There is perhaps no better circumstance for it."

"You would forego your gallop to accompany me?"

"Certainly."

She squared her shoulders. "Very well then. I shall ride."

Reynolds brought both horses around as soon as they were outside. The Empress shot Darcy a pointed look.

"You are correct," he said. "It was presumptuous of me to have Willow saddled before we spoke. Your sister explained my error in deciding on your behalf, in the strongest possible manner."

The Empress's gaze sharpened further. "Jane feels things very deeply, though most people would never guess it. She is not one for displays of emotion, and she is the most selfless creature I know. I cannot wonder that she would speak more strongly on my behalf — or her husband's — than her own."

"It is my fate to be properly humbled this morning, I see," Darcy said, boosting the Empress into the saddle and placing her foot carefully into the stirrup. "At the time I believed my motives to be just, but I was entirely wrong where your sister and Bingley were concerned. I have apologized to them both for my interference."

Her gaze softened. "I applaud you for so thoroughly owning your mistakes, Mr. Darcy. It takes a strong person to do it. Changing one's behavior is difficult enough; changing one's beliefs requires great fortitude."

"I had not considered that perspective," he said, settling onto Caesar's back. "Changeableness is usually thought to be a sign of weakness."

"There is a great gulf between the man who can settle on nothing and the one who can allow his views to be properly molded by experience."

Before he could reply, their attention was caught by the sound of racing hoof-beats. An express rider appeared.

Dear God, what is it now? An express rider never carried good news, in Darcy's experience.

The rider pulled up alongside him. "Is there a Mr. Darcy within?"

"I am Mr. Darcy." His stomach felt leaden as he took the letter. It was from Pemberley, in Harwood's hand.

The missive was short. He read it once — blood seeming to drain from his entire body — then again, uncomprehending. Had he not already been seated on Caesar's broad back, his legs would certainly have collapsed under him.

"Mr. Darcy? Are you well? What has happened?" The Empress clasped his arm, looking worriedly into his face. "Mr. Darcy, please tell me! What is the matter?"

His voice sounded to his own ears like it was coming from a mile away. "I must return home immediately. Pemberley has burned."

Twenty

Return to Pemberley

ARCY WATCHED the town of Lambton pass by the carriage windows. *Not five miles now.*

It had been three endless days since the devastating news had reached him; he felt disconnected from the world since reading Harwood's letter.

What will happen when I must face the reality of it? It had been difficult enough to do what was needed then.

"Pemberley has burned," he had said, not knowing how to say the rest.

The Empress had looked nearly as ashen as he felt. "What? Burned?" She had snatched up the proffered letter. "How can the kitchen have taken fire? Cook was always so careful! But thanks be to God that Georgiana was not at home! Her aunt will be a great comfort, I am sure…. What? No! No, no, no, not Mrs. Reynolds too!" She was weeping. "Mr. Darcy, this is dreadful!"

"How am I to tell him?" he had asked distantly. "After all I have done to him, how am I to tell Reynolds his mother has died?" The thought made him want to ride away and never return.

He had felt the strong grip of her hand taking his; he stared at her gloved fingers as his own reflexively closed around them. When he sought her eyes, her expression was a powerful mix of grief, compassion and determination.

"We shall tell him together," she had said. "Sarah must be there too. He will need her support."

Inside, Bingley had taken one look at his countenance and exclaimed in dismay. Bless the man — while Darcy and the Empress met with the Reynoldses, Bingley arranged for the carriage to be readied, trunks packed, and a basket of food prepared.

Reynolds's wariness had turned to fear as he met Darcy's eyes. "What is it, Mr. Darcy?"

"I have grievous news to share. I have just had an express from Harwood. Two nights ago, a fire started in Pemberley's kitchens. It destroyed the west wing of the house."

"Good God!" Reynolds had cried. "That's all of the family rooms and servant's quarters! Is everyone well? My mother, is she —?"

Darcy shook his head. "No. Cook perished, and two of the kitchen staff. Jill and Hester. And your mother."

"No! No, it cannot be true." Reynolds looked pleadingly at the Empress. "Please, Mistress! Tell me it isn't true."

"I am so sorry," she had said gently. "You know how your mother cared for the staff. Harwood said she refused to leave until every person was accounted for. He had to carry her out of the house. By then she had inhaled too much smoke."

Reynolds had slumped in his chair, his weeping wife embracing him tightly.

What should I say? This was harder than almost anything Darcy had ever done. "You have my deepest condolences. Your mother is — was — one of the kindest people I know. She will be greatly missed."

Reynolds's face had been bleak. "Thank you, sir. I would go with you when you return to Pemberley."

"And me!" young Mrs. Reynolds added.

Reynolds had finally looked at his wife. "You should stay here, love. Think of the babe."

"Where you go, I go too. The babe shall be fine. There are three months yet."

"I should be happy to convey you both," Darcy had said. "We leave as soon as possible."

When the Reynoldses had gone, Darcy had looked at the Empress. "Will you come as well?"

"Come to Pemberley? Me? Mr. Darcy —"

"Please. I beg you. After all that happened there last year, the people adore you. They trust you. I... cannot think about the house now; it is too much. But my first responsibility is to my people." He had scrubbed a hand over his eyes, swiping away the tears that threatened. His voice was hollow. "I need your help, Empress. I cannot do this alone."

Please say yes, he had mentally beseeched her. *Please. This year has nearly broken me. If I am forced to face this without you, I shall fall to pieces.* He understood, for the first time, what had happened to his father when his mother died.

"Very well," she had said, extending her hand. "We shall go together."

He had gripped it tightly, finally allowing tears of horror and relief to fall. "Thank you," he had whispered.

* * *

They had traveled as swiftly as possible, stopping only to rest the horses or to snatch a few hours of sleep. Today Darcy was exhausted but riddled with nervous energy — ever since awakening in the dead of morning, heart hammering wildly. He could not put the nightmare out of his mind: he had been at Pemberley, pounding futilely on the Empress's door as fire raged around him.

What might have happened if she had not gone away? If we had both been there?

He looked at her across the carriage. Thick chestnut curls framed a delicate face with high cheekbones and a narrow chin. Her eyes — which had so captivated him, with their dark lashes and bright intelligence — spoke now of sadness and insufficient sleep.

He had cursed himself for a fool a thousand times since his mind was restored to him — had tortured himself for months with visions of what his life might have been like, if only he had set aside his pride from the beginning and treated her as he ought to have done. Now he ached for the comfort of her arms around him, her head against his chest, the scent of her perfume in his nose.

He returned his gaze to the window before he could be caught staring. *Be grateful she is here at all*, he admonished himself. *If things had been different — if she had been curled beside you in your bed when the fire started — you might both be dead now.*

They were near the house when he smelled it: the damp, acrid stench of a charred building after rain. The coachman pulled the horses to a stop as they crested the rise. The house would be fully in view now, though still a few hundred yards distant. Reynolds pulled the door open a moment later. His expression was all the warning Darcy got.

The family wing was an utter ruin. Above the kitchen in the northwest corner, the walls crumbled just above the first storey window frames. The panes themselves appeared to be entirely gone and the stone was black with char. Portions of the second storey rooms to the front of the house were still visible, but the third storey was entirely absent and half the house was open to the sky. The only hint of its former beauty was the east wing, which appeared largely intact.

"Oh! Mr. Darcy — I had no idea," said the Empress. He felt the pressure of her arm against his. "I am so sorry. I have no words to ease such a loss."

He opened his hand, nearly weeping with gratitude when hers slipped into it and clasped tight. His mind struggled to acknowledge the truth of what he saw: the library, the gallery, his study, all the family rooms — all vanished.

Surely something of my parents survived?

"I cannot see anybody about," Reynolds said. "I shall ride ahead and try to find Harwood."

Darcy nodded. "I should like to walk around the house to obtain a closer view." His voice was thick. "Will you walk with me, Empress, or would you prefer the carriage?"

"I shall walk with you. Sarah may ride the rest of the way."

They were peering through the empty frames of first-floor windows when Harwood found them. "Mr. Darcy! I am very glad to see you, sir. And — Mrs. Darcy!"

"It is Miss Bennet now," Darcy said quickly.

"Of course. I beg your pardon, Mistress," said Harwood. "I was merely surprised to see you."

"I have come in hope of being helpful," she said. "How is everyone?"

"As well as can be expected, ma'am. A few laid up with smoke in their lungs, but most everyone made it out in time. Some have family nearby. The rest have bunked up with me, Burrell, or the tenant families."

"Is everyone accounted for, then?" Darcy asked.

"Aye. We held the service yesterday for those who died. Most of the staff don't know what to do with themselves, if I'm honest. It finally stopped raining last night, but the house was still smoldering until this morning, so we haven't gone in yet. Tomorrow we shall start clearing out debris."

"The study looks like a loss."

"Aye, and the library too. The books that didn't burn are likely waterlogged. Had it not been raining on the night of the fire the whole house would surely have gone up. But — begging your pardon, Mr. Darcy — what most of us wish to know is, what happens to Pemberley after this?"

"We rebuild. My family home has stood on this spot for generations. It shall take some time — years, probably — but Pemberley shall be restored."

Harwood gave a satisfied nod. "Everyone will be grateful to hear it, I reckon. We none of us wanted to think of leaving. In the meantime, I had Mary Abbott open Pemberley Cottage for you, sir. She and Mr. Proctor are there with a few other servants."

"Has anybody notified my sister?"

"Aye, I sent a note to your uncle at Matlock. I asked him to keep Miss Darcy safe there until you returned."

By this time, they had made it to the front of the house. The stables, the hothouse and the other outbuildings were all intact, and from this side, the damage was only visible above the second storey.

"Thank you, Harwood. It is a relief, as ever, to know that Pemberley is in such capable hands." Darcy turned to the Empress. "I suppose we must make our way to the cottage, madam. There is a great deal to do tomorrow. I should like to ride. Is your ankle strong enough to join me, or do you prefer the carriage?"

"I shall ride, if you can bear not to gallop."

He gave an exaggerated sigh. "A great sacrifice, after three days in a coach, but I shall console myself with the pleasure of your company."

She rolled her eyes, but the corners of her mouth turned up. Harwood gaped at them openly, closing his mouth with a snap as Darcy's attention returned to him.

He has never seen us this way, Darcy realized. The best he had managed before he fell ill was awkward pleasantries, and the Empress had already been miserable — even he, in all his jealous indignation, had recognized that. *Harwood has never once seen me compliment her, nor known her to be happy or playful. Neither has anybody else here.*

"Are you for home soon, Harwood?"

"Aye, sir."

"Excellent. On your way, please tell Burrell Miss Bennet and I have arrived. I shall meet you here in the morning to discuss the plan for clearing the house."

"Certainly, sir."

* * *

It felt good to be on a horse. "I thank you again for agreeing to come, Empress," Darcy said.

"I am glad to be here. What would you have me do?"

"Do I ask too much if I beg you to decide what is to be done about the household servants — the women, most particularly — and assist me in seeing to the tenants? I shall also want your opinion about what ought to be salvaged from the guest wing. I never bothered to redecorate, and it is not at all to my taste."

"You would have me be the mistress?" Her brow lifted and there was a dangerous glint in her eyes.

Yes, he thought. *From this day forward I would have you stand beside me as the mistress of Pemberley.*

Aloud he said, "With Mrs. Reynolds gone, you are the only person I trust to manage these things. I know little of Mary Abbott's abilities, and I have no notion if anyone remains who can cook. Georgiana can certainly see to the tenants, but I would never permit her to decorate the house. Her taste is far too feminine and frilly."

The Empress laughed. "On that we agree. I remember her rooms. But you have no notion of my taste, sir. I have had no hand in any place you have ever seen me."

"A valid point." He considered her. "Why did you never redecorate any of Pemberley's rooms?"

She colored. "There was no need — they were already so elegant! But even had I wished to, I did not believe you would approve."

"I am ashamed to say you were probably correct. But you must have known you were free to alter the mistress's rooms to your liking. Were they to your taste?" He privately thought them overdone — he had removed nearly one item in three from every other room his mother had decorated — but the Empress had changed nothing.

Her blush deepened. "They were not. I prefer a less ornate decorating scheme, especially for a bedchamber. In this case, however... at the risk of seeming ungrateful, I did not believe myself entitled to the mistress's suite."

"Is that why you moved to Fitzwilliam's room?"

"Nay. I could no longer bear to hear you shouting." She looked apologetic. "I am sorry to pain you."

He stopped so he could look her full in the face. "Do not apologize, Empress. We may both own a share of blame for the events of last year, but mine is by far the greater. It was my fault you felt unwelcome and undeserving. You need not shield me from it."

Her smile was sad. "Very well, but we cannot properly be friends if you are constantly apologizing for the past. I was selfish and mercenary, you were resentful and horrible, we are both exceedingly sorry, and there's an end on it."

"As you wish. I shall keep my castigation to myself. But I must say, I am reassured on the matter of your taste. I shall therefore reiterate my request for your assistance."

She chuckled. "If the alternative is Georgiana's, I suppose I must help you."

Archibald Proctor, Pemberley's butler for over a decade, opened the door of the cottage as Darcy was lifting the Empress down from the saddle. "Welcome home, sir. Mistress."

"Shall I ever convince them to call me Miss Bennet?" she murmured.

Darcy allowed himself a small smile. "Unlikely."

They were greeted by the sound of feminine laughter as they entered the house. Frowning, Darcy stepped past the Empress. At the entry to the sitting-room, he was brought up short: a pleasingly rounded young woman in a white cap and pinafore sat, giggling, on the knee of a familiar dark-haired man in uniform. The man lounged insouciantly, drink in one hand, boot resting on the chair opposite.

When he caught sight of Darcy, a wide grin spread across his features. "Well, if it isn't the lord of the manor! Welcome home, old man!"

The girl squeaked and jumped up, bobbing a curtsey and running from the room.

Darcy ignored her. "What in the ███ are you doing here, Wickham?"

Wickham shrugged. "I heard about the fire and wished to help. After all, it was my home too." His grin widened. "Ah, my lovely sister! Mrs. Wickham will be delighted to know you are again in Darcy's good graces."

Darcy was not willing to bandy words with him. "Get out of my house."

"Is that any way to treat a member of the family? Besides, for years this was my house."

"You are not welcome anywhere on this estate. Get out."

Wickham sighed dramatically. "I see you are as proud and disagreeable as ever." He stopped so near that Darcy's fingers itched to close around his wretched throat. "I am a generous man, however, so I shall give you a warning: when you tiptoe about the house at night, avoid the center of the hallway. The boards creak frightfully." He sent a meaningful glance in the Empress's direction.

"Get out," Darcy growled, "before I throw you out."

It was not an idle threat. Darcy stood half a head taller and outweighed Wickham by nearly fifty pounds, and just at that moment he would have been grateful for an excuse to thrash the blackguard.

"As you command." Wickham smirked. "But you should not get too comfortable. This is not where you belong, and we both know it." He bowed gallantly to the Empress. "Sister. I hope to see you again soon."

"Proctor!" Darcy barked when the front door had closed behind him. "How did George Wickham get into this house?"

"I am not certain, sir." The butler was visibly distressed. "I discovered his presence only moments before your arrival."

"It was me, sir," said the young woman, eyes down. Darcy finally looked at her: Mary Abbott, the head housemaid. "He said you were friends as boys, and he wished to surprise you. I'm sorry if I did wrong to let him in, sir."

Not technically a lie, of course. Darcy sighed. "I see. Our friendship is long since over, Mary. He is not to be admitted to this house again."

"Yes, sir. Welcome home, sir." She bobbed a quick curtsey. "Welcome, Mistress. I've made up a room for you and Sarah has unpacked your things. Shall I have a bath prepared?"

"Er… yes, thank you, Mary."

Darcy chuckled inwardly. *Naturally the mistress must take precedence. Nay, Empress, you shall not be 'Miss Bennet' here.*

"I shall need Caesar saddled again immediately," he told Proctor before turning to the Empress. "I hope you shall treat my home as though it were your own. Please rest and refresh yourself. I shall not be gone long, but now I know Wickham has been here, I must speak to Harwood. We must discover if there is any possibility he was responsible for the fire."

Twenty-one

A New Normal

ARCY HAD ample opportunity, over the following week, to vent his frustration and grief in physical labor. Each day he stripped to his shirtsleeves and shifted sections of roof, blocks of stone, and chunks of plaster until he was exhausted. The other men were initially discomfited by the master working alongside them, but Darcy willingly shouldered his share of the burden and in time they seemed to accept him — perhaps even to respect him. His labors left him covered daily with fresh bruises, cuts and blisters, but performing such difficult and dangerous work held a singular advantage: it allowed Darcy not to think.

When he was not working, his mind returned again and again to what — and who — had been lost, how the fire could have started in the first place, and what Wickham had been doing there. Harwood had found no evidence that Wickham had been in the neighborhood until the day before Darcy's arrival. Wickham had not set the fire, then, but it left open the question of what the reprobate was planning.

The Empress made quick work of organizing the household servants, leaving Mary Abbott in charge of the maids and advising Darcy to bring a cook up from his house in London. The tenants were all delighted to see the mistress again; with Georgiana's return, the two women soon settled into a visiting routine.

With the worst of the debris cleared, the men set to work sifting through the rooms of the family wing. Harwood was right; the entire first floor — including Darcy's study and the library — was a loss. What few books remained seemed to crumble in his hands. His great-grandfather's highly polished oak desk had been reduced to cinders, and the trunk where every important document from five generations had been stored was a block of charred wood.

On the second storey, Darcy was overjoyed to discover a surviving portrait of his parents in a rarely used sitting room. The frame had broken and one corner of the canvas was torn, but the image was intact. Unfortunately, the gallery had been in the northwest corridor; generations of Darcys were now gone forever.

The Empress and Georgiana were permitted to enter the undamaged guest wing, where they selected the items to be preserved and those to be sold or discarded. The undamaged pieces from the family bedchambers were brought for their inspection, but between the rain and the roof collapse, most of the furnishings joined the discard pile.

Their sole argument ensued over Georgiana's requests to install her pianoforte at the cottage. The Broadwood Grand,

Darcy's gift for her sixteenth birthday, was her most precious possession. To her great delight, it remained intact — it was, in fact, the only instrument to survive — and she begged him to transport it.

"Georgiana, your pianoforte is too large for the cottage," he said. "It shall take up half the sitting-room! I am delighted it was not damaged, but it must remain in storage."

"Please, brother! We need not place it in the sitting-room. Elizabeth shall support me — dear Elizabeth, please tell him! We can certainly find room for it!"

"It is not my house, Georgiana. If Mr. Darcy does not want it moved, then it must stay where it is."

He lifted a brow. "A politic response indeed. Tell me, then: can you find room for it?"

"I can." The Empress shrugged. "The morning-room sees little use. If you convert the family parlor into your study and the morning-room into a music-room, the sitting-room shall remain quite comfortable. There are not bedrooms enough to host a party of guests, so you need not worry about rooms for entertaining, I should think."

She is correct, of course. While the three of them occupied every available bedchamber, there would be no guests at all; he refused to think of the Empress as anything but a member of their family party. He sighed. "Very well, then. I shall ask Harwood to arrange it."

"Hooray! Thank you, Fitzwilliam!" Impulsively Georgiana kissed his cheek and ran to the morning-room to decide on the placement of the instrument.

The Empress smiled. "A wise decision. She shall be much happier here with her music. I must admit to selfish motives, however. Georgiana's influence was such that I have missed playing, these past weeks."

"If we are admitting to selfish motives, then I shall confess I allowed it so I might hear you play and sing. And before you say a word about your paltry skill," he said, raising a hand to forestall her, "I claim the right to my opinion. Which is that I prefer the performance of a person who enjoys music to that of a person with technical mastery but no feeling."

"Then I shall not argue the point. Though, as Mr. Burrell has just arrived, I should not have done so in any case."

Burrell had called almost daily, often staying through supper at the Empress's request. Darcy knew what the man was about. Burrell had never forgiven Darcy for mistreating her.

"Reynolds tells me you found his mother's chatelaine underneath all the rubble," Burrell said over dinner.

"We did," Darcy said. "I was glad it survived, for his sake. He seemed greatly comforted to have such a memento."

Burrell appeared surprised. "I did not know you thought so well of him."

"My mind no longer harbors the delusions it did before." He gave Burrell a direct look. "I have seen for myself how he adores his wife, and he is doing great things at Netherfield. Bingley is lucky to have him."

"Yes, well… I am delighted to hear it. He has asked me to hold a memorial at his mother's grave site on the morrow. I hope you will all join us."

"We shall be honored."

"Do Mr. and Mrs. Reynolds return to Hertfordshire on the morrow, then?" Georgiana asked.

Darcy shook his head. "Nay, I have asked them to remain until after the harvest festival."

245

The Empress's brows knit. "Harvest festival?"

"We host a festival for the tenants every year, to celebrate a successful harvest," Darcy said. "It has been a Pemberley tradition since my great-grandfather's day."

"I had no idea! Nobody mentioned it last year."

"There were many more important items requiring your attention, madam," said Burrell. "The wedding-breakfast for the Reynoldses more than made up for the lack."

Georgiana reached for the Empress's hand. "Will you help me, Elizabeth? I have never planned so large a party!"

"Certainly! But first you must tell me all about it."

The remainder of the meal was spent reminiscing. When the ladies left the table Burrell bowed, but made no move to follow.

What is this about? Darcy wondered.

Burrell regarded him with an expression that was equal parts curiosity and challenge. "When the Reynoldses leave, shall Miss Bennet go with them?"

"That is her decision, not mine."

"What are you playing at? You have made her the mistress in all but name."

"I am now without a housekeeper. I asked for her help."

Burrell raised a skeptical brow. "Shall you ask her to select new furnishings and decoration for Pemberley, too?"

"I should be glad to have her assistance. Her uncle Gardiner recommended an excellent architect. Mr. Barclay arrives the week after next."

"Have a care, young man. I have known far too many men who pursued a woman solely because the lady showed no inclination for them. It never ended well."

Darcy sobered. "I believe I have already made that error," he said quietly. "Now I hope I have learned better. If I must, I shall content myself with her friendship. I think too highly of her to ask for anything greater, if she does not reciprocate my affections."

"Do you believe she does?"

"Hardly. It has not been two months since I threw myself on her mercy. At present I hope only to convince her I can be amiable and just."

The older man nodded. "Then I shall not impede you, but be warned: I shall not tolerate any harm to her."

"Have no fear, Burrell. If I mistreat her again, I shall no doubt be drawn and quartered by her uncle, her sister, *my* sister, my cousin, Bingley, Mr. and Mrs. Reynolds, and you. She is well defended."

* * *

Their good luck with the weather held. The day of the festival dawned clear and bright, and by luncheon every tenant on the estate made their way to the lawn before the great house. The gardens were open for all to enjoy, and the children who braved the hedge-maze were met with prizes at its center. Musicians played, and a few spontaneous dances had broken out. Georgiana helped the smallest children braid the manes and tails of the ponies with gaily colored ribbons, after which Reynolds drove them around the lake in the low phaeton; childish laughter and shouts filled the air.

The Empress's uncle had supplied bolts of cloth, sturdy and well-made, as gifts for the women. Darcy had procured an excellent ale to hand around to the men, and the tables were filled with cold meats, cheeses, soups and bread.

Everywhere he looked Darcy saw smiling faces. He made a point of greeting every person present and even permitted himself to be drawn into a reel by a widow twice his age, to the raucous hoots and encouragement of the onlookers. The Empress clapped along, dark eyes sparkling merrily, before Burrell pulled her into the line.

"The mistress!" went up the cry. She danced with a light and graceful step, curls bouncing and cheeks flushed. When it was Darcy's turn to partner her, he found himself unable to stop grinning, despite the whistles and knowing shouts that followed their procession down the line.

It was only after the music had stopped, as she rose from an elegant curtsey, that he properly noticed her gown. *Russet,* he thought. *Not black.* She had dressed in full mourning for seven months. *Did she wear black yesterday?* he wondered. *Yes, she did,* he realized, but today the only black he saw was the ribbon on her bonnet.

She caught him staring; his perplexity was surely written on his face because she smiled. "My father would have loved this. He would have grumbled about the noise and expense and silliness of it all, but so long as he could sit at the edge of the crowd, watching everything and laughing to himself, he would have enjoyed it enormously." She surveyed the revels. "He would not wish me to wear black today."

"You look lovely, but I think he would have been proud no matter what color you wore." Darcy glanced up to see the musicians setting down their instruments. "If you will excuse me, I must say a few words."

"People of Pemberley!" he cried as the crowd assembled, "this has truly been an extraordinary year." There was a loud murmur of assent. "I am grateful to you all for your presence today. This year we have endured flood, fire, and grievous illness that took too many of our loved ones from us. Let us hold them in our hearts as we gather in celebration of a plentiful harvest and the promise of better days to come."

"Hear, hear!" came a shout. "To better days!"

"Pemberley shall be rebuilt, and I would hire as many of you as I may to build it. I shall invest in modern equipment for your farms and fields. My sister shall support the modest enterprises of the women. Together we survived tragedy, and together we shall know prosperity." There were more shouts of agreement.

Darcy held up his hands for quiet. "I take no credit for the diligence and care that shepherded our people through the worst time in recent memory. As you know, I was myself too ill. I must thank Mr. Harwood and Mr. Burrell for their many efforts." There was enthusiastic applause. "But we must all be grateful to one person above all others. Had Pemberley no mistress last autumn, many more would have suffered and died — myself included, I believe."

The reaction was deafening. The crowd pushed their furiously blushing Mistress forward until she stood before the stage. Darcy bowed deeply over her hand, unable to speak for the noise and his own emotion.

"I thank you all," she said. "You made me welcome when I was a stranger, and you banded together when your fellows were in need. I could have done nothing without you, and I celebrate you as you should celebrate yourselves!"

With that she attempted to melt back into the press of people, though she found herself stopped and thanked with every step. Darcy could not help marveling at the sight. *I am known as a good master, but the people have never looked at me that way,* he thought.

Georgiana took Darcy's arm as the tenants returned to the festivities. "Well said, brother. I do hope Elizabeth decides to remain, rather than return to Hertfordshire." She nodded to where the Empress smiled warmly at Reynolds and his wife, her countenance giving no hint of her intentions. "You look at her properly now, you know, and I should like to have her as a sister again."

He glanced down sharply, uncertain which of his swirling thoughts to voice first.

"Have no fear," she said, "I shall not try to sway her. Either she will come to love you on her own or not. I only wish you to know I pray for your success."

* * *

The days were increasingly difficult after that, but the nights even more so. In the daytime, at least, Darcy had numerous tasks to occupy his mind. At night there was no escaping his thoughts.

I am a fool. How did I ever believe I could content myself with her friendship?

None of Darcy's previous self-torture, envisioning what his life might have been had he treated the Empress properly from the outset, compared with his present reality. This was impossibly better — and worse.

How can such idyllic domesticity cause such misery?

The Empress had elected to remain with them. She now managed his household with quiet efficiency and provided sisterly guidance to Georgiana; she heard his difficulties and gently offered her advice; she suffered him to lecture her on

Roman history and read novels to him in return. She teased and challenged him, never pandering, and still she served his favorite foods, played his favorite songs, and presented him with cups of tea prepared exactly to his liking.

The nights were an abyss of longing. As silence descended over the cottage, Darcy could not help recalling Wickham's suggestive glance — *'Avoid the center of the hallway,'* he had said. Her door stood twenty feet down the corridor. Behind it she lay with her unbound hair around her in a cloud, dark lashes brushing her cheeks, chest rising and falling with slow breaths. Or so Darcy imagined; he had no notion what she looked like as she slept, much less the shape of her body beneath the coverlet.

Has she seen me? She knows my face in sleep, surely, but... did she ever aid Simmons to bathe or dress me? He could not remember.

His eyes strayed to the corner where his strongbox was concealed. He had found it, whole and firmly locked, in the ruins of his chambers at Pemberley. None but Simmons knew of its existence. Giving up on sleep, Darcy opened it, fingers seeking the slim rectangular box within.

After the Empress departed, he had been fiercely glad to see this sapphire necklace and ring. It had been weeks before he knew enough to feel differently, and months before he found the note. It was his own, addressed to her — though not by name; he had not given her even that courtesy — on the morning of their ill-fated wedding.

'She feared it a test she would fail,' her sister had said.

Darcy's chest ached. He rubbed at it, distantly aware that the jagged shards were fewer and less deadly but also that the reparation of his heart was fragile, not to be relied upon. The great sapphire was dark, swallowing the room's meager light. His thumb brushed it and he frowned.

Somehow this one jewel embodies every mistake I made. I was wrong to give it to her. He knew this to be so, though he could not have explained why, precisely. He considered the necklace for long minutes.

Eventually he closed the lid on the rectangular box. He would not look at the sapphire again. His decision made, he placed it back into the strongbox and tossed the note into the fire, watching the paper slowly turn to ash before taking up his pen.

Twenty-two

House Plans

W HAT YOU ARE ASKING cannot be done, Mr. Darcy."

How does he manage to appear both pugnacious and regretful at once? Darcy wondered. "Explain."

The young architect shrugged. "Too much of the original stonework is gone — whether burned or broken, it makes no difference. You cannot use what's whole to rebuild even the second storey, much less the third."

"Can you not quarry more?"

"Certainly, but it won't have been exposed to wind and rain for two hundred years, like the stones of the house. You could pick out the new stone from half a mile away."

"Mr. Barclay, you have been over every inch of the house in the past two days. I do not wish to hear it cannot be rebuilt as it was. I wish to hear how it may be accomplished," Darcy said. *And do not look at me as though I were a simpleton.*

Edward Gardiner had given Simon Barclay his highest recommendation. The architect's other references described him invariably as a "genius," with "very modern sensibilities" and "a talent for achieving the impossible." None thought to mention that the Scotsman was no older than Bingley, nor that "genius" was merely a kinder way of saying "impervious to reason."

Barclay smiled tightly. "To rebuild exactly as it was — all of the same stone — requires demolishing the entire building and beginning afresh. You might also use whole stones from the east wing to replace the damaged ones on the north and west sides of the first storey, then build the second and third storeys complete with new stone. If you used a contrasting color to create a division between each storey, the difference would not be so obvious."

"But that is not your recommendation."

"What you are asking of me, Mr. Darcy, is to duplicate every error in design and construction made two hundred years ago, so the west side looks like the east. If this is truly your desire, I shall recommend another architect. But you have an opportunity to build anew with the most innovative techniques available! *That* house I will design for you."

Darcy frowned, regarding the ruins of his home. *He asks the unthinkable.*

"What errors, Mr. Barclay?" The Empress had been silent up to this point, though she listened intently.

"I'm glad you asked, Miss Bennet," Barclay said with a winning smile. He was an exceedingly handsome man. "First, the roof collects water. The attics are beginning to rot on the east side, and if you look very closely you can see cracks forming above the windows of the third storey. Second, the foundation has settled. See the cracks near the ground there? My guess is they could not find bedrock in that corner."

"What does that mean for the east wing?" Darcy asked.

"It means you need a new roof that drains properly, and your children will likely need to rebuild the entire front face."

"Are there other considerations?" the Empress asked.

"Aye — the whole building is a great, heavy box, isn't it? No arches or round edges anywhere! It's curves that allow us to build structures both tall and graceful. An arched window supports the wall above it better than a rectangular one, and lets in more light to boot."

She smiled delightedly. "I do not believe I have ever seen windows like that except in a church."

"Oh, aye, in this country the Catholics were the pioneers in building. But I've been to India, Turkey, France, Bavaria — much of the world, really — and the Ottomans and Mughals were building light, airy palaces over two hundred years ago, while we were building boxes."

Pemberley is a perfectly elegant English country house!

Darcy forced himself to examine the east wing, with its heavy stone base and tall, rectangular windows, as though he were a stranger. He sighed inwardly. *And it is also a box.*

The Empress had moved on to the interior improvements Barclay proposed, her eager eyes wide. "And you can truly build a tub that fills itself?"

"Nearly so. You build pipes into the walls that carry water, and spouts where you want it to pour. You can also heat the water in one pipe but not the other."

"Mr. Darcy! Imagine not having to wait for the water to be carried up to have a hot bath!"

"That is tempting indeed," he admitted.

"There have been many advancements in recent years to make kitchens much safer, Mr. Darcy," Barclay said seriously. "Even if you choose another architect to rebuild Pemberley as it was, I recommend modernizing the kitchen at the very least."

Darcy nodded slowly, silence falling as he again regarded what remained of the west wing. The Empress watched him closely, lower lip caught between her teeth. He laughed. "You appear fit to burst if you remain silent a moment longer, madam! Very well, then: how would you advise me?"

"Nay, Mr. Darcy, Pemberley is your home. You must choose what most pleases you for its restoration."

"I shall certainly do so. But I asked you to hear Mr. Barclay because I desire your opinion. I am satisfied on the matter of your taste, but more to the purpose, you did not spend your life within Pemberley's walls. You therefore possess what I do not: a fresh perspective. I beg you, tell me your thoughts on Mr. Barclay's recommendation."

"Very well, then. I believe you should allow Mr. Barclay to propose a design for an entirely new house — one which maintains the elements you most admire about the present building, but with a more elegant aesthetic. If you dislike it, you have lost only a few weeks."

Barclay looked between them speculatively; his admiration for the Empress was obvious, and Darcy had introduced her only as a friend. When Barclay's expectant gaze settled on Darcy, it contained an element of challenge.

I could send him packing and hire another man twice his age, Darcy thought. But the Empress's enthusiasm — for the man's ideas and nothing more, he hoped — was infectious.

What might Pemberley look like as a light and airy English country house?

"No turrets," he said. "I have no desire for a castle. And I should prefer the house to remain where it is."

"Done," said Barclay. "I can have the first drawings ready for your examination in ten days."

Darcy smiled — the smile he reserved for opponents at his fencing club. "I look forward to it."

* * *

After Barclay's departure, Darcy determined to make the fullest possible use of his primary advantage: proximity. It seemed the heavens conspired to aid him, for the rains were too heavy in the next several days for anybody to venture out. The Empress already spent mornings in the study; Darcy had instructed that two desks be placed there, so his challenge was to find a topic on which he required her advice.

He finally hit on the ideal candidate. "With every volume in my library either drenched or cinders, I must start anew. I believe you felt it to be missing something before. What do you recommend I purchase?"

For the next three days they debated the merits of dozens of titles — prose and poetry, history and science, atlases and encyclopedias — and together they crafted a truly prodigious list for his London bookseller.

"I cannot fathom the cost of this," she said, laughing quietly. "Much less the cost of rebuilding Pemberley." She smiled with disarming frankness. "Nothing about my life at Longbourn prepared me to be the mistress of Pemberley, you know. This cottage is easy, but Pemberley was not. Did I ever tell you how I learned my way through the house?"

He grinned. "Nay, you did not."

"I instructed Sarah to name a place for me to find. She could only correct me if I went entirely the wrong direction." The Empress shook her head, smiling. "I thought the maids must be laughing behind my back, I was so often lost in the beginning."

Darcy smiled at the image of the Empress dragging Sarah about the house with her, but it was tinged with regret. *I paid no heed to what I asked of her — even had we not begun as we did, it must certainly have been overwhelming. But I promised to stop apologizing!*

"Well, you shall have no such excuse in future," he said, "as you have bullied me into having new plans drawn."

"Bullied, is it?" Her eyes took on a mischievous gleam. "I declare, if a smile is all that is required to bully you, sir, you are on dangerous ground indeed. I shall deploy my weapon at every opportunity."

He frowned with exaggerated concern. "Oh dear. I appear to have made a tactical error."

A knock at the door interrupted her laughter. "Who can that be, in this weather?"

Proctor entered the study, mouth pressed into a line. "Mr. Burrell, Mayor Davies, and Mr. Wickham to see you, sir."

What the ███ *What is Wickham doing here, and with the magistrate?*

Hoping to send them speedily away, Darcy strode into the entrance hall. "Good morning, gentlemen. How may I be of service?"

"We have come to take you into custody, Mr. Darcy," said Mr. Davies gravely.

Darcy scarcely knew the man — he had been the mayor of Lambton and the local magistrate for just over a year — but he seemed to be eyeing Darcy nervously.

Wickham, on the other hand, looked insufferably smug. Darcy ignored him. "On what charge, magistrate?"

"I have here a decree of insanity, sir. You are to be transported to Manchester Lunatic Hospital."

"What?" His astonishment was echoed by the Empress and, he was pleased to see, Burrell. "I demand to see this decree," Darcy said.

"Sir... I do not believe I am permitted to —"

"Davies, I have not been examined by a physician in six months. I shall not tear it to pieces, if that is your concern, but I have the right to know the contents of the accusation and the identities of the physicians."

Still the man hesitated, looking about anxiously as though an answer would be forthcoming from the air.

"May I see the decree, sir?" It was the Empress. "I do not believe Mr. Darcy will take it from me."

"Are you Miss Bennet?"

"I am."

"The allegations in the decree primarily concern your prior relationship with Mr. Darcy, madam. Are you entirely certain you wish to —"

"I am well able to endure whatever might be contained in that document, sir," she said calmly. "Please come with me, gentlemen."

She led the way to her desk in the study, where Davies put the decree into her waiting hand with visible relief. Darcy itched to station himself at her shoulder, but the magistrate would never allow it. Instead, Darcy contented himself with watching her subtle shifts of expression as she read.

"I know nothing of the law, so I may only tell you what is written here," she said at length. "The allegations are that you believe me — without foundation — to be a thief and an adulteress, and that you are being poisoned by the use of laudanum at my hand and Simmons's; that you see and speak to a woman who is not there, whose name is Elizabeth but who is *not* me; that you are exceedingly agitated and threatening to myself, Simmons, Reynolds, and Dr. Lindley; and that you pose a risk of physical violence toward all of those named, but myself in particular."

She is extraordinary, Darcy thought. Her tone remained flat and even, her face expressionless. He thought her cheeks had pinked at the mention of his hallucinating another Elizabeth — he had only the vaguest recall of such a woman; damn his treacherous memories! — but he doubted any other man would have noticed.

She looked directly at Burrell and went on in the same tone. "Witnesses whose information was relied upon for these allegations include Mr. Burrell and Mary Abbott, as presented by Mr. Wickham. The physicians who attest to these allegations are a Dr. Rutherford Gilmour and Dr. Philip Lindley. The decree was signed in London three days ago, on the eleventh of October."

"I beg your pardon!" Burrell bellowed. "Wickham, what perfidy is this?"

"I related precisely what you told me, Burrell," Wickham said easily. "Your concern for my dear sister and for the management of the estate was so compelling, I felt obliged to act."

"I had no knowledge of this, Darcy," said Burrell. "And I do not support it, Davies."

Davies looked at the others uncertainly. "Miss Bennet?"

"I was never consulted in this matter, nor do I support it."

Wickham smirked. "Sister, your fear for your safety was so great you fled to Hertfordshire and annulled your marriage. Your support, or the lack of it, makes no difference."

"Please allow me to conduct this inquiry, Mr. Wickham," Davies said. "Mr. Darcy?"

"I contest the legality of this decree. I demand the right to have my solicitor review the document and to a judicial hearing in the matter. I have never heard of this Dr. Gilmour and I last saw Dr. Lindley in April, at which time he declared me fully recovered from my illness of last autumn."

Darcy had apparently said what was necessary to soothe Davies's nerves, for the magistrate suddenly seemed more assured. "Very well, Mr. Darcy. I shall delay the execution of this decree pending the determination of the court. You are to remain under house arrest. You may not leave Pemberley Cottage until such time as a judicial hearing is convened."

"I will comply with those terms. Meanwhile I request you acknowledge my right to bar Mr. Wickham from any part of the Pemberley estate."

"You remain its master, sir. You have that right."

"Then kindly remove him from my property forthwith."

Twenty-three

Waiting Game

BEFORE THE FRONT DOOR closed, Darcy stalked to the window, glaring hard at Wickham's retreating back. "Damn Wickham!" he spat. "Apologies, Empress." Finally the three men disappeared. "What can he be planning?"

"You need not apologize," she said dryly. "I have heard far worse from your lips. I must see to one important task before we speculate about Mr. Wickham's plans, however. Proctor, please send Mary Abbott in."

"Yes, Mistress?" The maid was all wide-eyed innocence as she entered the study. Her expression shifted to worry when she caught sight of the Empress.

"To whom do you owe your loyalty, Mary?"

"Why... to you, Mistress — and the master, of course."

"Excellent. What, then, did Mr. Wickham promise you in exchange for information about Mr. Darcy's illness?"

Likely nothing more than his undying affection, Darcy thought, but the maid's eyes widened in fear. "I — I beg your pardon, Mistress?"

"You clearly know your duty," said the Empress. "For you to violate it, he must have promised something handsome indeed." At the girl's silence she added, "I hope it required more than empty flattery to purchase your disloyalty. I never took you for a fool."

The Empress's face and voice remained expressionless. Darcy sympathized with the girl.

Mary shrugged. "Am I to be dismissed, then?"

The Empress said nothing. She simply waited, expression fixed. Darcy was nearly to the point of shouting at the maid, but the Empress's stillness silenced him.

"He said a pretty girl like me deserved a proper dowry," said Mary defiantly. "That's more than Mr. Darcy would ever give me."

The Empress barked a humorless laugh. "You took that as a promise? You *are* a fool, Mary, and a disloyal one. You are dismissed as of this moment."

"Wickham has no money to make such promises," Darcy said when the girl was gone. "I can make no sense of this."

"What does he gain if you are no longer the master of Pemberley?" the Empress asked. "If you are declared insane, I must assume you will lose the estate."

"Yes. Even if I do not spend my life in an asylum, I should certainly not be permitted to remain its master, nor Georgiana's guardian." He shook his head. "But Wickham would gain nothing. Uncle Henry would oversee Pemberley until Georgiana's son comes of age, and my cousin Richard shares her guardianship with me."

The Empress nodded thoughtfully. "Would he descend to such malicious revenge as this, with naught else to gain?"

"Perhaps. He believes I blasted his prospects by forcing him to marry your sister."

She was silent for a long moment. "Why did you never call in his debts?"

"What do you know of his debts?"

"I found the receipts in that great trunk in your study — gone now, more's the pity — but why not have him arrested and thrown into debtor's prison long ago?"

Darcy smiled grimly. *If she has seen the trunk, there is no point in keeping secrets.* "He was my father's favorite. It would have caused a scandal, even before he attempted to seduce Georgiana these two years past. Then he was my brother-in-law."

The Empress did not appear in the least surprised by his mention of Georgiana's greatest shame. *She can only have learned of it from Georgiana. They are truly like sisters.*

"He is no longer your brother-in-law," she said, "but with the receipts burned nothing can be done, I suppose."

"You would have me imprison your sister's husband?"

"I believe Lydia sufficiently disenchanted to welcome the opportunity to be free of him." She shrugged. "But as nothing can be done about it, and we cannot know what he might be planning, I suggest we turn our thoughts to a less distressing topic."

"What might that be?"

She grinned. "How shall you decorate the not-castle Mr. Barclay shall design for you?"

* * *

The enforced isolation was maddening. After only four days, Darcy would have paid an alarmingly large sum just to be permitted to ride the estate for a day. Those around him did everything they could. Georgiana and the Empress diverted him with music, books, cards, and tales of their adventures with the tenant families. Burrell and Harwood both visited the cottage at least once daily.

Darcy had it out with Burrell the day after Wickham's visit with the magistrate.

"You were a spoiled, selfish child who became a proud, selfish man," Burrell had said, "and that lovely young woman did not deserve any of the misery you caused her."

"Agreed. On all counts," Darcy had said. At Burrell's look of surprise, he added, "You are a man of the cloth, Burrell. Do you not believe a man might repent his sins and strive to do better?"

"Well — yes, of course."

"Unless that man is me, it seems." Darcy had leveled a challenging gaze at the vicar. "Or do you merely believe her too weak-willed to be permitted to forgive? Must you carry resentment on her behalf?"

Burrell had stared into his teacup for an agonizingly long time. "You are right, Mr. Darcy. I love that girl like a daughter, and it hurt me to see her injured so. I thought her foolish to forgive you. But I thought her foolish to give any credence to Lindley's assertions that your mind might recover in time, too." He smiled wryly. "I did not hesitate to speak the truth in the harshest possible terms last January because I did not expect you to believe me."

"Had you been gentler I might not have done so."

Burrell's answering smile was fond. "She has proved to be the superior of us both, it seems. I am sorry, Darcy. I should never have spoken so to Wickham."

"If you will testify before the judge to what you have seen in recent weeks — months, even — then your testimony to Wickham shall lose most of its power."

They had shaken hands and parted friends. Darcy had since found he greatly enjoyed the man's company; Burrell could be relied upon for a spirited debate on any topic and was a fierce opponent at chess. This would have made him a valuable acquaintance under any circumstance, but particularly now.

On one topic, however, Darcy could not bring himself to speak to Burrell.

Did I truly see a woman who was not there? An Elizabeth who was not the Empress? He could not recall it. *But it must be so. The Empress blushed — did she witness it?*

It was mortifying to consider.

Simmons blushed as well, Darcy suddenly recalled. *When he told me of it. Just after she left.*

"Simmons," he said that evening, "I have been unable to recall an element of my illness, and I require you to tell me the truth of it: what woman did I see?"

Simmons kept his eyes on the jacket he was brushing. "I do not understand why this should be of importance now, sir. You have not seen any such thing in many months."

"Did Mrs. Darcy witness it? Me speaking to a woman who was not present, that is?"

"Yes, sir." A muscle twitched in Simmons's jaw.

"More than once?"

"Yes, sir." He grimaced at Darcy's expectant look. "Every night for at least a week, sir."

"I need to know." Darcy spoke quietly. "I believe I have heard all the ways I injured her but this."

Simmons sighed heavily. "You called her 'My Elizabeth.' We thought at first you were asking for the mistress; you were both just recovering from influenza, and she had not been with you in a week." He turned bleak eyes to Darcy. "She stood at your bedside and Burrell said, 'Elizabeth is here.' You looked directly at her and said, 'No.' Then you started talking to the window as though there were another woman there." He swallowed hard, eyes on the ground. "You... begged the other woman to come to your bed, sir."

Dear God. Can I wonder he did not wish to tell me? Darcy's face was aflame. "And I spoke to this woman often?"

"Every night, sir. It got worse after that."

"Worse?" *How could it be worse?*

"You sang to her, the mistress told me. Recited poetry. She would not tell me any more of what she heard, but if it was as... well, as explicit, sir... as what you said when I was there..." Simmons shifted uncomfortably. "I did not believe you kept another woman, sir, but the mistress likely did."

"She believes I did not want her." Darcy's voice was hollow with shock. *That I wanted — had — another woman in my bed, whose name was also Elizabeth.* Nothing could be farther from the truth. *But how may I say such a thing to her?*

"Thank you, Simmons." He sucked in a deep breath. "It is better I know."

"Yes, sir." Simmons hesitated. "Begging your pardon, sir, I know this is none of my affair —"

"Say what you must. After the last year, very little is out of bounds to you."

"Thank you, sir. I only meant to say — I hope you patch things up with the mistress, sir. You are happier now than I have seen you in years, despite all that has happened."

"Thank you, Simmons. I share your hope, but she must be happy too. I have caused her sufficient misery for one lifetime."

"Well, sir, she seems happy now. Almost like she was, as I recall, these two years past in Hertfordshire. I need not tell you she was unhappy last year, even before you were ill. We all worried for her."

"I am grateful for your honesty. Good night, Simmons."

"Good night, sir."

It is so easy to forget how much the servants see. Simmons's view — that the Empress seemed nearly back to herself — was reassuring. Her teasing wit had returned, though with a softer edge, and she laughed often. She did not appear to be avoiding him, either. On the contrary, Darcy had taken care not to let on how frequently he noticed her looking at him, her gaze most often thoughtful or amused.

I could hardly keep my eyes from her when we first knew each other in Hertfordshire, he recalled. *Did she find it as disconcerting then as I do now? At least she is not wary of me.*

Might she even feel some affection for me? He opened his strongbox and lifted out the papers inside. His copy of the annulment decree was here; it was so painful to read he hid it with the other documents he wanted no other eyes to see.

What was I thinking? He had signed the register "F.D.," knowing it was not legal. He had not planned it but had also made no attempt to talk himself out of it.

Did I hope for an excuse to rid myself of her? Part of him had, if he was honest. But by the time he appeared before the bishop in February, he had been so overcome with shame and guilt he wanted nothing more than to crawl into a hole and disappear forever.

God, I beg you would grant me the opportunity to be the husband she deserves, he prayed, setting aside the annulment decree and taking up the letter at the top of the stack. It had come today, a response to his inquiry ten days ago; he had plucked it from the salver and pocketed it without the Empress being the wiser, he hoped.

He read it through, closely examining the enclosed sketch. Smiling with satisfaction, he composed his approval and set it aside for Simmons to add to the outgoing mail on the morrow.

* * *

Simon Barclay returned to the cottage the next morning, a thick roll of papers under one arm. Darcy settled between the Empress and Georgiana in the dining-room with some trepidation, but the ladies were all excitement as Barclay spread out his drawings, placing the first — a front elevation of the house — before Darcy.

No turrets, at least. Barclay had not designed a castle, but neither did this building possess the clean, regular lines of Pemberley. It boasted steeply pitched slate roofs; pairs of tall, narrow windows, each topped by a peaked arch; an elegant conservatory just off the entrance hall; the broad, sweeping curve of a grand circular staircase; and a set of great bronze doors set in a peaked-arch frame. The front face was made up of a series of recesses and prominences that were entirely asymmetrical, yet somehow pleasing to the eye. Darcy had never seen a home like it.

"Mr. Barclay," the Empress said, "this is an extraordinary design! What inspired you?"

"Primarily the Gothic cathedrals, Miss Bennet. I greatly admire the tall, pointed arches that make their way into the windows and rib-vaulted ceilings. A new style that marries those elements with the greater simplicity we now favor is becoming quite fashionable. In this design I have added elements of the Gothic in the roof decorations, for example, but nothing so excessive as in the fourteenth century."

Next came the side and rear elevations, followed by floor plans and interior sketches. The great hall, dining-room and ballroom all shared the same soaring, intricately patterned rib-vaulted ceiling.

"It looks like a snowflake!" Georgiana exclaimed, closely examining the pattern.

"And see, the ribs which support the conservatory's glass ceiling are on the same plan," the Empress pointed out.

The most innovative features were entirely hidden from public view, however. Heating was provided by coal-burning furnaces "to more evenly and inexpensively heat the rooms, Mr. Darcy." Every bathing chamber had piped-in water — even a chamber pot that rinsed and drained itself! — and the master's bath included a standing shower.

"A series of semi-circular pipes force jets of water toward the body from above and all sides. An efficient way to clean oneself, sir," Barclay said.

The kitchens were a marvel, with their own piped-in water and the enormous brick Rumford cook-stove, which boasted adjustable temperature controls for each cook-pot, a baking oven, and a separate chimney. The man had even proposed an indoor pool for swimming!

This house will be the talk of London, Darcy thought. *But is it Pemberley?*

"Why do you frown, brother?" Georgiana's expression was incredulous.

Darcy schooled his features. "It is an extraordinary design, to be sure. But the Darcys have long stood for stability and tradition. We are unpretentious and —"

"Stodgy," Georgiana declared, rolling her eyes. "You are stodgy, Fitzwilliam. For once, look to the future instead of the past! Why do you cling to the image of a house that could easily be mistaken for Chatsworth?"

She set the front elevation before him again. "This is not pretentious. It is elegant and understated, just as you prefer. I would wish for crenellations and round towers and elaborate carvings, which you would call frippery. Mr. Barclay has not given you frippery, brother. But neither has he given you the starched, stodgy box you so love."

Darcy stared into the sweetly earnest face of his sister. She blushed, realizing all eyes were on her, but she lifted her chin and stabbed at the drawing with her finger. Darcy turned to find the Empress grinning proudly.

"Well, madam? What say you?"

"I adore the exterior, but I find it difficult to imagine what the interior shall look like. How large are these rooms?"

Barclay gave her his most winning smile. "Perhaps we should go to the great house, Miss Bennet. I believe I can use the exposed rooms to demonstrate."

To Barclay's evident chagrin, Darcy applied to the magistrate for permission to accompany them. Mr. Davies himself returned with Harwood to ensure Darcy's good behavior. They spent the next hour circling the ruined house with drawings in hand, attempting to envision something entirely new in its stead. Harwood was visibly impressed; even the magistrate found it difficult to remain aloof.

Darcy observed as Barclay led the Empress to the spot where the northeast hallway crumbled into nothingness. Barclay leaned close, animatedly pointing to where each of the new rooms would be positioned. The Empress's interest was obvious, but Darcy fancied she looked at the plans and the building far more often, and with greater pleasure, than the architect.

Reassured, he strode down the opposite hall to the corner, picturing the grand entrance which would be visible from this side. Glancing around, he found himself looking at the window in the master's bedchamber.

Who was this other Elizabeth I saw? Even with Simmons's description, no memory of the imaginary woman's face had surfaced. Darcy entered the chamber, walking on the planks that had been laid across the floor. The room was nearly empty; would this have been easier if it were still furnished? He stared at the window for a full minute, but nothing came to him.

I am in the wrong spot. He was standing beside where the bed would have been. Taking a step onto the bare wood floor, he tried again. *Nearly there.* One more step. *Yes, this is it.*

He remained still, eyes unfocused as he faced the window. He ignored a distant creaking noise. At length the vague hints of an image began to form in his mind: dark curls, sparkling brown eyes, laughing mouth.

Elizabeth. My Elizabeth.

Suddenly the creaking became a loud snapping, and the boards beneath him gave way. His hands scrabbled against the floor, finding no purchase. He was going to fall twenty feet to the library floor below.

Empress! He could not have said if his voice echoed his mind's cry.

Swiftly — much too swiftly — he slammed against something hard and unyielding. Pain exploded in his ribcage. Then his body seemed to bounce away and he was falling again.

Balustrade. Desperately Darcy reached for the railing; his hand closed around an iron post and his body jerked to a stop. He nearly lost consciousness from the sudden shock of agony in his shoulder and ribs, but he snatched at the railing with his other hand and hung there, unable to pull himself over.

Please come quickly, he prayed, light-headed with pain. *Please come before I fall.*

Twenty-four

Testimony

DARCY KEPT HIS BACK as straight as possible, teeth gritted, breathing slowly through his nose. They had been traveling for three hours over uneven roads; even in his well-sprung carriage, the jostling was more than his cracked ribs could withstand.

In the two weeks since he had fallen through his own bedchamber floor, pain had been his constant companion. "I am sorry to say there is nothing to be done for a fractured rib, Mr. Darcy," Dr. Pierce had said. "You must give the bones time to knit and try not to move too much." Simmons wrapped his ribs each morning so tightly he could not take a full breath. Not that he wished to; it hurt too badly.

He had diverted himself with conversation, primarily with Barclay. They spent several days dickering over the details of the plans, but ultimately Darcy had approved the design. Not out of gratitude, though he was certainly grateful to the other man; the architect's quick thinking had saved him.

While Davies and the Empress had run to the master's chambers, Barclay — understanding what the crashing sound meant — had come barreling at full tilt into the library, Harwood not far behind. The two men had succeeded in pulling Darcy up over the balustrade, where he promptly vomited from pain and shock.

It should not have surprised him that the Empress had taken this in stride, just as she tolerated his difficulty moving and his fraying temper. She had attended every meeting with Barclay, quietly anticipating Darcy's needs and teasing him out of his quarrelsome moods.

She rarely gave her own opinion, but still she succeeded in bringing him around — in the end, Darcy felt pride in the idea of a Pemberley at once so elegant and unusual. Barclay's sharp eyes missed nothing that passed between them; as Darcy shook the architect's hand to seal their agreement, he saw in the other man's gaze the calm resignation of one who has graciously conceded the field.

Following that, Darcy spent his time dickering with the Empress over furnishings and decoration for the new house, considering each room in detail. He was careful to avoid any discussion of the master's and mistress's chambers, but all the principal rooms had been thoroughly debated by the day they departed for Sheffield.

He was grateful the nearest court which could hear such a petition was 30 miles from Pemberley; there were no tenants to witness this ignominy or spread idle gossip. Instead, Darcy trusted every person he knew in this courtroom to defend him, save one.

Wickham's ploy soon became clear. The wretch smirked as his solicitor addressed the judge.

"My Lord, we petition the court to uphold the finding that Fitzwilliam Darcy is insane, a danger to all those around him, and that he requires confinement in an asylum. And, further, to remand the estate of Pemberley to the custodianship and care of George Wickham until such time as a legal heir is of age, per the late George Darcy's will."

The Empress turned assessing eyes to Darcy. "Would your father have entrusted Pemberley to him?" she whispered. "I did not see anything of this in the will."

"Nay. There is no such stipulation. I cannot fathom how, but Wickham must have fabricated it."

"There must be more than one copy of the will."

Darcy nodded. "Three. Mine, of course, has burned. My solicitor has a copy, and my uncle."

Mary Abbott was called first to testify, tossing the Empress a defiant grin as she took the witness's chair. The solicitor's questions were canny — "did you ever observe" and "tell the court what you witnessed," with no mention whatsoever of the dates of the occurrences. Her tale was harrowing, all the more so for being true.

She was the head housemaid, Darcy realized. *The only one permitted to clean my chamber for all those months.*

She recounted his rages and suspicion with lowered eyes and tightly clenched hands, her voice small and trembling.

Jaw set at a determined angle, the Empress quietly slipped out of the courtroom.

Where can she be going? Darcy felt a brief, irrational panic that she would not return. Had Wickham's lie and this mummer's display convinced her to flee from him?

No, he told himself sternly. *Were she intending to flee she might have done so a dozen times before this.*

When Wickham's solicitor finished his questions, Darcy's solicitor gave the former housemaid a knowing look. "Miss Abbot, on what date did you last witness this behavior?"

"I don't know the exact date, sir."

"What month, then?"

She hesitated. "It's been a bit, I'd say."

"Did you witness Mr. Darcy make these accusations after Miss Bennet departed?"

"Aye, sir."

"Did you witness him make these accusations after Easter? Which was the twenty-ninth of March, you recall."

She was silent, biting her lip.

"Miss Abbot?"

"Nay, sir."

He nodded. "Is it safe to say that Mr. Darcy had ceased to behave in the manner you describe well before Easter?"

She was silent again.

"You are under oath, Miss Abbot."

"Aye, sir." She sighed.

"How would you describe his behavior in recent months?"

"It's hard to say. He was gone for some weeks, sir."

"In the weeks since his return to Pemberley, then."

She shrugged. "Normal, I suppose."

"Have you seen him shout or threaten anybody?"

"He was upset to see Mr. Wickham in the house when he returned to Pemberley, sir."

"Have you heard him accuse Miss Bennet of anything?"

"Nay, sir."

He lifted an eyebrow. "How does he treat Miss Bennet?"

"Like she's the mistress." Mary Abbot's tone was sour.

"Is he respectful toward her?"

"Oh, aye." She snorted. "He moons over her, if you want the truth."

There were knowing chuckles from many in attendance. Darcy kept his eyes forward.

His solicitor waited for the laughter to cease. "I believe we are all interested in the truth, Miss Abbot. Only one question more: what did Mr. Wickham say you deserved, if the court grants him custodianship of Pemberley?"

Her eyes widened and flicked briefly to Wickham, but the question was too carefully worded for her to deflect it. "He — he said —" She swallowed. "He said I deserve a dowry."

"Thank you, Miss Abbot. I have nothing further."

Burrell was called next, then Simmons and Harwood. All told the same tale: for months they witnessed the master of Pemberley bedridden and screaming, incapable of making the most basic decisions, speaking to an imaginary woman, viciously accusing his wife of adultery and theft. Then they saw him gradually recover his body and mind — becoming, indeed, a more generous and humble man than he had been. The judge began to look annoyed.

The Empress returned just after Burrell took the witness's chair, her expression resolute. She handed Darcy's solicitor a folded note; he gave her the barest nod before calling her to the stand.

"Did you hear the testimony of Mr. Burrell, Mr. Simmons, and Mr. Harwood?"

"Yes, I did."

"Do you agree with their characterization of Mr. Darcy's behavior last autumn?"

"Yes."

"Was his behavior the reason you sought an annulment of your marriage?"

She nodded. "At the time he still hated me without reason, although much of his strength had returned and he was not agitated. I believed his mind would never recover." Her voice was steady, even as she glanced apologetically at Darcy.

Nobody could blame you for believing as you did, Darcy thought. *Least of all myself.*

"When did you leave Pemberley, Miss Bennet?"

"The thirty-first of December, 1812."

"When did you next see Mr. Darcy?"

"At the annulment trial. That was the ninth of February, 1813."

"Did you speak to him?"

She shook her head. "No. I avoided him."

"Why did you avoid him?"

"I did not wish to hear his accusations against me."

"Were you aware he was no longer suspicious of you?"

"I was not." She directed another glance at Darcy.

He had told her the complete story of his recovery during her convalescence at Netherfield. She had been gratified to hear how Burrell's anger and Lindley's rationality had broken through Darcy's false beliefs and surprised by how soon after her departure it had happened. It had been necessary to reassure her that she had been right to leave. Had she stayed, Darcy insisted, Burrell would never have confronted him and he might never have learned the full truth.

Darcy's solicitor gave the Empress a brisk nod. "After the trial, when and where did you next see Mr. Darcy?"

"He came to Hertfordshire. I saw him at Netherfield — my sister's house — on the thirty-first of July."

"And how did he behave?"

"He just stared at me that first time, until I ran out of the room." A ghost of a smile crossed her lips.

"Were you afraid of him?"

"I did not know what to expect." She looked at Darcy. "His cousin had told us of his recovery, but I could not be sure of his opinion of me."

"When did you discover his opinion?"

"A week later. I came upon him when I was riding, and he apologized for everything he had ever done to hurt me." She smiled. "He was quite thorough."

There were chuckles again; this time Darcy joined them.

"Tell us about his behavior since then."

With all eyes upon her, hands folded delicately in her lap and countenance filled with angelic compassion, she told a tale the court had not yet heard — of humility, regret, consideration and penance which made her forgiveness seem the most natural thing in the world. There was a small silence when she finished.

"Thank you, Miss Bennet. Nothing further."

"Did you not fear for your safety last year, Miss Bennet?" Wickham's solicitor asked.

"At the time I did."

"And do you not fear the same might occur again?"

She looked at him levelly. "No more than I fear such a thing happening to myself. Were I to suffer the same terrible confluence of illness, pain and laudanum, who is to say my mind could survive it any better? It might happen to any of us. But I fear it least of all from Mr. Darcy."

"Why?" It was the judge.

"He sits there with two broken ribs, My Lord. He suffers tremendous pain, but he will not consider taking laudanum because of the effect it might have on his mind." She favored Darcy with a brief, fond smile. "I do not fear him because he rates his own suffering as less important than my safety."

The judge nodded, smiling, and it seemed to Darcy it cost Wickham something to maintain his insouciant posture. When Dr. Lindley strode into the courtroom after the midday recess, the smirk vanished entirely, replaced with surprise.

The Empress eyed Wickham in disbelief. "Could he truly have believed Dr. Lindley would not come?"

"This is an exceedingly foolish gambit otherwise," Darcy murmured. "Of course, I expect he thought he could produce an insanity decree and that would be the last anybody ever saw of me. That *is* how it usually happens. He may also have believed you and Burrell would support him."

As Darcy had anticipated, Lindley's testimony was even more decimating than that of the Empress. The petition was verbatim from his note written on the twelfth of November 1812. Dr. Lindley testified that he had recently been visited by a Dr. Gilmour, who wished to consult about symptoms of insanity in severe illness, and with whom he had shared his notes. He had been unaware of the insanity petition before Darcy's solicitor contacted him.

At the request of Darcy's solicitor Lindley read his notes aloud, from November 1812 through April 1813, when he had declared Darcy to be fully recovered. "I have not examined him since."

The judge was not amused. "Dr. Lindley, would you be so good as to conduct an examination now?"

"Certainly, My Lord, though if I am to do it properly there must not be so extensive an audience."

"This court is in recess until tomorrow at ten o'clock." The gavel banged. "Dr. Lindley and Mr. Darcy, please accompany me."

In the judge's chambers, Lindley subjected Darcy to the same exhaustive physical and mental examination he had performed dozens of times over the long months of Darcy's illness and recovery. Darcy — under oath — readily admitted to his previous delusions, his hazy memories, his combined longing and loathing for the laudanum. He detailed the slow, painful experience of discovering the truth, and the lengths to which he would now go to protect the woman he loved.

"I wish you luck, sir," the judge said when he had finished, his handshake firm. "A man is not often afforded a second opportunity."

"I thank you, My Lord."

* * *

"It is my medical opinion that Fitzwilliam Darcy is of sound mind, and that his difficulties last autumn were entirely due to delirium."

Wickham's expression was sullenly resigned; the morning was beginning with an obvious defeat at Lindley's hand.

"Please explain, Dr. Lindley," said Darcy's solicitor. "What is delirium?"

"It is a condition of temporary mental incapacity, usually due to an illness or the influence of chemicals, such as those found in some medicines. It typically causes the sufferer to lose track of the date, and sometimes even where or who he is. He has difficulty remaining alert. His memory suffers, as does his ability to think rationally. He may hallucinate — see or hear things which are not present in reality. He may be intensely suspicious and agitated. It looks very much like insanity to those who do not understand it."

"You said it is temporary."

"Yes, it typically resolves once the illness or chemical is no longer present."

"Does it recur?"

"It is possible but not certain. Many sufferers experience it only once."

"You said it is caused by illness or chemicals. Does that mean any person could experience it?"

"Certainly."

Darcy's solicitor raised his voice a fraction. "Doctor, does the medical community consider delirium to be a form of insanity?"

"No."

"Would you recommend a delirious person be committed to an asylum?"

"I would not."

"Do you mean to say that you did *not* sign this petition to declare Mr. Darcy insane?" His solicitor held up the paper.

"That is correct."

"Would you have signed such a petition last November, when Mr. Darcy's agitation and suspiciousness caused his wife to fear for her safety?"

"No, I would not. As evidenced by the fact that I did not. I did insist Mrs. Darcy — Miss Bennet, now — avoid entering Mr. Darcy's chambers until his health improved."

Wickham's solicitor asked no questions and began stacking his papers, but Darcy's solicitor remained where he was.

"I call Henry Fitzwilliam, the Earl of Matlock."

Wickham whirled about, the color draining from his face, as Darcy's uncle came forward from the shadowed corner at the rear of the courtroom. Wickham's eyes darted frantically, and he looked ready to vault from his chair until an officer came to stand at his elbow, hand on his baton.

"What document do you hold, my lord?" Darcy's solicitor asked the earl.

"My copy of George Darcy's will. I was his executor."

"When did Mr. Darcy die?"

"Six years past."

"And where has this copy been since then?"

"In the strongbox in my study."

Darcy's solicitor handed the earl an apparently identical document. "Please examine the final page, my lord. Have you ever seen this codicil?"

The earl frowned. "No."

"Can you read the date?"

"The eighth of August, 1807. Two days before he died."

"And which solicitor's signature is on the page?"

"Ambrose Barnes."

"Was Mr. Barnes George Darcy's solicitor, my lord?"

"He was, until his death. He was also mine. Afterward you assumed that duty for both me and my brother."

"And do you happen to know when Mr. Barnes died, my lord?"

"I do not recall exactly, but it was before Christmas 1805."

"Do you not think it unlikely that Mr. Barnes signed this codicil in 1807?"

"It is not possible, sir."

"Thank you, my lord. Nothing further."

"I have heard enough," said the judge. "Mr. Darcy is sane. This decree is clearly fraudulent, as is the codicil to the late Mr. Darcy's will. Bailiff, please take Mr. Wickham and his solicitor into custody."

Darcy's solicitor stood quickly. "Mr. Darcy would also ask the court to consider the matter of Mr. Wickham's unpaid debts, which Mr. Darcy owns, amounting to one thousand three hundred seventy-six pounds."

Wickham's laugh was mocking, despite the bailiff's hand clamped around his elbow. "You have no proof, Darcy! Your study is naught but ash!"

"These predate my father's death," Darcy said, holding up the receipts. It took all his self-control to keep from grinning at the change in Wickham's countenance. "I kept them from his knowledge. They were never in the study." He shrugged. "It so happens nothing in my bedchamber was burned."

"Enough!" snapped the judge. "Mr. Wickham. Can you pay these debts?"

Wickham's voice had lost all its bravado. "No, My Lord."

"What remedy do you seek, Mr. Darcy?"

"Imprisonment, My Lord."

Wickham's expression was suddenly canny. "You would not dare, Darcy! You know what tales I may tell!"

"Who would believe them? You are a known liar."

"I am your brother-in-law!"

"As I am presently unmarried, I cannot agree with you."

Wickham turned his eyes to the Empress. "My dear sister! You cannot permit this!"

"I certainly can, sir. My sister shall be better off without you. Her family shall protect her."

The judge rolled his eyes. "I have done! Mr. Wickham, you shall face charges for attempting to defraud this court. When that is finished, you shall be remanded to debtors' prison." The gavel banged.

Darcy threw up a hand to ward off the congratulatory clap on the back Burrell nearly landed. "I beg you, sir. I shall be most pleased to accept your verbal congratulations."

"Ah! Sorry, Darcy." Burrell grinned. "That was quite the show your solicitor put on. Worth every penny you pay him, I wager."

"That and more. Thank you, Burrell. And my thanks to you all." Darcy shook the hand of every man there — including Simmons and Harwood — and kissed the Empress's fingers.

"So, this is the exceptional Miss Elizabeth Bennet," his uncle said, smiling widely. "I have long wished to meet you, madam. My wife and son cannot say enough in your favor, and a woman who can capture the attention of my famously recalcitrant nephew is sure to be worth knowing."

The Empress blushed. "I thank you, my lord. I am very pleased to meet you, and grateful you were able to come so quickly."

He laughed. "My wife fairly kicked me out the front door after reading your express, my dear. When the mistress issues a command, a sensible man steps to it."

"Hear, hear," said Darcy and Burrell together.

Darcy caught Simmons and Harwood attempting to stifle grins. "Come," he said. "We must celebrate. Let us see if the inn has any champagne."

Twenty-five

Second Chances

DARCY WAS ALMOST able to forget the pain in his ribs on the journey back to Pemberley. He had drunk a bit too much champagne, which typically made him surly. It was a testament, then, to his unalloyed excitement that he felt lighter than he had in years — decades, even.

Wickham. He was the specter hanging over me.

Even as boys, Wickham had been charming where Darcy was reticent. Petted and indulged by his own parents and by Darcy's father, Wickham had always been skilled at robbing Darcy of whatever happiness he might find, eager to claim every advantage Darcy had. Even during the years they never saw each other, Darcy could not be certain Wickham was gone from his life for good.

The Empress was right — he knew I loved her. He likely ran off with her sister just when he did to prevent our marriage.

287

But now he could carry out no such schemes. Conditions in the prison were tolerable only if a man had money to bribe the guards, and Darcy was not inclined to be so generous.

Darcy had not truly been worried, once he convinced the magistrate to bring the matter before a judge, that he would be dragged away to the madhouse. But now that threat was gone, Wickham was gone, and Pemberley would be rebuilt more spectacular than before.

I need only one thing more to be perfectly happy.

He looked across the carriage at the Empress. He had been stealing glances as surreptitiously as possible. It was unlikely Burrell had actually missed them, but it would not do to be too brazen. In this instance, however, he caught her looking at him. Her eyes dropped instantly, face flushing, but he had seen her expression — speculative, mostly, but had that been yearning?

He did not look away this time. Dark lashes fanned across high cheekbones that retained spots of pink. Her lower lip was plump and reddened where she had bitten it. Her hands sat demurely in her lap, but her thumb worried her opposite palm.

She is anxious. Her hands always did that when she was unsettled. *Why would she be anxious?* He carefully turned the question over, attempting to see things as she might.

It hit him like a hammer. *There is no longer any reason for her to stay. The house and tenants have been seen to, and I am no longer in any danger. She will be wondering how to tell me she wishes to leave… or wishes not to.*

But which is it? They had settled into a comfortable routine together — she was the mistress in all but name, it was true — but was that what she desired?

Jane Bingley's words came back to him. *'You do not make a woman love you,'* she had said. *'You invite her to do so. You must respect her right to choose.'*

The Empress had chosen to stay with him when the Reynoldses returned to Netherfield. Would she choose to stay with him now? It seemed to defy credulity that her feelings for him might transform from fear to love in three months.

But we have spent so much time together. Far more, in fact, than most couples before they wed. And the way she spoke of me — of us — at court.... Can it be?

Darcy's eyes remained fixed on the Empress; he was sure to be caught staring. *There is not a spot of black on her,* he suddenly realized. *Not even her bonnet. No gray, either, nor lavender. She is no longer in mourning.*

He could not keep the smile off his face. It could not be a coincidence that she had given up mourning entirely just at this time. She peeked up at him then, and her answering smile sent his heart beating wildly in his chest.

The carriage turned; they were approaching the ruins of the great house. Darcy thumped on the ceiling and they soon rolled to a stop.

"I have been sitting long enough. I should like to walk for a time. Empress, will you join me?"

"I shall be delighted, sir."

Burrell gave Darcy a small nod as he handed the Empress down. "Please take Mr. Burrell home," Darcy instructed his driver. "Then return to the carriage-house. Miss Bennet and I shall take the gig back to the cottage when we are ready."

He stood for a long moment as the carriage drove away, regarding the scorched and crumbling walls of his former home in the fading light. He remembered running through the halls as a boy, Mrs. Reynolds trying not to laugh as she scolded him; Cook sneaking him biscuits before chasing him away, whenever he came in covered in dirt from climbing trees; hours spent with his mother in the music-room, her patience endless as he fumbled at the keys of the pianoforte; sitting next to his father in the study, poring over the account-books, discussing investments and estate management.

"Why do you do that?" the Empress asked.

Darcy looked down; he had been rubbing at his chest. "It is a recent habit. Whenever I think of that which I have loved and lost, my chest aches." He nodded toward the house. "They shall begin pulling it all down tomorrow, you know. Barclay hopes to have the walls down before the weather turns."

She nodded. "And after they are done, you shall have a lifetime of memories though nothing else remains." She took his arm. "Let us walk through it one last time."

Once they were through the doors, however, Darcy found he did not need to go further. Standing in the silent hall, the breeze carrying the faint scent of charred wood and stone as it ruffled his hair, he discovered these walls no longer felt like his home. Home was the cottage, and the woman at his side.

Good-bye, he thought, and the lingering ache in his chest disappeared.

The Empress's face was pensive; she shivered in the chill breeze.

"Let us go to the hothouse," he said. "It is warm there." *And the memories are not so painful, particularly for her.*

The hothouse smelled of earth and roses. The Empress inhaled deeply, her whole body seeming to relax. He recalled how she always seemed to belong in that grove at Rosings, as though she were a wood-sprite. She looked like one now in the gathering dusk, the moonlight not quite bright enough to illuminate her features.

She regarded him curiously. "What is it, sir?"

"You seem otherworldly just now. If I turn my head even for a moment, you shall surely disappear."

"You would have me stay, then?" Her eyes were filled with questions and — yes, that might indeed be yearning.

"Yes. Stay with me." He lifted a trembling hand to cup her cheek. "We are not yet finished with the house. We must still decide on the decoration for my chambers — and yours." He smiled tenderly at her small gasp. "The mistress's chambers are yours, dearest. They have always been and shall only ever be yours."

"Truly? I thought…" She glanced away. "You never — and then when you were ill, you —"

The few remaining shards in his heart had not finished carving at him, it seemed. He gently turned her face back to him. "Empress. May I speak plainly?"

She swallowed hard but gave him a tiny nod.

"I have only ever wanted you. Ever. I nearly came to you that first night, after I returned to Pemberley. I had my hand on the doorknob, even. But I was angry and jealous, and I feared I would hurt you. I could not bear the thought of our marriage-bed as a place of violence. I vowed to wait until I was not angry, and you were not miserable. And then I fell, and everything became worse."

"I did not know —" Tears gathered in her eyes.

"I could not tell you. I feared you would shred my heart to ribbons; you have always had that power. And then, when I was ill…" He took a deep breath and instantly regretted it. Wincing, he said, "Do you know what I was doing when I fell through the floor?"

"Nay. I wondered, of course."

"Simmons told me what I said to that invisible Elizabeth. What he saw. What *you* saw. But I could not remember her." Her chin dropped; he lifted it again. "Empress, please look at me."

Eventually she did; he read shame in her eyes.

"I stood just where I had lain in my bed, and I finally remembered. It was you." He wanted desperately to kiss away the sudden crease of surprise and confusion between her brows. "It was always you, but as you were before — before Wickham. Before Rosings. As you were at Netherfield, when I found myself enchanted by a woman who refused to flatter me. I longed for you even then." He shook his head. "I cannot tell you why, in my delirium, I did not see that you and she were the same. Dearest, I am sorry I ever gave you cause to believe I did not desire you."

Her smile was gentle and sad. "You were ill, but you were not wrong. By then I was not the same woman you knew in Hertfordshire. And I am not now the same woman I was last year."

"Neither am I the same man. What has not changed is how very much I love you." He took her face in his hands. "My glorious Empress — I do not wish to imagine my life without you. Marry me, I beg you."

Hesitantly she reached up. "I cannot see your eyes," she said, lifting his hat off his head.

He allowed her to turn his body, shifting until the dim moonlight was in his face and returning her questioning gaze with every ounce of his passion. *Please, God, let her see how I love her.* He was suspended in her glittering dark eyes, feeling every seam between the newly joined pieces of his heart threaten to pull apart as the silence stretched.

"You are not the same man at all," she said at length. "When first you asked me to marry you... I could only hope this man existed. I prayed there might be warmth and generosity beneath that cold exterior, but I did not truly believe it could be so. Not until you returned to me this summer." Her hand came to rest on his cheek. "I am not certain how it happened — I was so afraid, Fitzwilliam! So afraid this man I saw would vanish, and the one who hurt me would return! — but he did not."

His head rang like a bell. *Fitzwilliam!* She had never called him by his name. It was so loud he nearly missed her next words.

"When you fell through the floor... I was terrified. I could not bear to lose you. It was only then I discovered how dearly I have come to love you." She smiled. "Then we planned Pemberley together, and I could no longer imagine myself anywhere else."

"Then —" his voice was raspy. "Will you —?"

"Yes!" Her face flooded with joy. "Yes, Fitzwilliam, I will marry you."

She might have said more but he could restrain himself no longer. He clasped her to him, the pain in his ribs no more than an annoyance as he kissed her hungrily. She was at first tentative and unsure, but he did not let up and her hesitation soon melted away. When he tugged at her bonnet-strings she broke away, giggling as she untied the ribbons. He flung the bonnet to the floor, his hat following, and reached for her again, only for her to ward him off with a raised hand.

"Wait," she said, glancing around. "Ah!" She snatched up a footstool a few yards away and carefully placed it before him; when she stood upon it their eyes were nearly level. "You have a very great debt of affection to pay me, sir. I shall not permit you to cry off due to injury."

"Clever wench," he murmured. It was some time before he could speak — or even think — again, but finally she pulled away, just far enough to look at him. Her lips were swollen, eyes wide and dark, hair and clothing in disarray.

I am likely no better, he thought with a wicked grin.

"Come to me tonight," she breathed.

His body surged with lust, even as his mind struggled to comprehend. "Empress... are you certain? We are not yet married, and — well —"

"We are and we are not. It hardly matters. I doubt anyone in that house will bat an eyelash. And I am absolutely certain I do not wish to wait another night for my husband to make me his wife in truth." She hesitated. "So long as your injury will not —"

"A few broken ribs will not keep me away," he interrupted, grinning again. "But I fear you must be more adventurous than most brides."

Her eyes flashed with a mixture of excitement and trepidation. "Nothing else about our marriage has been typical. Why should this be any different?"

Twenty-six

From This Day Forward

ARCY KNOCKED on the Empress's door, pausing only a moment before he let himself in. She sat perfectly still before her dressing-table. Her new lady's maid hardly spared him a glance, mouth full of pins as she twisted her mistress's hair into a complex knot.

The Empress met his eyes in the mirror. "Mr. Darcy, surely you recall I am to meet you at the church this morning? It is not done for the groom to invade the bride's chambers, sir."

"When have we ever benefited by following such absurd rules? There is something I must speak to you about before we go to church, but it can wait until Betsy is finished."

He settled himself on her favorite window-seat, which gave him an excellent view of her lovely face. He had missed her fiercely last night; she had not permitted him to come to her, despite his pleas. "Your bride must sleep tonight if she is to be prepared for her wedding-night," she had said with an arch smile.

That first night — seventeen days ago, now — after Georgiana's delighted embraces and what felt like an interminable evening in the music-room, the Empress had excused herself early. "Remember," she had murmured as she passed by him, "avoid the center of the hallway."

Darcy had waited until the servants were upstairs, trusting to the sound of their movements to disguise his own, before creeping down the hall. The Empress had answered his soft knock in a diaphanous gown that stole his breath entirely. It was as well he succeeded in quashing his first instinct, which was to tear it from her body; he had since come to adore that gown. Instead, he had buried his hands in her unbound hair and kissed her hard, whispering her name — "My glorious Empress" — in her ear.

"Elizabeth," she had said. It had stilled him utterly. Her voice soft and sultry, her eyes knowing, she said, "When you visit my bed, I am Elizabeth."

Neither of them had slept that night. The following night he had nearly been caught in her bed, so loathe was he to leave their warm cocoon. Simmons — good man! — made no mention of the fact that his own bed had obviously not been slept in.

Their journey to London, brief as it was, had been torture. His bed was vast and empty; he dared not visit her in the inns, and for the sake of propriety she had stayed with her aunt and uncle.

The days were filled with errands: Darcy convinced the Archbishop to issue a second special license — itself no small feat — then negotiated a new settlement with the Empress's uncle Gardiner, visited the jeweler and the bookseller, and finally escorted the Empress to a dizzying array of shops to purchase new clothes, shoes, and other accesssories. He took her through Darcy House, giving her a proper introduction to the servants, and she invited Betsy and the head housemaid to return with them to Pemberley Cottage.

All necessary activities, of course. But after nearly two weeks with no more than brief, stolen kisses, Darcy had been exceedingly gratified to see Barclay had promptly attended to his request: beside the wardrobe in his bedchamber, a door now opened directly into the Empress's room.

No more sneaking through the halls, he thought.

That night she had slipped into his chamber wearing only that translucent gown — though not for long. After very little sleep, Darcy had been awakened before dawn by Simmons's soft voice outside the bed-curtains: "Good morning, sir. The maids shall soon be stoking the fires, I imagine. Will you take breakfast in your room?"

"Yes, thank you, Simmons."

When the door had closed quietly behind the valet, Elizabeth had uncurled from Darcy's side and gasped at the sight of her night-rail draped neatly over the back of a chair.

"You did say nobody would bat an eyelash. Besides, there are only two more days until we marry." He had chuckled at her expression, a mix of chagrin and triumph. "Come now, give me a kiss and go to your own bed, if you truly think Betsy remains ignorant."

That night he had instructed Simmons to prepare a bath and depart until morning. The man had left a dozen towels and several bottles of delicately scented oil beside the oversize tub Darcy had rescued from the great house.

Elizabeth had laughed. "Do you prefer to smell like roses or lavender, sir?"

"I am at your mercy, madam. Choose what pleases you." What had pleased *him* was the way her soapy hands glided over his body and the supple softness of her clean, damp skin against his. Once again, he had slept little.

After two such nights Darcy had been badly tempted to go to her bed despite her refusal, but her sister's warning came to him in time. *You must respect her right to choose.* Sighing, he had resigned himself to his empty bed, vowing it would be his last night alone. After today he would wake each morning beside her, the warmth of her body entwined with his.

She must have felt the weight of his thoughts; she eyed him sidelong, her lips curving into a tiny smile as the last curl was pinned. "Thank you, Betsy. You may go now."

The Empress was effortlessly beautiful in a gown of ivory satin trimmed with lace and tiny seed pearls, her garnet cross around her throat. Darcy had deliberately chosen an entirely different ensemble today than he had worn at their first wedding: burgundy jacket, fawn trousers, and ivory waistcoat.

"You matched your waistcoat to my gown again," she said.

He shrugged. "Georgiana's doing. She was quite insistent." Darcy gently kissed his almost-wife. "I have one thing to add to your ensemble, Empress."

"Your mother's necklace?" Her voice and expression were carefully neutral.

"Nay. That was a mistake on my part. You need never wear it again." He waited as her expression shifted — first to relief, then to curiosity — then spoke softly. "You have brought light into every part of my life, Elizabeth. Even when things were at their darkest, you somehow held tight to that spark inside you." He held out a sumptuous velvet box. "You brighten the lives of everyone around you, my love. You must have something that shines as you do."

She gasped as the box opened to reveal the necklace he had commissioned for her. The morning sun sent a thousand sparkling rays across her face and around the room as the stones reflected its light.

"Fitzwilliam! Are these —?"

"Diamonds? Yes. If you will allow me?" He gently removed her garnet cross and fastened the glittering circlet about her neck. Each round, perfect stone was nestled in a delicate gold rosette, the diamonds gradually increasing in size as they neared the hollow of her throat, where a large pear-shaped diamond hung cradled in its own golden petal.

She gazed at her reflection, touching the diamonds with trembling fingers. "It is so beautiful," she whispered. "Thank you!" She whirled and kissed him fiercely. "I love you, Fitzwilliam."

He gently brushed the tears from her cheeks. "I love you, Empress. Now we must go, or Burrell will have my hide for keeping him waiting. I shall send your sister to you."

In the front hall he greeted the Bingleys warmly, accepting Jane's kiss on his cheek and allowing himself to be hurried into the carriage.

"Second time's the charm," said a grinning Bingley. "You are positively incandescent, Darcy."

Darcy smiled. "You had it right from the very beginning, my friend. Love makes all the difference."

The church was crowded. In addition to the Bingleys, the Empress's mother and younger sisters had made the journey with the Collinses. Her aunt and uncle Gardiner, who Darcy had come to greatly admire, waited at the back of the church. His own aunt and uncle were flanked by his cousin Richard and a beaming Georgiana. Lady Catherine was not there, of course; she had cut him after he announced his engagement last year and he had never attempted to heal the breach. The part of him that desired happiness for his cousin Anne was sorry, but otherwise he could not regret his aunt's absence.

The rest of the pews — and the aisles and every other possible space — were filled by the people of Pemberley. Mrs. Bennet was clearly delighted by the substantial turnout, and for once Darcy could not object to the presence of so large a crowd. The excitement was palpable. He took his place with Bingley at the front of the church, Burrell giving him a smile that felt like a benediction.

The doors soon opened, and a young blond girl began to make her way up the aisle, sprinkling rose petals as she went. Martha Wright — nine years old now, Darcy recalled — was rosy-cheeked and almost giddy as she stepped to the side, making room for Jane Bingley, who followed her.

There was a collective gasp as the Empress stopped in the doorway beside her uncle Gardiner. She was truly glorious: her dress glowed softly in the morning sun and her hair seemed to shine with glints of gold, the diamonds encircling her throat catching and reflecting the light in all directions. Once again Darcy saw only his bride as she glided toward him, but this time his heart was near to bursting with joy.

Mr. Gardiner nodded his approval as he placed the Empress's hand in Darcy's. Unable to help himself, Darcy kissed it before she took another step. A rumble of amusement rose from the congregation, but he saw only her indulgent smile and felt only the press of her fingers against his.

He truly listened to the words of the ceremony this time, feeling them settle into his bones. He vowed to love, honor and cherish the woman before him — for better for worse, in sickness and in health — making his promise to her, and to God, with a fervency he had never before felt.

Her eyes were bright, unwavering pools as she made her own vows, and it seemed as though the last jagged shards in his chest settled back into place and fused together, leaving his heart truly whole for the first time.

Finally, he slid the ring onto her slender finger — a pear-shaped diamond set in gold at the center of a row of round diamonds — and pledged to her his heart, his body, and all his worldly goods.

How could I have said these words before? he wondered. His happiness had been a tiny, fragile thing then — so frail it had survived only a few hours. Now it was strong, deeply rooted and inextricably entwined with hers. So long as they were together it would continue to grow.

"You may kiss your bride, son," Burrell said.

Without hesitation Darcy did so, capturing her lips for a space of time that edged past indecent into the nearly scandalous. Not that anybody seemed to mind; the cheers were raucous, even from some of the ladies, and Elizabeth made no move to pull away.

Finally, he released her with a grin. Pitching his voice for her ears alone he said, "Welcome to Pemberley, Mrs. Darcy."

"Thank you, Mr. Darcy. When may we leave?"

"Eager to flee your adoring subjects, Empress?"

She laughed softly. "You have no idea."

"On the contrary," he chuckled. After a small wedding-breakfast with family they were to depart for Bath, where his uncle had a house. They would return just before Christmas, if the weather held; if not, Darcy was entirely willing to have his wife to himself for the next few months.

"Before you lovebirds fly away, I have a small matter of business for you," Burrell said. "Once you have accepted all your congratulations, come find me in the vicarage."

It took some time to leave the churchyard; every tenant, it seemed, wished to give the mistress their best. The Empress embraced Susan Wright and her children, giving her bouquet of flowers to Martha as Darcy gallantly bowed over the girl's hand. Then Darcy and the Empress distributed kisses to all their relations, with a promise to see them at the cottage in very good time. Finally, they knocked on Burrell's door.

"Come in, Mr. Darcy. Mrs. Darcy." Burrell smiled. "I have here the register, if you please." He gave Darcy a shrewd look.

"Of course, Mr. Burrell." Beneath the entry in Burrell's bold hand, declaring them married at Pemberley on the twenty-sixth of November 1813, he signed his name with a flourish: *Fitzwilliam George Darcy.*

Epilogue

"WHAT NEWS from Netherfield?"

Elizabeth smiled mischievously at her husband. "Bingley's handwriting is unreadable as ever, I take it?"

"Hopeless. He is also not half the gossip your sisters are. If we are ever to learn what is happening in Meryton, I must rely on you." He waved his sheet of paper dramatically. "All I can glean from this is he will be bringing one of Caesar's get with him next month."

"That is excellent news, brother!" Georgiana said, looking up from her pile of correspondence. "I know how you miss that great brute."

"Yes, well. Caesar was a fine horse in all ways but one. I understand his progeny inherited much of his strength and stamina and are generally better-behaved, so I may be getting the superior end of the bargain, when all is said and done."

Fitzwilliam had remained devoted to his ill-tempered stallion until the day Caesar attempted to kick Elizabeth, just over a year past. Philippa had begun crying in her arms while they were visiting the stables, which Caesar evidently found intolerable. Elizabeth had fortunately been swift enough to remove herself and Pippa from the vicinity without injury, but her husband set nothing above the safety of his wife and daughter. He had written Charles Bingley with an offer to sell the horse that very morning; Mr. Reynolds had arrived to collect Caesar two weeks later.

Elizabeth flashed a teasing grin. "I have no doubt we shall all be delighted by whichever horse Mr. Reynolds has chosen for you, my dear."

"It is well I am now on good terms with Reynolds, then, I suppose," Fitzwilliam said, returning her grin. The breeding program was Charles's venture, but they all knew no decision was final until Mr. Reynolds approved.

"Indeed so." Elizabeth returned her attention to her letter. "Very well, here is the news: Jane writes that Beth fancies herself very grown-up indeed now she is three, and insists on being allowed to hold little Charles. Charles, of course, would much rather be crawling than sitting on his sister's lap, and Jane cannot decide which of them is more dissatisfied with the other."

Fitzwilliam laughed. "Aye, that is a dilemma. I imagine we shall have much the same, eventually."

They shared a private smile. Elizabeth's courses had not come for three months now, but until she felt the quickening, she was unwilling to speak a word of it to any but him.

"Kitty was wed last Tuesday, and they are already gone off to Newmarket," Elizabeth went on. "Mr. Milton could not miss another Sunday, it seems, though Mamma wished them to stay in Meryton another week. His parish is busy, and the curacy is vacant, but of course dear Mamma thinks nothing of *that*."

"Does not your mother go to visit Mrs. Grantham?" Georgiana asked.

"She and Mary go to the Granthams in October and shall stay until the new year. I suspect Lydia would happily keep Mamma longer, but Colonel Grantham put his foot down." Elizabeth shook her head. "That poor, dear man! He knew not what he did, I think, when he married Lydia."

"Many men do not look past a pretty face and high spirits, I fear," Fitzwilliam said wryly. "It was good of him to adopt Lydia's boys."

"He is certainly a good-hearted man. Such a husband, I must hope, shall settle Lydia somewhat." Elizabeth glanced at Georgiana's pensive face. "What is it, dearest?"

"It is awful of me, I know, but… I cannot help thinking it is better for all concerned that she was widowed so soon. Imagine if Wickham had lingered in prison for months — years, even!" Georgiana shuddered.

Elizabeth put a comforting arm about her shoulders. "I believe we have all had such a thought at one time or another. None of us wished his death, of course — and certainly not in such a manner! — but you are correct. A pretty young widow receives a great deal more sympathy than does the wife of an inmate."

Fitzwilliam nodded, and Elizabeth met his eyes above Georgiana's head. Generous as Fitzwilliam was, he had been prepared to support Elizabeth's wayward sister for years. He had offered to do so before they were married again — before the insanity trial, even, after he discovered a collection of receipts in his strongbox and revived their discussion of calling in Wickham's debts.

None of them had been prepared for Wickham to be murdered in prison within a week of his arrival. The husband of one of Wickham's paramours — already sentenced to death for the murder of another man — did not hesitate to take vengeance for his cuckolding.

Afterward, Lydia had played the role of wronged, innocent widow for all it was worth. Colonel Grantham, a war-weary bachelor more than twice Lydia's age, had been sufficiently captivated to overlook her modest fortune and the scandal of her first marriage.

There was a commotion in the hall. A small dark-haired, dark-eyed girl with dimpled cheeks barrelled into the study, followed by her harried nurse.

"Mamma, Mamma! Look!"

Elizabeth swung her daughter into her arms. "What do you have there, Pippa?"

"Look! My cup!" The girl held up a large cup. It held two smaller ones, neatly stacked.

"That is an excellent cup, dearest. But you must go with Hannah now and put on your shoes so we may see our new house."

A quizzical expression crossed the child's face. "This my house!"

"Yes, this is your house. But tomorrow we shall move to the new house. Would you like to see your new room? Yes? Then you must wear shoes." Elizabeth kissed her daughter's forehead and set her on her feet. Philippa ran past Hannah; moments later they heard her heavy footsteps on the stairs.

Georgiana grinned impishly at her brother. "Fitzwilliam, you shall spoil that child rotten. Imagine! How often does a toddler receive a house for her second birthday?"

"Nothing is too good for my little girl," Fitzwilliam said easily. "Come now, we are all eager to see the house. Your applications must wait, sister."

Georgiana closed her desk. The study was cramped with all three of them, but they had long since accustomed themselves to it. Georgiana's lending project had been such an unqualified success that now, three years on, she corresponded with great ladies all over England who wished to duplicate her approach with their own tenants. Elizabeth would assume responsibility for Pemberley's program after Georgiana married next month and removed to Plymouth, where Captain Somerset's ship was being refitted.

Fitzwilliam had been every bit as ruthless as he had once promised when the captain applied for Georgiana's hand. Despite being the third son of a duke and nearly Fitzwilliam's age, Captain Somerset was subjected to rigorous questioning about his prospects, his plans for the future, the strength of his affection for Georgiana and his philosophy on married life.

Elizabeth had taken care to prepare Georgiana for this. "It is nothing at all to do with whether Fitzwilliam likes Captain Somerset or not. My Papa did the same to him," she had told her sister, smiling fondly as she recalled Papa's reaction to her first engagement to Mr. Darcy. It was a pity, she thought, Papa had not lived to see their current happiness together.

"Fitzwilliam was entirely unprepared for it, he said, but he bore it well, and he vowed to do the same whenever a young man came to him about you."

The captain's answers had been more than satisfactory, Fitzwilliam had later told Elizabeth, and the two men were now great friends.

Mr. Burrell had also been particular about the intended husband of Miss Darcy; this was to be the last wedding he performed. Shortly thereafter he would retire to Manchester, to live out his days with the family of his youngest daughter. Elizabeth was overjoyed for both Burrell and Georgiana, and equally saddened to see them depart. She hardly knew how she would manage without them!

With her mind thus occupied, they were nearly to the great house before Elizabeth realized it. Much as she enjoyed riding, she was grateful she had elected to take the gig this morning along with Hannah and Pippa while Fitzwilliam and Georgiana went on horseback. It meant she could fix her attention on the building as they approached. Although she had seen it many times before, her belly still fluttered with anticipation as the new Pemberley came into view.

It had been just over four years ago that she looked upon the old Pemberley's staid walls as she returned from her first visit to the tenants. Then, she had felt an interloper in the house, undeserving and unwelcome. Now she looked upon pale, gleaming stone with elegant arches and a steep, slate-gray roof, and her heart soared — *this* was home. Here, she was meant to be mistress.

Elizabeth paused just inside the great bronze doors and turned slowly, taking it all in. The smell of flowers and earth reached her from the conservatory just off the entrance hall. Light poured in from many windows, setting the marble of the central staircase ablaze and warming the rich brown of the shining woodwork.

Mr. Barclay was waiting for them. He bowed politely over Elizabeth's hand and shook hands firmly with Fitzwilliam.

The two men had gotten off to a rocky start; Elizabeth suspected Fitzwilliam of some jealous inclinations at that time. They also had altogether different visions of what an elegant English country house should be, but after much discussion and a few outright rows during construction, they had come to a genuine accord.

Some of the rooms — the library, study, billiard-room and master's chambers — maintained the darker, traditional look her husband favored, while the other public rooms were airy and light-filled. Elizabeth particularly adored the spectacular rib-vaulted ceilings, and Mr. Barclay had added them to the design for her chambers and her favorite sitting-room.

Fitzwilliam carried Pippa on his shoulders through all the rooms on the main floor, whispering the secrets of each as they moved along. "A family of owls lives just outside the window in that tree," he said as they peeked out the window of the blue sitting room, and "This room is as tall as our entire cottage!" as they stood in the center of the ballroom.

Pippa looked about with interest, but her eyes went wide with excitement as her Papa set her down to explore her new playroom with Hannah.

"I should like to investigate the acoustics of the music-room," Georgiana said, skipping down the marble steps after giving her own chamber a cursory examination.

"Go ahead, dearest," Elizabeth called after her, laughing. Georgiana's piano had been moved last week and was just tuned; it was a wonder the girl had patience for any other part of the house. Besides, Elizabeth desired to keep her husband to herself for the next little while.

They entered the mistress's bedchamber together. Their only real argument had been about this room: since Pippa's birth Elizabeth had shared the master's chamber with Fitz-william, and he saw no point to a mistress's suite.

It had taken some doing to convince him not to alter the design. She had pointedly reminded him it was impossible that every future occupant would be as felicitously married as they, and she had fully required her own chamber during and after Pippa's birth.

What had finally mollified him was her insistence that the room would serve more as her study than her bedchamber. "I very much enjoy spending our mornings together," she had told him, "but the years in the cottage have highlighted how frequently we shall require our own work-spaces. Besides, your study is entirely too much a cave for my liking."

They passed through the sitting-room that adjoined both chambers and Elizabeth peeked into the master's bathing chamber. She had been positively giddy when Mr. Barclay first demonstrated the taps that filled the bath with steaming water in only minutes. She had not told Fitzwilliam she also intended to take full advantage of the shower; he would be delighted to discover it on his own.

The master's bedchamber was not as dark as Fitzwilliam preferred, in deference to her taste, but the light was still sub-dued. Elizabeth threw open the doors that led onto the wide balcony overlooking the lake, lifting her face to luxuriate in the warmth of the midday sun — unusual for late September. Fitzwilliam's arms came around her and his breath tickled her ear.

"Empress — or is it Elizabeth just now? — how do you like the house?"

"I shall not be Elizabeth here until we have had sufficient time to properly enjoy that enormous bed. And the house is perfect. I *belong* here."

"You do." He kissed her jaw lightly. "You are the first and greatest mistress of this house, if I do say so myself. My only concern is for poor Pippa. She will not know what to do when she cannot run directly into our bedchamber each morning."

Elizabeth nodded. "I have been thinking — perhaps she should sleep in the sitting room between our chambers until she becomes accustomed to the nursery. We shall move her to the nursery proper when her brother or sister may also go with her."

He stilled, but his voice held barely contained joy. "You are certain?"

"Yes. I felt it during the ride in the gig this morning, but it was not until we entered the house, and my belly would not stop fluttering, that I recognized it for what it was."

Fitzwilliam grinned. "My glorious Empress." He rested his hand tenderly on her belly as he kissed her, long and deep. "Welcome home, my love."

THE END

Afterword

What was wrong with Mr. Darcy?

Mr. Darcy suffered from delirium, caused by a combination of several overlapping medical factors. The explanation Dr. Lindley gives the court is a good layperson's description of severe delirium. It should always be suspected if a person with no prior history of psychosis is experiencing visual hallucinations, confusion, disorientation (losing track of the date or where they are), agitation, or paranoia — especially if there is a new medical condition or a new medication or drug in the picture.

Delirium is so common in critically ill patients that it is sometimes called "ICU psychosis." However, even minor medical illnesses can cause it: in older adults, something as simple as a urinary tract infection can cause delirium that persists long after the infection itself has been treated.

In Mr. Darcy's case, the first condition to present itself is Guillain-Barré Syndrome. GBS is a rapidly progressive auto-immune disorder, in which the body's immune system attacks the peripheral nerves. This causes muscle weakness and paralysis, which can be life-threatening when it involves the respiratory muscles. It also causes numbness, tingling, and pain. The most common trigger is an infection, usually of the respiratory or gastrointestinal system. (Mr. Darcy suffered a gastrointestinal infection.)

In a majority of GBS cases the symptoms resolve over weeks to months, though a third of sufferers do not fully recover their muscle strength. In 1812 this disorder did not yet have a name; French neurologists Georges Guillain and Jean Alexandre Barré described it, including a key diagnostic feature of the spinal fluid, in 1916.

Dr. Lindley's hypothesis, that weakness of the legs caused Mr. Darcy to fall, is correct. Mr. Darcy had exhausted his already-affected muscles by galloping across Pemberley's grounds just that morning. In the fall he suffered a fracture of the right tibia and fibula (the lower leg bones, which are often broken together), followed by a concussion when his head struck first a massive porcelain vase and then the floor.

To treat the pain, Mr. Darcy was given laudanum, which is opium dissolved in alcohol. This was a commonly prescribed medicine at the time, used for a variety of ailments. Both of its primary components cause physiologic dependence, in which the body becomes accustomed to the substance and higher doses become necessary to achieve the same effect.

It can also cause addiction through complex changes in gene expression and neurochemical signaling in the brain. Chronic opioid use can cause difficulties with emotion regulation and pain tolerance. Agitation and anxiety are common in withdrawal, and both overdose and withdrawal can be fatal.

Mr. Darcy experienced both dependence and addiction. Dr. Lindley's insistence on a careful and unvarying tapered dosing schedule was the key to weaning him off the drug. (Mr. Darcy's later caution about taking laudanum to treat the pain of his broken ribs was also wise.)

Added to all this, Mr. Darcy was infected with influenza, a common virus that kills up to 650,000 people worldwide every year. The most common complication is pneumonia, but it can also cause inflammation affecting the heart or nervous system. (It may even lead to Guillain-Barré Syndrome, though this is uncommon.) While most people recover without complications, Mr. Darcy's risk of death was high, given his condition at the time he became infected.

Influenza is generally passed through respiratory droplets from coughing or sneezing, so strategies such as wearing masks when ill, covering one's cough, and regularly washing hands and sanitizing surfaces are important for infection prevention. In 1812, however, these strategies would not have been widely recommended. The dominant theory of infection in Europe at the time was the miasma theory, which held that bad air from decaying organic matter caused disease. Germ theory was not well accepted until much later in the 19th century.

What happened to Mr. Darcy, then? His delirium began due to GBS and laudanum use, worsened significantly after he was infected with influenza, and subsequently took more than two months to resolve.

Were Mr. Darcy alive today, he would likely be hospitalized and receiving a variety of treatments for GBS, pain, and influenza. He might require mechanical ventilation to support his breathing, given that his respiratory muscles were affected. He would likely also receive IV nutrition, since his tongue was affected, making it difficult for him to swallow without aspirating fluid or food particles into his lungs. He would certainly receive extensive physical and occupational therapy as he recovered.

In addition, given the severity of Mr. Darcy's agitation, paranoia and visual hallucinations during the height of his delirium, a modern psychiatrist would likely recommend a temporary course of an antipsychotic medication. As Dr. Lindley explained, however, Mr. Darcy would not be considered mentally ill, and his family members would be advised to expect eventual recovery of both his mental and physical symptoms.

Acknowledgments

No book is ever a truly solo project, and this one is no exception. Despite it being only my second novel, a pattern is already emerging: Darcy has a miles-deep hole out of which he must climb.

Thanks, then, to my beta readers Carla Vera Ries and Craig & Suzanne Sheumaker, who were unflinching in telling me, "That's too deep a hole. Give the man some stairs to get partway up, at least." A special shout-out to Carla for catching me whenever I used medical terminology that was not yet common parlance in the Regency era.

Thanks also to Micky Logan, for teaching me how lawyers think, and foregoing a well-deserved nitpicking when I deviated from strict courtroom procedure.

Thanks, as always, to my husband Bruce, who has stuck by me through the ups and downs of more than twenty years of marriage.

Finally, thanks to the many sages through the centuries who made the observation that drove this book, known colloquially as Murphy's Law: "Anything that can go wrong will go wrong."

About the Author

Alexa Douglas is an inveterate bluestocking. Her interests include science, psychology, traveling and crafts; just don't ask her to sing in public or do anything requiring athletic prowess.

As with any good reader, there are dozens of books patiently waiting for her attention. Since she took up writing, however, they've become suspicious she'll never get to them at all. This doesn't faze her; in her years working with people suffering from psychosis, delirium, and substance dependence, Alexa has been called worse things than a "fornicating toad," so she considers such polite suspicion to be pretty benign.

Find her at **www.alexadouglas.com**.

Also by Alexa Douglas

Alexa Douglas delights in sending Jane Austen's beloved characters on startling new adventures.

The Re-education of Mr. Darcy

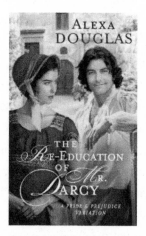

Elizabeth Bennet is the daughter of one of New York's first families. When her grandparents take her and her sisters on a journey abroad, she is not surprised to encounter anti-American prejudice among the members of the English upper class. If only her new friend's brother was not the most offensive of the lot!

Fitzwilliam Darcy is grateful that his sister is coming out of her shell. If only her new friend was not a brash American who gets the better of him at every encounter! And if only he could stop thinking about her...

When Elizabeth and her family depart for Italy, she is happy to leave Mr. Darcy and his disdainful cruelty behind. Darcy is not prepared to let her walk out of his life for good, but how is he to win a woman who despises him and challenges everything he was taught to believe?

Available in paperback or Kindle at amazon.com

Made in the USA
Monee, IL
04 September 2021

77384157R00194